The Omega Challenge

I0670404

Omegas of The New South Book Two

Sharilyn Skye

Copyright 2020 by Sharilyn Skye
All Rights Reserved
EBook ISBN 9781736133705
Paperback ISBN 9781736133712
First Edition: November 2020 updated 2/18/26
Cover Design: PaigeLCro Photography
Cover Photo: Depositphoto/Julenochek/doodko
Dark Horse Publishing Morgantown, WV

Table of Contents

Quotes:

Southern women see no contradiction in mixing strength with gentleness.

~Sharon McKern

In the South, perhaps more than any other region, we go back to our home in dreams and memories, hoping it remains what it was on a lazy, still summer's day twenty years ago.

~Unknown

A woman's horse will see her soul way before you ever will. He can smell her miles away when we spend $100 on Chanel to smell her just a few feet away. Her horse knows her secrets. He can dry her tears. She can wrap her arms around his neck, and he can take her to the nearest water when we can't even open her car door. And we wonder why, in a lady's darkest hour, she runs to the barn.
When we fail her, her horse won't.
~Unknown

Trigger Warning:

This is an Omegaverse novel and contains all the triggers you might expect, plus a few more. This book is not recommended for anyone with triggers. Any trigger. Though there is a HEA ending, the road is quite long.

~Sharilyn

Prologue

After decades of uncertainty and strife, in 2072, the Great War finally happened. As the victor often writes history, no one knows what precipitated the warheads flying from continent to continent, but the truth is that they did. The entire west coast of the United States disappeared within minutes, as did choice targets on the eastern seaboard. The missile defense network saved parts of the country. Still, not all, and the areas not destroyed by bombs were altered forever by the fallout.

In retaliation, any place suspected of launching those warheads was turned to ash, glass, or rock, depending on its original landmass's makeup. The last order from the dying central government was to push every button on every missile silo in existence.

No victor was declared.

Afterward, the United States fell upon itself, ripping and tearing apart what remained. Factions split the remainder of the country into three areas containing a few hundred thousand residents each. The New North, New South, and Middle West's total population is estimated at less than two million souls.

Deep divisions within the military began the split, and civil war finalized it. The Army ruled the West, the Navy, the North, and the Marines the South. The Air Force as an entity did not survive the Great War, and remaining members chose which country they wanted to call home. Most of those individuals settled into post-military life without looking back. An uneasy peace followed.

It took decades to rebuild the power grids and a century for technology to begin to recover. Due to the atmosphere's damage, air travel was restricted to three thousand feet or less and limited to smaller shuttlecrafts or helicopters.

High walls separate the three new countries, and their cities are encapsulated by smaller, less ominous walls. They were an attempt to keep citizens safe from the wild things unleashed during this troubled time. Although life outside of the walls was viewed as impossible by those living within them, it does go on.

Everything changed.

Exposure to unknown agents caused a shift in the human genome. From a population comprised of what would become genetic Betas came Alphas and Omegas. The pre-war world had used the term Alpha Male like they knew what it was all about.

They did not.

Not that all alphas are male, and alpha females are known to be particularly vicious and wickedly smart. The rarest of all creatures is the Omega. Small of frame and gentle of spirit, they bear the burden of creating more Alphas and Omegas. Their bodies call specifically to the Alpha, providing something that is not only necessary for them but to all else who remain as well.

Fertility rates among all dynamics are abysmal. Still, enough are born to keep the wheels turning, even if just barely.

A huge help to Alpha and Omega alike, Betas keep the status quo, and everyone is grateful for that if nothing els

Chapter 1

Kill one damn Alpha male and one stupid Beta male, and that mess follows you forever. Lorelei sat at a table, glaring at the crowd and thinking about what bullshit it was that no one would dance with her.

Alphas and Omegas mixed and mingled on the dancefloor, in dark corners, and at tables loaded with food, trying to see if they would be a good fit.

NS304, signed into law by her best friend's mate, made it possible for the Omegas of The New South to have a choice in these matters, and she applauded that. Lukas, The Alpha with a capital T, capital A, was a decent enough fellow after Eve whipped him into shape by almost dying. But he was still an Alpha. His influence over other Alphas was unqualified, and he often spoke kindly to her in front of others. Still, none of this helped Lorelei. Not really.

Technically, it was two bodies, but in her defense, she thought, it was one incident. To her, the distinction is essential. Like having one bad day in a string of good days, she felt that killing those men was justified and that she shouldn't still be paying for it; yet, there she was. Alone.

Men and women moved about her like she was a rock in the middle of a river, and maybe she was. That's certainly what she felt like. After a few weeks of angry fallout from Alphas all over the New South, there had been relative peace. So far, things had gone well; no one wanted to challenge The Alpha on NS304, at least not yet.

A few of her sisters and brothers had already found someone to mate with and accepted the claiming mark that meant forever. Because once you got it on your body, wherever these lunkheaded alphas chose to place it, you were theirs. Not that they weren't yours, too, but the fact remained it was for life; she didn't really want that mark. The thin white scar on her neck notwithstanding.

The Alpha she allowed to see her through that fateful estrous had been killed before whatever magic that makes the bond permanent could solidify. The mark itself had healed wonderfully, leaving only a tiny scar. He barely broke her skin or drew blood. The feel of his teeth had set her off immediately. She had known what was coming as soon as his lips brushed her neck. Now, you couldn't even tell that teeth had made it.

In her fury over the placement of his teeth on her neck, she had torn him apart. Never piss off an Omega. What they lack in size and strength, they make up for in determination and fury. That Alpha hadn't seen it coming. The dead Beta was just an unhappy accident. Halfway through her estrous, she'd had no choice but to take him to her nest. She couldn't help that he wasn't up to the task. He'd died with a smile on his face if that counted for anything.

Eve and Lukas swayed to a slow song while those around gave them a wide berth and cautious glances. The Alpha was known to be overly protective of his mate, and no one wanted to push their luck. The gentle swell of her belly under a white dress proved their mating had been successful, and his constant purr calmed the wild emotions pregnancy brought. That purring would calm her Omega body, giving the baby the best chance of being born at term. Lorelei loved her sister, but she thought the whole thing was ridiculous.

If only she'd been born an Alpha female. Shaking her head, she sipped her tequila sunrise and smirked at her best friend until Lukas whipped his head around and glared at her. He couldn't help it, not really. Alphas are slaves to their biology as much as an Omega; no one doubted that. Well, Alphas doubted that, but those around them knew better.

She gave The Alpha a snarky look and blew him a kiss, raising her eyebrow in challenge to prove he didn't scare her. Maybe everyone else in this room, but not Lorelei.

She was Eve's second-best fighter in their small but capable Omega Force, which had been instrumental in bringing rebels in the Seventh district to heel. She had earned that place fair and square. She'd gone toe to toe with more Alphas than most, and

3

they didn't scare her. She could fight with the best of them. No, she wasn't a match for their size and strength, but she made up for it in speed and stealth, and she was a hell of a marksman. Markswoman. Whatever.

At the heart of it all, Alphas thought with their cocks, and a cock can be controlled. If the cock is controlled, the beast is controlled; it's that simple. The problem with Alphas is that their instincts demand they possess and claim an Omega. Omegas are no better in that they are blinded by estrous caused by lust four times a year. And hers was coming soon.

"Fuck," she said to herself, looking around the room at the available Alphas.

"I mean, I was just going to ask you to dance, but if you want to go straight to fucking, I'm okay with that." The voice whispering in her ear was deep Fifth district, making her wonder what a Georgia boy was doing in the capital. His strong southern accent told a truth about him that no amount of civilized clothing and proper enunciation could hide.

Although the states no longer existed, she had spent a lot of time in the district once known as Georgia. She and Eve had finished grad school there before returning to the Seventh to work.

Lorelei wrenched her head around to see who owned the hot breath, making her shiver as she cursed the nearness of her heat. If she wanted to stay single, she needed to hunker down soon or go sign up at the Omega House for a brief stint as one of their rentals.

"James," he said, offering his hand. "Jameson, actually, but I prefer James." Dark brown eyes, framed by thick black lashes, looked out from a strong face softened by a brush of red freckles across his light brown nose. "You know, like James Bond," he laughed.

"James Bond?" she laughed, tilting her head back so that her light blonde hair fell down her back. "More like Jimbo." She stopped, giving him a salty wink. "Jameson Beauregard Battle, age twenty-six, unmated. Seventh District's Chief of Cyberwarfare; it's nice to meet you." She grasped his hand in a firm handshake and gave him a knowing smile.

"Interesting," he chuckled. "I heard you were wicked smart. I didn't know you were a stalker too." One side of his thick lips quirked up in a smile, but his dark eyes narrowed as he spoke.

He leaned down, scenting the top of her head. The light caught the splash of freckles that played across his nose, making his skin look warm and inviting. His dark brown hair was cut in a way that the tousled mop of curls on the top faded to nothing down the sides. He smelled terrific, like most Alphas do, but instead of something woodsy, his scent was heavy with exotic spice. She liked it. That was the moment she figured out she was in trouble.

"I graduated near the top of my class," she whispered. "Plus, we received files on all the single Alpha males in the District. Eve made sure of it," she finished so quietly he had to strain to hear her.

Straightening her back, she leveled him with a look. Jameson, she liked that name better than James, as Jameson was also her favorite whiskey. Per his file, he was not a bad guy, not for an Alpha.

He was around seven feet tall, as most Alphas are, and built like a tank. Broad shoulders narrowed to a trim waist, and his tight black shirt did nothing to hide the thick Adonis belt that caught Lorelei's eye and kept it.

He was an Alpha, though, and she knew what that meant. She'd been on a few 'dates' since NS304 had gone into effect. Still, she wasn't interested in commitment, and Alphas wanted their Omegas firmly committed, despite legislation giving them a choice. No, she hadn't been raped like days past, but she'd definitely been pressured.

"I like smart women," Jameson said. "I like beautiful women, too; you're both. My eyes are up here, though, Lorel," he chuckled low and deep, almost purring.

The sound went straight to Lorelei's core, sending a trickle of slick into the pine tar and flower-filled thing she used to keep her Omega scent and flow of slick suppressed. It also skirted a subsection of NS304 that stated an Alpha cannot use purrs, growls, or his cum to incite an unclaimed Omega.

Who would have thought such a thing would happen?

Eve had. Eve had believed all along that Omegas could obtain some measure of choice in a land dominated by men who did not much care for it. And they had.

Their fight had lasted years, but once Eve had hooked Lukas Jennings, The Alpha of The New South, the fight had been quick, vicious, and over.

Now she sat at a table on the edge of a dancefloor, looking at one of the most beautiful men she had ever seen in her life, and realized she could say yes...or no. It was freeing.

Sipping her drink, she met nearly black eyes with her own. "I would love to dance, but my name is Lorelei," she said, rising slowly. She was taller than Eve, maybe even tall for an Omega. At around five feet even, she had to look down to see most of her friends, but she was nearly minuscule next to Jameson. The thought made her chuckle sweetly up at him; she never chuckled sweetly. It wasn't in her genetic makeup. What was the matter with her? Her thoughts were wild as she tried to get control of herself.

Narrowing her eyes and glancing at the table to ensure there were only two straws there, she shook her head at her girlishness. Due in about ten days, her estrous was far too near for her to have left her quarters. Her impending heat was making her stupid.

Lorelei took the hand he offered, following him to the dancefloor. During these events, there was a two-drink limit to minimize the risk of couples doing something ill-advised, like placing claiming marks on the dancefloor or knotting Omegas in the corners. Once rooted, the bond was unbreakable, and the rule made sense to ensure that step wasn't taken lightly or while wearing whiskey glasses.

The thing was, she and Eve, along with most of the Omegas from West Virginia, could down moonshine with the best of them. She didn't understand why her tequila sunrise was making her giddy. Maybe it was her nearing cycle. Or maybe it was the fact that her pregnant bestie was no longer sipping moonshine with her in secret.

Damnit, she needed better friends- or worse ones. She was slipping.

Jameson gathered her into his arms and spun her around the dancefloor to the DJ's beat. He was a good dancer; she liked that. Maybe she would hire him to serve her through this stupid estrous. He would have to agree not to place his claiming mark on her. That, or agree not to hold her liable when she ripped him apart if he did. It's all about compromise.

Smiling up into his face, she tried to count the cinnamon freckles that dotted his nose and cheeks. His brilliant white teeth flashed down at her as he maneuvered her through the crowd. The song changed, and he shifted, slowing his pace and matching time with the song perfectly.

"I was a dancer," he laughed, catching her puzzled look.

"You were a what?" she asked, her voice rising with incredulity.

"A dancer," he said, giving a firm nod of his head. His dark eyes gleamed with such mischief that she believed he was lying. "I'm not lying," he added, seeming to know her train of thought. "My mom was convinced, I mean convinced with a capital C, that I was going to be an Omega." His smile widened as most southern boys will when they talked about their mamas.

"I wasn't huge, like most Alpha babies. I didn't hit my growth spurt until later. My dynamic didn't reveal until I was in my teens, and she never got the blood test. She said she just knew that I would be her one Omega son. I had dance, piano, cooking, and sewing classes. I am the most well-rounded Alpha you will find; that's why you should pick me," he said with a wink. "I make a mean sweet potato casserole. Plus, with seven older Alpha brothers, I can take a lot of punishment and have a decent sense of humor, you know, for an Alpha."

She shook her head at his arrogance. But then, they were all arrogant. Funny that the twist of a gene could cause such differences in the dynamics. She smiled at him despite herself.

Maybe she could grow to like him; he certainly wasn't any worse than the rest, and maybe he was a little bit better. Most of the other Alphas she talked to spoke down to her, patronized her, and tried to push her into being claimed. Maybe his mama had done a thorough job with his home training. Not all Omega moms drank that particular Kool-Aid. That was a lot of maybes, but she had to make a choice sometime. With a sigh, she smiled up at him.

Chapter 2

He'd never seen anything more lovely. Perched on the edge of a chair and growling quietly at the surrounding couples, she lit the room. Her natural, light blonde hair contrasted with the dusted cinnamon shade of her skin, while deep eyes that were almost black glinted around the room. Lorelei Nash was a legend, and he couldn't believe she was sitting alone.

Jameson knew about the unfortunate incident with some backwoods Alpha from The Seventh, and he didn't care. Of course, she fucked a Beta to death. If she hadn't, he'd have been worried. Estrous is a powerful thing. Fighting that instinct would be like swimming upstream in the Chattahoochee when the water is running- it can't be done. He applauded her viciousness and wanted her to give birth to his children.

He watched as another Alpha brought her a drink. It was her second one, and she pulled the straw out, placing it on the table in front of her before dismissing the Alpha with a wave of her hand like he was a waiter.

Jameson's grin widened as the other man stomped off with a dark glare over his shoulder at the pretty little Omega. Lorelei knew he was beneath her and barely noticed.

Unable to keep the predatory stalk of his stride in check, Jameson approached her from behind. Moving into the slight breeze from large paddle fans that scattered the faint scent of her approaching estrous through the air, he breathed deep. She smelled like honeysuckle, sunshine, and whatever crap these wild Omegas used to hide their natural scent. It was delicious.

Would she dance with him? He didn't know. She was a wildcard. Since the Omegas from the Seventh moved into the Capitol building, he'd watched her. He'd hunted game all his life and knew that one had to know their prey to be successful.

Lukas warned him away from her, saying that Lorelei was too volatile and better left alone. It wasn't that The Alpha didn't like volatile women; he just didn't think Jameson was up to the task of keeping an Omega like Lorelei safe. Jameson knew better.

When she brought her dark eyes up to his, and he saw the little chill bumps that rose on her arm, he knew there was no future where she would not accept his claim. He'd bake cakes, casseroles, tap-dance, and write her sonnets if need be. He'd get his mama involved; no one could resist that woman. He knew the rules; he would dance around them, on them, and over them until she was his.

Her pupils were buried in the darkness of her eyes, but the faint outline showed them to be wider than they should be. He narrowed his eyes, wondering about that. Then the beat of the song changed, and he watched as she downed the last of her drink before stepping into his arms.

"Sweet potato casseroles?" she asked, her smile so wide it showed her sharp canines.

"Yes," he answered, his tone leaving no doubt that he was serious.

"Okay, I have a follow-up question," she said, her eyes narrowing to angry slits, and he knew that whatever she asked, it was crunch time.

"Shoot," he said. He slowed his steps and stared at Lorelei intently.

"Marshmallows or brown sugar?" Her voice had an edge of steel, and he knew that if he answered incorrectly, it was over.

"Brown sugar," he said firmly.

"Hmmm. Vinegar or tomato based?

"Duh, Vinegar," he answered, noting she hadn't slapped him and stormed away yet. He was winning.

"Fried or grilled?" she asked with a growl.

"Fucking fried, of course," he answered. "In bacon grease," he finished, feeling the slight trickle of sweat run down his back, worrying that maybe he shouldn't have gone for the bonus points.

"Country ham or pork loin?"

"I can't believe you even asked that one," Jameson responded with a huff, threatening to pull away from the little Omega.

"Boiled peanuts or dry roasted?" she asked with finality.

"I believe this conversation is over. There are two types of people, those who like boiled peanuts and those who are wrong," he said with a laugh, spinning her into the beat of a faster song.

She threw her head back, exposing the thin curve of her neck, then laughed so loud that others turned their heads. She muttered something under her breath that sounded like, 'maybe he isn't a bastard after all.'

It was his turn to smile; he had passed the first test.

She wobbled a little in his arms, and her eyes grew hazy. "I think I need a minute. It's sweltering in here." She stopped dancing and shook her head. "Don't run off; I want to talk about music next," she said, trailing her hand along his as she moved away towards the hall that led to the bathrooms with a soft smile on her face.

Oh God, Jameson thought; music was a tough one because he liked many genres.

He went to the bar to get a drink while he waited for Lorelei to return, not noticing that she was followed as she left.

Chapter 3

Something was wrong, Lorelei thought as she stumbled down the hall to the bathroom. She felt hot and dizzy. She was attracted to Jameson, sure, but slick was pooling in her cup and threatening to run over. She had more self-control than this. She had ten days before her estrous; this was not normal. Her estrous was like clockwork; it never came early.

Her head spun as she dashed toward the bathroom, feeling the beginnings of a cramp coil in her uterus. A vise closed around her arm, jerking her back into a wall of pure muscle. A palm clamped over her mouth, silencing her scream. Lorelei felt a hand rip the shirt out of her waistband, then grope her nipple in a hard pinch. Her mind wild, she kicked and scrambled to get away from the man behind her. The hand over her mouth held relentless pressure against her nose and mouth, not allowing her to breathe. Her dizziness intensified, and fear spiked madly.

Fighting harder, her chest heaved against the iron grip. She was shoved into the bathroom and heard the click of the lock. She looked into the mirror above the sink and did not recognize the Alpha that had her pinned. His green eyes met her brown ones, and the grin on his face took away and trace of what might have made him handsome.

"About time, Omega. You lasted longer than you should have; I'll give you that. The first drink should've had you running down the hall with your legs soaked." He sneered at her as he ripped the front of her pants open and jerked them down.

She struggled harder against him, but he had her hips pinned against the sink. Her breathing was fast and shallow, and she couldn't get enough air. She felt the cool temperature of the room wash against her hot sex, and she groaned.

"That's it. That's a girl. It'll be over soon. Don't fight it. Take my knot and my claim, and it will be fine, I promise. I've wanted you since I saw you; pretty little thing." One swipe of his fingers and her cup was gone, letting free the waterfall of slick it once held back.

"Goddamn, that pill works wonders. Brings on your heat and will make you accept me as your Alpha," he said, loosening his belt with one hand.

Lorelei fought harder, screaming from behind his fingers. She did not want this. Her body cramped, bringing a groan from her lips as her back bowed into him against her will. Tears fell hard and fast against the hold of his hand, and she shook her head as fast as she could, trying to dislodge it from her mouth. She tasted the blood from her lips; his grip was so tight.

She fought against the first push of his cock into her, screaming louder with each thrust, but with no air in her lungs, she couldn't make a sound.

"God, this is how it should be. The Omega Rule is bullshit. If an Alpha wants an Omega, they take it. God, yeah," he said, thrusting deep inside her. "Fuck, you feel good. Take my Alpha cock. You're mine now," he said, thrusting harder and harder into her. Her hipbones crashed into the sink, splitting the skin, and the sweet scent of Lorelei's blood scented the air.

In her mind, she started to let go. All their fighting, all their struggles, everything they had fought for, and here she was, getting rutted in a bathroom. This wouldn't have happened in the Seventh. Only that was a lie; she knew it had. It had happened to Eve, the sister of her heart. The Omegas hadn't won anything and never would.

"That's it, baby. Let go; accept it. It's natural," he said when he felt the struggle leave her. His thrusts became harsher and more rapid. Slick ran down her legs and coated the balls that slapped against her ass. Despite the slick and her cramps, this Alpha brought her no pleasure, no orgasm; he offered her nothing.

Lorelei felt him tighten and knew what was coming. She had never been knotted, had never allowed that. An alpha could serve her through estrous, but the knot was personal. She didn't want personal and never had. Bucking against him, she finally got out a loud scream from between his fingers.

The Alpha bent to her, clamping his teeth into her shoulder and shaking his head so that blood went flying, and her screams turned frantic. "It's too late now, baby, too late." He bit down hard, and she felt the knot begin to form.

All she could think was no, no, no.

A bellow of rage sounded from the hall, and the door ripped free of its hinges. Light from the hall caused a giant shadow to fall over the man fucking her, and she felt his hot cum splash across her back as he was ripped away before the knot could bind them. A second bellow joined the first, and she sank to the ground, sliding under the sink in fear.

Then the fear changed, and she felt that coil of that unknown Alpha's claim sinking into her. Her screams grew louder as she felt it snap into place. Voices and shouts raised in the air, but Lorelei could hear none of it. She clamped her hands over her ears.

"No! No! No!" Her screams echoed down the long hallway and out onto the dancefloor, where the music soon stopped.

The sounds of Alphas fighting were drowned out by her cries and the roar of fury echoing through her head. Fists on flesh and animal grunts did nothing to cover it. Blood splashed onto the floor at her feet, sending splatters up onto her face. It ran in rivulets down her cheeks, and her screams grew frantic.

"Stop!" The Alpha's voice rang, his command clear. The power The Alpha held forced the fighters to freeze.

Jameson's hands twitched, straining towards the other man despite Lukas's warning. A fierce growl sounded deep in his throat, causing The Alpha to cast an appraising eye over his computer guru. He had not known the other Alpha to be quite so strong; he hid it well.

The Alpha crouched low in front of Lorelei. "Did you consent?" he asked, softening his growl to a purr so she would feel safe in answering.

Try as she might, the words would not come out. Tears splashed from her cheeks onto the floor, and she shrank deeper under the sink.

"Lukas Alexander Jennings, move over," Eve said, slipping into the small space between her mate and her best friend. "Sweetie, answer him. It's okay; it'll be okay." Eve cradled the larger Omega, rocking her from side to side.

Lorelei shook her head rapidly, unable to say the words. Still, she brought her eyes to meet his as she did, dropping them when she caught sight of the two bloodied Alphas frozen behind him.

Jameson's growl intensified, and he strained forward. Lukas shut him down with a glare.

"Is the claim solidified?" The Alpha asked, forcing his voice to be calm and not filled with the rage he felt.

Lorelei let out a howl that chilled the room, and Jameson snapped free of The Alpha's command, pummeling the other man twice before Lukas could stop him.

"I will handle this. If he is to die, it will be by my hand, friend; otherwise, the same sentence will apply to you. Do you understand?" Lukas did growl now. Jameson's show of strength against The Alpha's command could be seen as a challenge. Under the circumstances, he would overlook it, but it ended now. Jameson stilled, but his low growl continued.

"By the provisions outlined in NS304, Xander Hollins, you are sentenced to death," The Alpha started, his voice booming into the silence of the rooms beyond. Eve rocked Lorelei faster, and the girl's wails quieted to strained silence. "I remind you all that it is unlawful to force, coerce, or blackmail an Omega into submission. It is punishable by death to claim an Omega without her full consent. That consent cannot be obtained unless the Omega is of a clear mind." Looking down at his mate, Lukas could see the sense of urgency in her eyes and wanted nothing more than to get her out of there.

Lorelei felt the claim growing close to her heart, and her howl rent the air. Rubbing her chest against it, she started screaming again. Jameson pushed through The Alpha's will and sank next to her, ripping Lorelei away from Eve. He began to purr to her, his chest rumbling, and she calmed. He wasn't her Alpha, though. It wasn't he who could help her now.

"You would kill me and force this Omega to suffer, Alpha?" Xander snarled at Lukas, his expression haughty; he knew the worth of these Omegas. He was banking on it.

He'd thought that The Alpha wouldn't actually follow through on his threats to enforce NS304. How could he? Lorelei was ruined now. Mated to him, she couldn't have another. She would suffer without him; she was suffering now. The Alpha needed to be brought to heel on this matter. There was no room in the Alpha-Omega relationship for legislation.

"Lorelei," The Alpha said, calling her tear-stained face to his. "Do you want this bond? You must answer."

"No!" she yelled, shrinking into Jameson but clutching Eve.

"Then it can be broken." Lukas turned to Xander and, in one swift movement, snapped his neck. The man sank to his knees, then onto his side, his dead eyes staring at Lorelei in accusation.

Only the claim didn't break. Lorelei felt the cord of it thrashing around in her chest like a live wire. It snapped and popped, making her cry out and clutch at her shirt, trying to rip it off. The cramps started again, and her cries of frustration could be heard by all.

"Jameson," The Alpha spoke, and Jameson rose with Lorelei in his arms. Their eyes met over the thrashing Omega held firmly in his grasp. Their faces grim, Jameson nodded once and carried Lorelei away.

Frantically, Eve jumped up, grasping at her friend. "Give her to me," she said. "I can get her through this, Lukas!" she shouted, trying to pull Lorelei from the much taller man's grasp.

"Settle, mate," Lukas said, trying to calm her. "You can't help her. Only an Alpha stronger than Xander can stop the bond from taking hold; let him try. The alternative is to allow the strongest Alphas to fight for the right to do it, and that is not going to happen. It's the only way, EJ."

Eve's growl deepened, and she struck at Jameson to try to get to her friend. "Lorelei managed just fine when the last asshole tried to bite her; let her go," she demanded. "She doesn't want this!"

"According to the report, Lorelei killed that Alpha before his teeth fully broke her skin, Eve. It makes a difference. The bonding magic didn't happen then. It's happening now," Lukas gathered his struggling wife in his arms and purred loudly, pulling at the long strands of her red hair to settle her. Though she was mostly beyond the danger pregnancy in an Omega presented, he didn't want to take any chances. She went limp in his arms. "Give your friend a chance at something over a life of nothing, or worse, death. It's all you can do. The longer he waits, the harder it will be," he whispered to her. "This gathering is over," The Alpha boomed so he could be heard. "All further gatherings are suspended until an investigation can be completed." Stepping over the dead Alpha, Lukas carried Eve away.

Chapter 4

Jameson hurried Lorelei out of the building and into his truck, noting the lingering males' heated looks. He didn't live far from the capital and could have easily walked, but if he was honest, he had hoped the night would end with her at his side. But not like this. God, not like this. He'd taken the truck so that she wouldn't be exposed to danger if she had decided to go with him to his house on the outskirts of town. Despite everything, the city streets could still be dangerous.

He pushed back the seat of the pre-war beast and slid into it. The old diesel engine started with a clatter, then hummed loudly as he adjusted her on his lap. She had fallen silent and curled into a tiny ball around herself. Her body trembled, and the scent of another alpha's cum and estrous gone wrong filled the air. What had that motherfucker done to her?

He felt the hair on his body rise in anger. He never should have let her go down that hall alone. He should have recognized that something wasn't right; he could see it in the way her eyes glazed over.

The Omegas from the Seventh could pound alcohol- all of them. For God's sake, they drank jet fuel and called it moonshine. They were an urban legend in town. He should have known. But they had demanded freedom, and he thought he was being enlightened by giving her space. He had fucked that one up.

Guilt chewed away at him as he jammed the truck into gear and threw black smoke as he made a U-turn out of town. Now what? She was going to fucking hate him for what he had to do.

He'd known from the jump that she was going to be a tough nut to crack. From what he knew, she hadn't had much interest in the Alphas of the capital, choosing instead to spend her time with friends. She wouldn't want any of this, but what choice did he have? What choice did any of them have? She wouldn't want to be tied to that son-of-a-bitch forever.

Fuck. He pounded his steering wheel in frustration and felt the plastic give. The little thing on his lap gave a startled cry, and he issued a broken purr for her. The purr grew steady, and they both calmed.

It would be okay; somehow, it would be okay.

He slammed the truck into first gear in his drive and set the parking brake before clutching her to him and lifting her out. Holding the silent Omega in one arm, he unlocked the door to the little bungalow he called home. He didn't flip on the lights as he walked through the small sitting room to the stairs. They creaked with his weight as he took them slowly, not wanting to jostle Lorelei more than necessary.

The house was hundreds of years old and had withstood the test of time. The war had not been kind to the old place, but he had restored it, loving the grace and beauty in the old girl's bones. Dim light shone through original stained glass as he made the turn on the landing to the second floor.

Lorelei's face was tucked into her chest, but he wished he could see it all the same. The master was on the second floor, and Jameson had taken several of the smaller rooms to make it larger. A decent-sized master bath adjoined the bedroom, and that is where he took her.

Jameson turned the water on hot without setting her down and eased his clothes off one-handed around her. Carefully, he stripped her before stepping under the hot spray. Jameson didn't have all night; he knew that. The bond would solidify, and he had a better chance of breaking it before it did. He wanted her to accept him. He wanted her to understand, but he also wanted the scent of that fucker off her.

A tiled bench ran the width of the shower, and he placed her on it, unfolding her stiff limbs so that the water could reach her. He dumped half a bottle of his shampoo into her hair and gently soaped it. Having never done this before, he didn't know how much to use, but she had a lot of hair, so he figured more was better. The suds took over, and he realized his mistake, but he washed her body free of the blood and gore of the night using the extra.

She was exquisite, and he felt his cock respond. The gentle curve of her breast slid under his palms, and the soft planes of her stomach ignited a fire in him he didn't want to put out, circumstances be damned. He'd wanted her before, and he wanted her still.

She said nothing, just stared straight ahead; her unseeing eyes didn't meet his. Not even when he slid his fingers between her delicate folds did she respond. Slick dripped steadily around them as he washed the last traces of Xander away.

"Lorelei," he purred at her, trying to draw her eye. "It's the only way. I don't want to hurt you, but I won't allow you to be tied to him forever. It's not fair to you. I know none of this is fair," he added when a growl started deep in her chest. "But you liked me earlier. We clicked. I made you smile and laugh, even if only for a little while. We could have had something; we could have. We still can. Please, just try to understand. Please," he begged.

Unable to look at her face, he pulled her to her feet, turned her around, and entered her from behind. He sank into her depths in one stroke, feeling the surge of hot slick surround him. He groaned at the tight feel of her.

She howled at his intrusion and began to fight him. He held her with one arm and eased deeper into her. He would do it because it had to be done, but he wouldn't hurt her if he could help it.

Her tight walls clenched around him, and his purr turned to a growl, causing more slick to flow. Her back came up, and she pushed against him, unable to fight the feeling of his body in hers.

Her fist pounded on the walls, and her cries echoed through the small space, and he knew he needed this first time to be quick. He didn't want her to hurt herself fighting him, and until he broke Xander's claim and placed his own, things were tricky.

Reaching down, he thrummed across her hard nub, sending an unwanted spasm through her. He sank to the hilt, her body taking his cock as it should.

He pressed her core until she cried out her orgasm and gripped him like a vise. Unable to help himself, he sped up. Her back arched, and she angled her hips so that his tip edged past her cervix. He hit that spot once, and she growled, pushing against him to take more and more of it. Using the wall of the shower, she pounded onto his cock harder and harder until a second, deeper orgasm shook her body. He used her hair to pull her to him, and when her walls clamped tight, he pushed his growing knot deeper and bathed her with his cum, his knot exploding into her. At that moment, he lined up and bit savagely into her flesh, eradicating the other man's mark.

She fought him for real, then. She bucked and screamed and tried to free herself from the grip of his teeth. Jameson would not be moved. With his knot and his teeth buried deep in her, he pulled her onto his lap on the bench. Tugging at the strands of her hair, he purred until she stopped fighting him and went limp.

He had never knotted an Omega. He didn't know exactly how long that tie would bind them together. He'd fucked plenty of Omegas at the Omega House in town, but he'd never knotted one. To him, that knot was just as much of a bond as the claiming bite was. He rocked her against him, feeling the shallow, rapid rise and fall of her ribs. He could feel their tie. It wasn't strong yet, but it would be. After a long night, it would be. He'd make sure of that.

When the water ran cold, the knot abated, and a combination of their fluids rushed out of her. Rising with her in his grip, he opened the door, grabbed a towel, and walked to the bed. The smell of them together had his cock rising again.

"I don't want this," she whispered, not meeting his eyes.

"What would you rather I do? Do you want to live an empty life with a dead man's claim on you? Worse yet, do you want to die?"

"Kill me," she said. "Please, just kill me." Her eyes finally found his. They were so black that no pupil showed. Round and wild, her eyes held his. "I can't do this," she finished.

"I won't kill you, Lorelei; you're mine now. Just as I am yours. I won't do it. I would never have done it, no matter what."

She screamed into his face, letting all her fury bleed onto him. Pushing her back, Jameson held her down with one hand and buried his tongue in her sex until her cries of rage changed. Slick oozed from her as the cramps from induced estrous hit her again.

Jameson ate it up like a man starving, flicking his tongue along her seam and around to her hardened clit. With his tongue, he forced another orgasm from her; her body shaking and limp when he finished.

Belly full of her pleasure, he slid up her body and entered her again. This time, he wasn't gentle. No, not this time. Gripping her leg under his arm, he slid in, making her feel every contour of him. Eyes closed, she cried out. She needed this; needed him. He was her Alpha now, and he would give her what she needed.

Plunging his cock straight to that spot, he pulled another orgasm from her, her walls tightening around him, trying to milk his own orgasm free, but he wasn't going to be quick. He slid his hand to her throat and his lips to hers while grinding his hips into her. She moaned, arching into him.

He teased her lips apart with his tongue, loving the way her hot mouth felt. Moving his grip from the front of her neck to the back, he massaged until she opened for him. He kissed her, even though she didn't kiss him back. He swept his tongue across her lips; she tasted like heaven. She would accept him. In time, she would.

The bond was designed to make them both happy; she just needed to accept it.

He rose on both arms, enjoying the view below. Her long, blonde hair played across the midnight blue of his sheets. Her big eyes were closed, and long lashes lay across her cheeks. He refused to regret a single event that had brought her to this moment. Yeah, it could've happened differently, but it happened. She was his now. With a groan, he arched into her. Her body responded, tilting to accommodate him. Unable to take another minute, he hit that spot until she clenched around him again, only this time he gave her his knot and his seed.

She was perfection. She would come to understand that. As the last stream of cum left him, he sank his teeth into her again and felt his claim grow as the other weakened.

Chapter 5

When his teeth sank into her, Lorelei couldn't believe it. All her life, she had fought against this. Now she had been claimed by two Alphas on the same night. The feel of his knot behind her pubic bone should have been unbearable, but it wasn't. The rounded apex of her uterus was filled with his seed and stretched pleasantly by his body. She hated every second of it. She lay limp and unmoving under his weight, closing her eyes to feign sleep.

She had to get out of here. She'd go back to West Virginia and live in one of the thousands of abandoned hollows. No one would ever find her. Or, she'd jump off that damn rock Eve had fallen from. With no one around to save her, she'd die, and this could end. She just wanted it to end.

The cramps hit again, and the need caused by whatever poison that man fed her struck. She hadn't known there was anything that could induce estrous. If she had, she would have been more careful. How could this have happened under The Alpha's nose? Under all their noses?

Another cramp hit, and she groaned, pain racing through her like wildfire. Jameson responded, his lips finding hers. He wasn't a bad Alpha; he wasn't. Maybe he really believed that shit about this being the only way, but she hated him for what he'd done to her.

Nothing could fix this.

Her back arched, and he slid his hot mouth to her breast, pulling her nipple gently. He didn't gnaw on it like most men did, and she appreciated that. His rough tongue licked over her peak, causing her to cramp more and whimper into his neck. His body was the only thing that would ease this, but she refused to kiss him. Refused.

He could force his knot and inflict his bite, but he could not make her kiss him. He slid to the other nipple, licking and teasing until slick puddled under her, and she begged for him. Opening her legs wide, she rubbed herself against his length, seeking relief.

He brought one hand down, slipping two fingers in and letting his thumb trail over her clit. She rode it, needing release. Had everything been different, she would have enjoyed having him serve her through an estrous, but not like this. He didn't tease her. He gave her what she needed when she asked for it. The minute her pain started, he eased it. It could've been perfect.

God, it could've been perfect.

She rode his hand and thumb until her orgasm blinded her. She clenched his fingers, trying to pull them deeper, needing to feel that knot. She needed that. How could she not have known? Had she known what that felt like, she never would have refused one. But the knot was a bond, wasn't it? She thought, furiously fighting the pleasure Jameson gave her.

His cock entered her one glorious inch at a time. All Alphas had big cocks, but Jameson's was huge and veined. It had a broad head, and the ridge of it was thicker than any she'd ever felt. The feel of it sliding in caused her walls to clench and slick to flow.

He hit the edge of her womb, and sparks flew behind her eyes; she groaned until it changed to a demanding growl. She needed him to give her more, and she snapped her teeth in irritation, trying to slam herself onto his cock for relief. Jameson brought his hand to her throat again and tightened it just enough. Pleasure coursed through her, and the fire leaped to new heights.

Her closed eyes rolled back in her head, and she came on his thick cock again. Bucking and writhing, she tried to force his own orgasm; she wanted that glorious knot. She needed it. Her walls clenched around him and tried to pull him into her core, tried to squeeze the seed from him.

He slid his heavy cock out, and her eyes sprang open, meeting his for the first time. One long strand of cum shot from him, and he rubbed it into her skin with one hand while clutching his cock in the other to stop his orgasm. He brought his cum streaked fingers to her lips. She sucked them hard, holding his eyes until she couldn't help but let hers roll back. Alpha cum was terrific, but this Alpha's cum was better.

Lorelei felt him tease her lips with his cock, and she opened. She needed him in her. The bond between them was settling, making her need all of him even more. Gripping his ass cheeks, she pulled him to her, roughly forcing his cock down her throat until he gave a surprised yelp, but she didn't care.

She slid her mouth up and down his cock and took him to the hilt. Omegas don't have a gag reflex; slobber coated his shaft, and it eased all the way in. She tilted her head so that it was comfortable, and mouth fucked him until he filled her belly with his seed, coming with a roar and gripping her hair hard. She grabbed his knot and squeezed it over and over again, forcing him to give her everything he had.

When his cum hit her belly, the last of the old claim faded, and Jameson's snapped into place. She hadn't known that would happen, but then she'd spent so long avoiding it. How could she? Tears fell hot and fast as she struggled away from his hard grip.

Unrelenting, he held her, his purr low and deep like an Alpha's should be. He tugged at her hair and massaged her skin until she was calm. The bond between them hummed; his side sure and hers angry, but it hummed all the same.

"Shhh, baby girl. I've got you; it's okay," he said. "I've got you." Wrapping her in his arms, he purred until she could feel only calm. Hating every second of it, she closed her eyes and drifted off.

She awoke a short time later. Jameson sat on the edge of the bed, watching her. Moonlight streamed through the windows, dancing off the glorious planes of his chest. His muscles danced and twitched, and that Adonis belt she had admired at the beginning of the night snagged her eyes again. She tried to turn away from his stare, but he snagged her, pulling her to him. "Drink," he said, wrestling her into position and bringing a cup to her lips.

She drank from the cup he held until it was empty. He set it down and brought a piece of cheese to her lips. "I don't want to eat," she said, trying to pull away.

"Do it anyway," he said, his voice gruff with emotion.

"I don't want any of this," she answered, pushing against the wall of muscle that held her to no avail.

"I understand that, but here we are. Take a bite."

"A bite is what got me into this mess," she whispered, drawing an angry growl from Jameson.

"A man raped you, then forced his claim on you, Lorelei. The Alpha killed that man, but the claim remained. It would have taken root. Does my bond feel no better than his?" he asked, his dark eyes sad.

Jameson's bond wasn't slimy and sick like Xander's. That much was true. She just hadn't wanted either of them.

"Maybe we could have had something, but we never will now, Jameson. I didn't get to choose. Maybe I would've chosen you, maybe not. But I didn't get to make that choice. I was wrong;

you're no better." She tried to get out of his arms, but he held tight. With a sigh, he turned her until she was under him.

"You would rape me too?" she asked, tears threatening again.

"I will do what it takes to get you to accept me and accept the bond, Lorel."

"Only my friends call me Lorel, Jameson. You're not my friend."

"I may not be your friend, but I am your bonded mate, and you need to accept that," he growled in her ear, and the mate bond and her body betrayed her, causing slick to flow for him. Then he was inside her again, pushing his cock to her core and making her body cry out.

He is your mate, the bond said. His body is magnificent, and look at how he serves you, it said again. The mate bond demanded to be heard, telling her over and over again that it would be okay if she just let it.

She lay unmoving beneath him as he kissed along her jawline and across her lips. His hands found her breast, and he gripped one, pulling his tongue across her taut nipple. He licked her breasts, then back to her neck again, finding her earlobe with his teeth. Her legs lay open, but she didn't move for him, not at all.

The bond in her chest chastised her for ignoring the beauty of the man above her. It railed at her for not accepting his strength, generosity, and prowess; he was her mate now, and it screamed at her to accept him, but she couldn't. He had saved her; she knew that. She didn't care. She hadn't wanted to be saved.

He tilted his hips and took her deeper, patiently drawing pleasure from her. Rising up, his thumb flicked across her core as the head of him breached the space behind her cervix. She cried out, the bond singing with happiness as she started to clench around him. She brought her hands up, placing them on his ass, but kept her eyes closed. She couldn't look at him.

"Open your eyes, wife," he growled. "Look at your mate when he is pleasing you."

"I am not your wife," she snarled.

"You are," he growled, making more slick come.

"You can't take a wife," she said, opening her eyes to glare at him.

"It doesn't matter how you got here; you're mine now. Look between us. Look!" Jameson shouted when she refused.

She jumped, and her eyes slid to where his cock was buried in her.

"This pussy is mine," he growled lower, making her back arch with need. "But that cock is yours too, mate; only yours. There can be no one else. How we got here is irrelevant; accept it and accept me."

"No. I'll fuck the first Alpha I find to get you out of me," she snarled, bringing her eyes to his and feeling their bond cry out in anguish.

He delved deeper, teasing the orgasm from her with his thumb. She felt her resolve crumble, and her walls tighten around him. He wasn't gentle, not like before. He had a point to prove. There would be no other Alphas for her; she knew that. Her body would respond to no other. She would sing for him and only him.

He growled and purred, plunging into her. He made her come even though tears ran down her face; he made her cry out his name and beg for his knot, but he wouldn't give it. Over and over, he made her come until she was limp underneath him.

Finally, he pulled out, jerking his cock until he covered her in his cum, then he rubbed it into her skin until all she felt was him, and all she smelled was him. She missed his knot and felt cheated without it. She felt empty. He rolled off her, grabbed his shirt, and stalked to the bathroom, slamming the door behind him.

Snagging the sheets, she pulled them to her chin and curled up, sobbing. The cord between them felt sad; it vibrated and wiggled in her chest to the point of discomfort. The shower ran for a long time, and when Jameson showed no signs of leaving the bathroom, she got up, walked to his closet, pulled out a T-shirt, and tugged it over her head and down past her thighs.

She could leave; she knew that. She could run. They'd never find her in West Virginia, and even if Eve could, she wouldn't. She'd let Lorelei make this choice if no other. Padding to the door, Lorelei opened it, taking in the house beyond.

Beautiful stained-glass windows dotted the second floor, and open doors down the hall beckoned. Slowly, she explored. It was a lovely house, not giant but not small either. Two other bedrooms and a full bathroom were down the stained walnut hall. Doorframes and crown moldings matched the hardwood floors and gleamed with loving care.

Trailing her hand on the banister, she went downstairs. The kitchen was modern, and stainless steel shone. She walked around, opening doors and looking into rooms before deciding that the house wasn't just nice- it was gorgeous. Well maintained and clean, it was nicer than anything she had lived in growing up. Her ratty single-wide in Wade's Run had been falling apart. She'd stayed with Eve after they met, her parents not really caring where she went. The care taken with this place showed what kind of man Jameson was.

Saddened by the fact that they hadn't had a chance, she slipped out the wide French doors and into the backyard. A bubbling Koi pond glimmered in the light of a fall moon. It was surrounded by a padded bench and brightly painted Adirondack chairs. Fall blooms lay sleeping in the dark, even though the night sky was lit with stars. A white picket fence surrounded the backyard, and beyond the flowers lay a manicured lawn.

There was money here. Lorelei could see that, but there was also love. She slipped into a yellow chair and pulled her knees to her chest, covering them with the shirt against the fall chill.

"This house was my grandmother's," Jameson said from behind her.

"It's beautiful," she said without looking back at him. She stared into the pond, catching glimpses of large orange and white fish as they swam.

"Coffee?" he asked, handing her a mug. Wordlessly, she took it, clutching it to her chest. "Its been in my family since it was built in nineteen-twenty," he continued. "After the war, it was a mess and was pretty much abandoned. I grew up near Taylors on a big farm; my mother had no interest in this place. But with my military contract and stuff, it was just easier to live here, and I actually love the old house. I did most of the remodeling myself."

"It shows the house is lovely," Lorelei said, still not looking at her Alpha. Sipping coffee, she let a long sigh leave her. "What now?"

The sun began painting the horizon, and she made out a firepit surrounded by camp chairs. There was a large enough empty space to the right where a pool would fit. She's always wanted her own pool. While post-war luxuries could be hard to find, they weren't impossible.

"Do you want to go for a ride?" he asked quietly, looking at his hands.

"I have no clothes," Lorelei answered.

"I washed yours from last night."

"I never want to see them again," she countered.

"Then let's get new ones," he tried.

"I can't do this," she said, taking a big drink of the marvelous dark roast.

"Lorelei," he said, coming to her chair and planting himself between her legs.

"Are you going to rape me again to shut me up?" she asked, turning her sad eyes to his. "Because I said I can't do this?"

"Just try Lorelei. Please, just try." His fingers found her clit and made her back arch.

"So, every time I say I can't do this, you're just going to make me come?" she asked.

"I told you I'll do what it takes to get you to accept me. I'm not a bad guy, Lorelei. You could've done a lot worse. I just want you to accept me. This," he said, tapping his chest. "This hurts; I don't like it. I want you to be happy because my happiness is tied to yours, and I'm a happy guy." He tried to make it come out light and funny, but it ended with a sob.

"Please let me go. Let me leave here and never come back," Lorelei said as Jameson slipped two fingers in and thrummed her clit to a climax. Clenching around him, she cried out, making the neighbor's curtains shutter closed.

"I can't do that," he whispered, purring as her body trembled from the aftershocks.

"Why not? You don't know me. I mean nothing to you."

"You're everything to me now, Lorelei. Everything. When you accept the bond, you'll see that." He crushed his mouth to hers, and she fought to get away from him. Lifting his tee-shirt from her legs, he unbuttoned his jeans and slid his cock all the way home.

He held her tightly as he moved inside her. Slow thrusts and deep groans covered the sound of the bubbling pond and happy birds. He clung to her, pulling her against him as he split her down the middle. The false estrous had worn off, but they were bonded now, and her slick responded to him, easing his violation of her.

He was tender in his caress and kind in his touch, but he demanded too much. She couldn't accept him; she couldn't accept this. She had fought for choice only to have hers taken. As he made love to her, begging her with his body to accept him, she thought she never could. He could make her cry out his name and clench his thick cock into her core, but he couldn't make her accept him.

"I need a shower," she said when he was done.

"No," he said simply, pulling her to his chest. "You need to smell like me."

"How could I not smell like you? Even after a shower, I will smell like you," she argued. "I'm not pregnant if that's your goal," Lorelei said, trying to push away from him. He hadn't given her his knot again, and it bothered her. She couldn't figure out why, but it did, and a tiny part of her hated herself for it.

"I know. That's not my goal, actually. You won't accept my seed until you accept me," Jameson said, sighing long and deep.

"Plenty of raped Omegas get pregnant," she taunted, her voice sharper than she intended.

"I'm not," he started forcefully, only to pause and soften his voice. "I haven't raped you, Lorel. You never said no."

She gave him an incredulous stare. "I haven't said no?"

"No."

"I've fought you, screamed at you, tried to escape you, but because I didn't say the word, then it's okay?" heavy tears formed on her lashes. "I can't believe this. I said no from the very beginning. I said I didn't want this. Me not spelling out N O is just some Alpha excuses bullshit. Let me go," she screamed, jumping from Jameson's lap. She turned and slapped him with every ounce of her fury before shoving him hard and sending him stumbling backward.

The pain in Lorelei's chest flared as she raced through the doors, up the stairs, and slammed the bedroom door. She turned the shower on as hot as it would go, locking the door while it heated.

Scrubbing herself until her skin was raw, she cried under the hot torrent of water until it went cold. But she was better than this. She was a warrior. She had fought off dozens of men in life, and in war, this was no different. She only needed to get away.

Chapter 6

Jameson listened to Lorelei cry from behind the locked bathroom door. It gutted him. He'd known this was the hard road; it would have been easier to let her go and try to find another Omega that suited him. But she was perfect; he knew that. Their personalities gelled, and he liked her spunk. Yeah, she was gorgeous, but beauty was one thing and compatibility another. It crushed him to do this to her.

The bond another Alpha places on an Omega is almost impossible to break. He was a much stronger Alpha than the dead man, but even now that his bond with her had taken root, he could feel Xander and would until Lorelei accepted him.

He wasn't asking her to place her own delicate claiming mark on him. He had hoped for it before this, but now he just wanted her not to hate him. Maybe he had fucked this up.

The first time Jameson looked into the deep pool of her eyes, he'd known they could be something. He'd longed for the type of relationship he envisioned with her. She was the one for him, and he could've been the one for her; he knew that in his soul. Then fucking Xander ruined it. He hadn't ruined Lorelei, no, not to Jameson. He had taken away his chance, though, and now he was left with an unhappy, volatile, crying, and possibly suicidal Omega mate.

He didn't want to break Lorelei, but he'd do what it took to get her through to the other side of this. Plenty of Omegas started off in worse situations, and it had ended well. He was going to ensure that happened this time too.

Knowing he needed to call out the big guns, he picked up his ComLink and dialed.

When Lorelei exited the bathroom, she found Jameson on the bed's edge with his hands in his lap. Wearing only a towel, she went to his closet and took out another shirt. This one was black and came to her knee. Using the belt she'd worn the night before, she made a dress of it. Jameson thought she looked adorable and that the black made her light hair pop against her dark eyes and lighter skin.

"Hey," he said, not rising from the bed.

"Hey," she answered, her face more relaxed than when she'd run from him. It was blank, though, and he hated that the fun-loving girl filled with laughter from the night before was gone. Her eyes were puffy and red, telling the tale of her emotions.

"Do you want to go for a ride? Maybe get out a little bit?" he asked, staying seated so that he didn't tower over her.

She sighed, her chest rising and falling heavily. With her eyebrows scrunched together, she surveyed the room. After hanging up the link, Jameson had changed the sheets on the bed, straightened up, and placed a laundry basket full of nesting material on the floor. Her eyes snagged on it before coming back to Jameson.

"Okay, I guess," she replied, moving to the door and sidestepping the bundle neatly.

Jameson waited until she was through to stand; he was trying to be less intimidating and softer. He knew how to dance, damnit. This was the most important dance of his life; he could do this.

She waited at the bottom of the stairs for him, looking small and lost. When he came to the landing, her face tilted up, melting his heart with its sadness.

He opened the door for her, locking it behind them. His truck sat waiting, and he unlocked it before lifting her up into the cab. Once upon a time, the truck had been lifted. It ran on oversized tires, and the running board would be a huge step up for her. She would struggle to get into it.

He slid in beside her, trying not to notice the speed at which she moved away from him, but the seatbelt on the passenger side was broken, so she was forced to slide back to buckle up. She pretended she hadn't meant to escape him, and he pretended not to notice. Shoving the truck into gear, Jameson backed out of the driveway and eased onto the street.

Some of the roadways were impassable, but most of those in and around Greenville were well maintained. Heading out of town, Jameson stopped at a strip mall that contained the shops they would need. Picking Lorelei up, he sat her feet on the ground. She left out an aggravated huff but did not complain. They walked towards the drugstore, and Lorelei slowed her steps, glancing around.

"Get what you need," Jameson said. "You know, toothbrush, toothpaste, makeup, whatever you want."

"I have money," she started. "Just not with me."

"I want to take care of you, Lorelei. I know you already have stuff. Eve is boxing everything up and will bring it over one night soon. She's demanding to see you anyway." Jameson smiled at that, his stern face cracking. Lukas Jennings had his hands full with that one; he didn't envy him in the slightest.

"I bet she is," Lorelei answered, giving a small smile of her own. Warm fall sunlight brought out the shine in her hair, making it gleam like platinum. "She's probably furious. I should call her."

"Once we get service, you can use my ComLink; this is a dead zone. It'll get better on the road." Jameson dropped his hand on Lorelei's head, thinking she looked better now that they were out. She'd lost a little of the haunted look in her eyes. "After you get stuff in here, we'll run into the other stores for clothes. Just for now," he added when he saw her shoulders slump. "Eve can bring the rest when we get back."

"Get back?" she asked, startled. "Where are we going, and how long are we going to be gone?"

"It's a surprise."

"I don't like surprises," she huffed, pulling away from his light touch.

"Somehow, I don't believe that," Jameson laughed and followed her into the store.

She picked out what she wanted, and he didn't complain. He didn't think she needed war paint, but she bought it anyway. She picked out lipstick colors he liked and added hair stuff and various items to the basket he carried. He hated that she bought her own soap because he wanted her to smell like him, but he understood. Softer, gentler, kinder; he could do this. If he could knit proper doilies, he could do this, and he knitted a mean doily.

In the clothing stores, she kept it simple, piling basic jeans and tees on the counter. The Alpha liked his mate to dress in oversized, shapeless sacks, but Jameson wasn't bothered by the form-fitting Beta outfits. She liked them, and he wasn't intimidated by it, so they worked. Whatever she wanted worked for him. Feeling hopeful for the first time since the party, he grabbed a pair of square-toed cowgirl boots to replace her dress shoes. She would need them. She looked askance at him when he added them to the pile, but said nothing.

"I appreciate that you're trying," Jameson started. "I see you, Lorelei; I do." They had left the stores and walked toward his truck when the need to say something overcame him.

"I don't have a choice, do I, Jameson? You took that away." Her shoulders slumped, and he wished he'd kept his mouth shut. He'd only wanted to acknowledge her effort. "I can run," she continued. "And maybe I will; I haven't decided," she said, and he knew she was speaking honestly. "But none of that changes today. I didn't want this. You're right; maybe we could have had something. I just don't see it now. Whatever it was is gone."

Jameson stopped just shy of his truck, leaving her to walk on without him. She could leave him; he knew that. He doubted he could keep her if she didn't want to stay. He'd seen her fight. Well, that was a lie. He'd seen their path of destruction and not much of them in action, but what he had seen was terrifying. The Omega Force moved like fog on a fall morning. Not one Marine had seen an entire Omega battle; they were almost mystical. All smoke, mirrors, and wildfires, they had crushed their enemy, mainly before the Marines could get a foothold in the territory. It was incredible.

He watched the tiny thing jump to reach his door handle; he'd have to put a lower running board or always be there to lift her in. He didn't think she'd appreciate that last option. She was independent and quietly fierce, not overtly dangerous like her sister, Eve, but dangerous nonetheless.

What would he do if she left him? Neither one of them would ever be satisfied by another; that was part of the bond. She could follow through on her threat and fuck any alpha she wanted, but it wouldn't satisfy her estrous. Eventually, she'd die the way that Eve had been willing to.

He watched her scrabble into the cab of his truck and slam the door. She didn't look over at him, just sat there staring straight ahead. He'd win this war; he had to. For him, a broken mating bond meant that he could never find satisfaction with another.

Jameson probably wouldn't die, but he would lead a lonely, miserable life. He could do that if he had to, but he wouldn't let her kill herself over this. He just couldn't. He'd wanted her from the beginning, and this twist of fate changed nothing. She was his mate, and the bond drove him to care for her. Jameson would fix this, he thought, resuming his walk to the truck, or die trying.

Chapter 7

Lorelei watched the scenery change as the truck headed out of town. She'd sat as far away from Jameson as she could get, not caring that the seatbelt didn't work. He'd slowed down about twenty miles per hour on average and begun taking the curves more slowly once she'd refused to sit next to him and buckle up.

She knew he was trying. Jameson was fighting the instinct to club her over the head and drag her into his cave by her hair. She knew that, too. It's not that Lorelei didn't appreciate it; she just couldn't care. Suburban townhomes changed to houses and wooded lots to farmland as she wondered where they were heading.

They said nothing, and she marveled at his restraint. The bond must be screaming at him to fix it, to fix her. She felt the pops and rattles in her chest the bond caused, like taking West Virginia potholes at high speed.

Sighing, she glanced at him from under her lashes; he was gorgeous. His unruly mop of hair disheveled, and his usually clean-shaven face covered in dark scruff. He really was beautiful. His sweet freckles and spicy scent were intoxicating.

He hadn't been unkind either; she knew that too. Still, he hadn't let her face her fate the way she'd wanted. He'd stolen another Alpha's claim and made it his own. Had it saved her life?

Probably in the short term, but the jury was out on what her future held.

The truck began to climb, and the trees grew thicker as they headed into the Blue Ridge Mountains. She loved the mountains, but she didn't know these hills, not like the Appalachians. She slid her window down, taking in the fresh scent of pine trees and clean air. Like Morgantown, these mountains had protected Greenville, leaving parts of it untouched by the ravages of war. Unlike herself.

The road narrowed and became one lane; offshoots went right and left every mile or so, but Lorelei never saw a house. Pointing the nose of the vehicle right, Jameson eased off the roadway and onto a narrow drive. The truck dipped into ruts and the well-worn tire tracks, bobbing and groaning as it went. If he traveled this route often, Lorelei saw the necessity of the truck's height.

Thick pine trees created a canopy five or six feet high; she could imagine walking under their shelter. She longed to get out and walk on the carpet of dried needles and smell the sweet scent of them, but the truck swayed on. The dim light of heavy forest lightened, and fence replaced trees. They burst through the gloom of the forest into the bright fall sun. Her breath left in a soft whoosh as she took in the sights before her.

A massive house lay at the end of a long, well-manicured drive. Three stories easily, it was white with gray shutters and expansive wrap-around porches. Curved stairs with elegant rails were spaced to allow easy access to entry points. Smooth, white columns supported balconies on the upper levels, and the place looked like a mansion from antebellum times. She'd seen them in the old books Eve kept hidden in her office and never realized any still existed.

Barns of different sizes were scattered across the farm's rolling hills, and in the distance, a tractor cut long grass into hay. Bright white rail fencing separated paddocks filled with horses, and that is where her eye stayed. Gripping the edge of the window, she pulled herself nearly out to get a better look, missing Jameson's big smile at her reaction.

The truck rolled to a stop in the drive that circled the mansion. Jameson jumped out to help Lorelei but found her door wide open and her small body plastered against the rail fence when he came around to her side.

"What are they?" she breathed, reaching her hand through the bars. Lorelei loved horses and had ridden the breed native to West Virginia hundreds of times. She'd never seen anything like the solid colored, well-muscled horses before her. Horses from the Seventh were mostly wild. They had run off or been turned loose during the Troubles. They had intermixed with one another and had settled into a small, wiry, Heinz fifty-seven of spots, colors, and heights.

"American Quarter Horses," a quiet voice answered.

Lorelei whipped around, readying herself for a fight. Already on edge, she had little patience for surprises. A woman had joined them, standing next to Jameson. Her arm wrapped around him as high as it could; she wasn't able to reach his waist without a chair. Curly black hair cascaded from the long tail she wore down her back, and huge emerald eyes watched Lorelei from under heavy dark lashes. The upward curve of full lips grew wider, and her small hand reached for Jameson's.

Lorelei growled, pulling her lips back to expose teeth as she wondered who this beautiful woman was and what right she had to touch her mate.

"My name is Annabelle, child. Jameson is my son," the other woman said, taking away Lorelei's ability to speak.

The woman looked no older than herself. Annabelle stepped forward, wrapping Lorelei in a hug; she stiffened, then slowly relaxed.

"I apologize, ma'am," she said. "I'm a little jumpy is all." Lorelei tried to step back but only got to the end of the smaller woman's arms so that the dark-haired beauty could examine her closely.

"She's beautiful, Jameson. That hair; you don't see that hair around here," she said, releasing Lorelei from her grip. Lorelei shuffled back until she hit the fence, her eyes rounded and wild.

"Thank you, ma'am," she said, glancing left and right.

"Don't call me ma'am," Annabelle said, "Call me mom." Her green eyes danced with joy when she looked up at her son. "I always wanted an Omega daughter, and finally, one of my Alpha sons has obliged me." Her accent was so thick, Lorelei had to parse it out to understand what she was saying. She must've been wrong about it being Fifth district. Perhaps they were deep Sixth instead. "I just knew little JB was an Omega; just knew it. Then fiddlesticks, he was an Alpha like his brothers," she said with a laugh that sounded like bells.

Lorelei watched as Jameson's face heated to a bright red. JB, huh? She'd known. Jimbo, Jimmy, or JB, she'd somehow known he'd have a shortened nickname. She laughed too, despite herself.

"Come on inside, and I'll get you a coke; we have orange ones. I have tea, too, if that's better."

With a longing look over her shoulder, she followed Annabelle up the stairs and into the house.

"You like horses, do you?" Annabelle asked once she was seated at the wooden farmhouse table with an orange coke in her hand. She hadn't had one in years, and the syrupy sweetness was like a slice of heaven on her tongue. Jameson and his mother sipped sweet tea as they watched her.

"Yes, ma'am," Lorelei answered.

"Now, what'd I say? Call me Annabelle, or mom."

"Okay, Miss Annabelle," Lorelei answered as best she could. Southern born simply do not call an elder by their first name; it's unseemly. "I do like horses. I've never seen ones like those."

"Ah yes, American Quarter Horses are a Heritage breed; that's why we can use the term 'American' when referring to them. They used to be very common, but few breeders breed for purity and bloodlines anymore. We strive to keep the breed from dying and its excellent attributes along with it," Annabelle said, taking a sip of her tea. Jameson said nothing. He leaned back casually with an ankle crossed over the opposite knee.

Unable to sit still, Lorelei rose, leaving her drink on the table. Moving slowly, she went around the open kitchen and into the large great room beyond. Looking at pictures and trailing her hands over furniture, she explored quietly, unsure why she was here or what to say. She'd never had a family, not like this.

Pictures scattered on walls and flat surfaces showed the Battle family in various stages of growth and development. School pictures, candid shots, and professional portraits of seven larger boys and one smaller one showed broad smiles and straight teeth.

She'd known people like this existed. Eve lived this life if Lorelei was honest, but now that she was a part of it, she didn't know how to act.

"Let me show you to your room, Lorelei," Annabelle said, rising.

"I can take her, ma." Jameson rose too, towering over his diminutive mother.

"She's not staying in your room, Jameson. I'll take her." Annabelle stepped forward, ushering Lorelei to the stairs, confusing her completely.

A deep growl sounded, and the floor practically vibrated with the Alpha's fury.

"Jameson Beauregard Battle, you did not just growl at your mother? I will get a wooden spoon and tan your hide. Don't think I won't nullify your birth certificate, young man."

The growl stopped, and Jameson dropped his eyes.

"Don't mind him, sugar; come this way. Bring her bags on up, son, then head out to help your pa," The dark-haired Omega took Lorelei up curved walnut stairs, raising an eyebrow in challenge to her son as she went.

"Yes, ma'am," he grumbled, the sullen stomp of his feet as he retreated through the kitchen made Lorelei smile. Annabelle noticed and was glad that her favorite son had called for help.

"Bless his heart, sugar, he does try. He doesn't have a lick of sense, though," Annabelle gave an exaggerated sigh as she rounded the landing, escorting Lorelei to a room at the end of the hall. Jameson had told her everything, leaving out nothing from the sordid story, and what a sordid story it was. All of it. Then she'd demanded he bring his broken Omega to her for fixing. She'd set this to rights. She'd done harder things.

"Yes, Miss Annabelle," Lorelei said as she stepped into the soft cream and vivid pink room she'd been guided to. The room took her by surprise, as she knew there were no daughters in this place.

Jameson said his mother had always wanted an Omega daughter; why Lorelei didn't know. Omegas did not lead the best lives. Perhaps she'd set this room up long before she'd birthed eight Alpha sons. Who knew?

Deep shag area rugs pulled at her bare feet as she crossed the floor to run her hands over the tall frame of the rice planter's bed. She'd seen one in a museum in Fairmont, a small town outside of Morgantown. These beds were hundreds of years old, and this one looked like it had always been in this house.

"The house is old and the furniture older. Please excuse any dust you find. It's just their dad and me now, and sometimes I forget to clean," she said with a wink.

Jameson crashed through the door, carrying Lorelei's bags and a scowl.

"Set those there, baby, and go on out," Annabelle said, dismissing him with a wave that made Lorelei chuckle inwardly. With one last glare over his shoulder that faded the second his mother caught it, Jameson left.

"Why don't you freshen up, dear? Make yourself at home. I'm going to head out to the big barn on the left and check on the mares. You're welcome to join me, Lorelei. And if I didn't say it before, I'll say it now; welcome to the family." Annabelle moved to the door, intending to close it behind her.

"You're just going to leave me alone?" Lorelei asked, her voice low and uncertain, her eyes cutting immediately to the door.

"You are not a prisoner, Lorelei." Annabelle turned, giving her the most confident smile, and left her baby's wife by herself.

Deep down, she hoped the girl would not run. Annabelle hoped the wild-eyed thing would settle, but in the end, it was her choice. She'd had no choice in how she came to be her son's mate, but Jameson was a good man. He would care for the fearful, exotically beautiful Omega better than any other.

Lorelei wandered around the space, looking at everything. The room was all frills and pink ribbons, with no hint of masculinity anywhere. A small private bath opened from the bedroom, and an oversized walk-in closet beckoned to be filled. She took what clothes she had and hung them up, not wanting them to wrinkle.

She hadn't been alone since this nightmare started, and she took a minute to just breathe. She'd never spent much time alone, if she was honest. Just those few short months in the woods outside the Seventh while they plotted and planned their revolution from afar. What fools they'd been to think they could change anything.

The Alpha could make whatever rules he wanted, and others would still break them. Was it worth it?

Eve nearly died, and they'd all suffered. Still, some of her brothers and sisters had chosen their mates. Even Eve, in her calculated measurements and research, had chosen Lukas Jennings. He was not the mate Eve had wanted, but he turned out to be what she needed, and instead of dying, Eve was now pregnant and happy.

So, was it worth it? Tears threatened, spilling across her lashes and down her cheeks. Allowing herself a moment of self-pity, Lorelei turned onto the bed, sobbing into the soft pink pillows.

Chapter 8

"Ma, is she okay?" Jameson asked, falling in step with his mother when she left the house and headed for the broodmare barn.

"Of course she's not okay, you dolt," Annabelle said, smacking her son as high as she could reach. "She's in there sobbing into a pillow. Good heavens, what a fine mess this is," she finished, hooking her arm through her son's so that he could escort her to the barns. "You did the right thing, Jameson. She's stronger than she feels right now; she'll get through this and come out better on the other side." Annabelle let out a heavy sigh, slowing her steps until she stopped. "Do you remember that bay mare, SuddenZ Loping?" she started.

"Good Lord, Lightning?" Jameson asked, stopping to stare down at his mother.

"Yep, Lightning," Anabelle chuckled.

"How could I forget that mare," Jameson groaned. "She broke my arm."

"No, you broke your arm trying to ride her. Lord, she was a tough one. Lorelei is like that. Wild and half ready to kill you, she doesn't know if she wants to run or stand and fight. Taming her will be no different than taming Lightning. You've been breaking horses your whole life; don't forget the lessons you learned.

"Sometimes you have to back up, let them get used to your smell, and stop trying to ride them every five minutes. You gotta give the hard ones a chance to come to you, Jameson.

"Lightning turned out to be the best mare we ever had, and her show record is unparalleled to this day. She came from a bad background, and eventually, you made her see that life could be good. Give your mate the same chance." Annabelle stepped away from Jameson's thoughtful gaze, walking into the barn.

Jameson looked back at his childhood home, hoping his mother was right. He didn't want an unhappy mate, but he wasn't letting Lorelei go either. Forcing down the desire to go in there and claim his mate again, he walked away to find his dad.

He helped in the hayfield, starting up the old diesel tractor to follow his father, Earl, with the hay rake. The cord in his chest screamed at him to go to his mate. He knew she was hurting, but he couldn't help that right now, he told himself as he made the turns around the field. He'd never felt anything like this, and he wondered how all Alphas didn't go crazy with worry over their mates.

As the afternoon sun moved into evening, the tractors were parked and chores completed. He wanted to ask his father about the challenge an Omega mate brought, but Earl wasn't much of a talker. He'd shaken his hand and congratulated him on finding an Omega mate, but that was all he'd said. Together, they walked toward the house. His father stopped suddenly, reaching a hand to stay his son. The older Alpha stood motionless, a look of worry on his face.

"What's she doing, boy?" Earl said, tipping his head toward a pen near the barn.

Lorelei leaned against the inside of the fence, staring at a sorrel mare. The mare stared back, the white of her eyes showing. She snorted loudly and pawed at the ground, shaking her head in irritation at Lorelei's nearness.

Lorelei simply dropped her arms and walked to the mare, neatly dodging the first strike of her hooves. The mare moved to whirl and kick out, but Lorelei stayed with her, gluing herself to the horse's side. All the while, she spoke in low tones, words Jameson couldn't hear.

"Annabelle!" Earl shouted, taking off at a dead run.

Jameson stood stock still, not understanding what was happening. He watched his mother race from the barn towards his mate with her arms outstretched.

Lorelei dodged another strike and placed her hand on the mare's shoulder, soothing the horse with her touch. "Hush now," she whispered. The mare stilled, whipping her head toward Lorelei. Her nostrils flared, and sides heaved, but she didn't fight the Omega anymore.

"Aren't you a beauty, red-haired like Eve. I bet you're a spitfire like she is too. A red-haired horse can't be a natural thing, but then they say that about her too."

Jameson's parents froze where they stood, their eyes and mouths wide.

The mare snorted through her nose, pawing at the ground again, shaking her long, tangled mane. "You sure are a pretty little thing. Omega sized, even." Lorelei smiled up at the animal's face, and it was the most beautiful thing Jameson had ever seen. It was the first real smile she'd given, and her features were extraordinary because of it.

"I could've used you a few weeks ago, I bet you and I would've made quite the team." Lorelei put her tiny hands to work, picking through the snarls and dreads of the red mare's mane.

There was only one reason a horse would be in that paddock and in that shape. The mare must have been one of Annabelle's rescues; she must also be dangerous. That pen was reinforced, and only the worst of the worst went into it as it had no access to cover. Lorelei talked low to the mare, unaware of any danger.

The mare stood still, eventually relaxing into the spell she wove with her voice. Time restarted, and his parents walked forward.

"Get out of that pen, Girl," his father demanded.

"Now, hush your mouth, Earl. She's fine. They're fine. Go on up to the house; I'll be along." Annabelle shooed her husband away.

"Annabelle," the older Alpha started.

"Go on, Earl. Dinner's in the crockpot."

Lorelei stopped, her hands stilling in the long red strands of the mare's mane. Wide eyes stared at Earl; lips spread to reveal her teeth. Shifting her weight, she moved just slightly in front of the small red mare. Jameson could see the pounding of her heart at the base of her neck, and he wondered if she would turn and run.

He couldn't tell if she was terrified or preparing to fight, but knew she could ride. He'd seen hints of it in the Seventh. All of those Omegas rode like they were born on a horse. He didn't trust her not to disappear into the woods forever on the back of that wild thing.

As his father turned and stomped away, he saw Lorelei release the breath she was holding and resume her steady picking of the mare's mane.

Annabelle raised a hand to stay her son's steps closer. "Sweetie, you hungry?" she asked as if nothing had happened.

"Yes, Miss Annabelle," Lorelei replied immediately, and Jameson kicked himself. He hadn't fed his Omega all day, and it was late. Maybe he wasn't cut out for this.

"Come along, dear, let's wipe our feet and wash up for supper. I imagine our men are hungry too."

Annabelle turned, walking toward the house. She intercepted Jameson and demanded his arm again. Together, they left Lorelei to make her decision.

"Jameson, that mare is pertnear dangerous. Pulled her off the trailer and haven't been able to get near her since. She's tried to kill your father twice. That girl of yours stood watching her for over an hour, then just walked right up to her like it was nothing. She's something special, that one. Pretty as a peach and with enough gumption to keep a good man in line once she's all fixed up.

"Keep walking and don't look back, son. This is part of it; let her come to you." Annabelle gripped his arm with the iron strength of an Omega mother who'd raised eight Alpha sons and walked calmly into the house.

Jameson's instincts screamed at him, demanding he go and save his mate from danger. They fought with him to pick her up, throw her over his shoulder, and lock her in a room for him and him alone, but his mother was right. He didn't want a broken female; he wanted that bright, shining, happy woman that accepted his request to dance.

He wanted the female who'd known his name on arrival and had reviewed his file, liking what she saw. He wanted the Omega who had ripped an Alpha to shreds because he dared to try to claim her against her will. He didn't want a frightened shadow of that person. Even though he'd take what he got because she was his now, he wanted her happy.

Relaxing when he saw her duck through the fence and follow, he led his mother into the house. His father was putting cornbread and cold fried chicken on the table when he walked in. He could smell beef roast, too. His mom was sneaky; at some point, she'd doubled back to the house and put on a Sunday spread. Annabelle washed her hands and began to help while Jameson loitered at the door, waiting for Lorelei.

He needed her. He needed to bury his cock into her and renew his claim. He felt like it was weakening, and Jameson couldn't stand that. He knew what his mother said was true, but he knew what his instincts said too. If he didn't calm them, he would snap and do something no one could fix.

"Jameson," his mother said, giving him a soft motherly purr. "Go on and wash up. Stop stalking that girl like she's prey. You have to have patience."

Growling under his breath so his mother couldn't hear, Jameson stomped into the powder room off of the kitchen to clean up.

When he was done, he stepped out to find Lorelei descending the stairs. She had washed her face and tied her hair back into a long tail; Jameson walked to the table, taking his customary place. Lorelei slid into the chair beside him, not looking over; her nearness was calming.

As dishes were passed, he filled her plate first, then his, thus soothing himself more. The first plate she ate almost immediately. She'd gone through a short estrous with little food or water. She had to be starving.

Loading her plate again, Jameson watched her devour everything he placed in front of her. Some of the pain in his chest eased, and finally, she sat up straighter and paid attention to the conversation. His father cast an occasional wary eye toward his little mate but said nothing about her table manners.

"That pack of coyotes got another calf off the Dillard's farm last night," Earl said idly as he buttered another slice of cornbread.

"Once they have the taste, there's nothing to do but hunt them down," Annabelle said, passing the plate of tender beef back to Jameson.

"You have a coyote problem?" Lorelei asked, sitting straighter in her seat. Her eyes sharpened on Earl, and her focus on him laserlike.

"Yes," Earl answered simply, noticing the change in Jameson's mate.

"They've been going after the foals and calves, taking down anything smaller than a yearling. It's been awful," Annabelle added.

"Do you have firearms?" Lorelei asked. "The antique stuff is better; a .45-70 or an old Glock 19 would be good. The laser stuff is okay, too, as long as the foliage isn't too dense." Lorelei's eyes lit up, and Jameson remembered something he shouldn't have forgotten.

"Lorelei is quite the marksman, dad," Jameson growled, casting a warning glance at his father. "She was involved in the conflict up north a while back."

"A bow would work even better, or a spear. If you have anything, I'd be happy to help with the coyotes."

It was the most Lorelei had spoken in days, and Jameson's heart tripped over several beats.

Earl leaned his head back and laughed out loud at the ceiling. Lorelei's shoulders slumped at the sound. "Little lady, I have an old .45-70 around here somewhere. In fact, I've got about every firearm you can imagine; you take your pick. I want to see this. JB, you did good, kid. Remember all the times I cursed you with a mate like your mother? Looks like I win."

A small smile graced Lorelei's lips, and Jameson sat back, relaxing into his chair as he enjoyed the sight of it.

"Your brothers are coming tomorrow with their various friends, partners, situationships, or whatever they are calling it these days," Earl snarled. "Nothing proper about any of this, I say, but they'll be here, and we'll commence to coyote hunting then."

"Tell us about yourself, Lorelei," Annabelle asked quietly, shifting the subject to something less violent.

"There's nothing to tell," Lorelei answered.

Jameson watched the excited gleam in her eyes sputter and die. He placed a piece of peanut butter pie on her plate, adding a clean spoon. "That's not true at all, Lorelei," he said. "Ma, Lorelei graduated at the top of her class. She majored in accounting and business. She worked for the Seventh District's Alpha." Jameson let the pride he felt show on his face as he looked down at his mate. She gave him a small but grateful smile.

"She's a hell of a little fighter. She's Eve Jennings's second in command of the incredibly efficient garrison that helped squelch the Seventh's uprising. I know this firsthand because The Alpha and I ate their smoke the whole way into those crazy ass mountains. The entire Marine corps did. They taught us a lot about guerrilla warfare," Jameson laughed, reaching over and pushing a strand of long hair out of Lorelei's eyes.

"I don't think that's true, Jameson," Lorelei said, looking at him for the first time in what felt like days. His heart soared, and that hopeful feeling returned as she met his eyes.

"It's absolutely true, Lorel," he said, trailing his hand down her face to trace across her lower lip. Pulling away quickly, he dropped his hand to his lap, noting the startled and not entirely happy expression on her face when he did so.

"Anyway, she's been working with Eve to make sure the other Omegas settle in. The Alpha is going to ask her to join his finance team when a position opens up," he added with a little laugh. "And a position will definitely open up," he said with a chuckle. "No one can put up with that man for long, except maybe his wife."

He didn't look at Lorelei when he shared that tidbit of news, but he saw her staring at him in shock from his peripheral vision. His mother was right, as always. He needed to go slowly. More than that, he needed to remind Lorelei of everything she had accomplished.

She needed to remember who she was and understand that another's actions, his included, did not change that. Yes, she was his mate. No, there was no way around that, but she could still be herself- even with the bond. He'd just remind her of that.

Jameson thought that if it came down to it, he could lock her in a room and knot her until she broke. He could take her over and over again, rubbing his scent into every pore in her body until all she knew was him.

He would if he had to, as a last-ditch effort to keep her with him. He'd enjoy it too, every fucking second of it. His cock hardened in his pants at the thought, but he wouldn't do that, not yet. He'd give her a chance to come to him, knowing their lives would both be better if she did.

Jameson thanked his mother silently for treating him like an Omega for half of his life. It had done wonders for his perception of things. He knew his brothers wouldn't have the restraint he showed, and in the typical Alpha way, he patted himself on the back for his compassion.

They talked as they finished their meal. Jameson's parents shared funny and embarrassing stories about their late-blooming son. As the night wore on, Jameson noted the way Lorelei relaxed. Finally, she gave real smiles and even a soft laugh at the things being shared. When he caught her eye, she didn't look away.

"Well, son," I'm turning in. It's going to be a long day in the hayfield, and I'm beat," his father said, rising from the table first.

"I'll just clean up and be along behind you, Earl." Annabelle rose, moving to get the dishes.

"I'll get those." Lorelei jumped up, rushing to take the plate from Jameson's mother.

"Now, dear. Guests don't clean up after supper."

"I'm not a guest, remember?" Lorelei answered, giving Jameson a shaky look.

"No, I suppose you aren't," Annabelle answered, letting Lorelei take the dishes from her.

"We've got it, ma. You'll be cooking all day for my idiot brothers; you'd better rest." Jameson piled dishes in his oversized arms and followed his mate into the kitchen.

Chapter 9

"I can get this, Jameson," Lorelei said, shouldering past the large Alpha in front of her.

"And I can help," Jameson answered. "I basically have a degree from the school of mom in Home Economics." He gave a little laugh and caught the curve of her lips when she smiled. "Mom has a dishwasher but doesn't think it gets her dishes clean," he added with a groan.

"That's okay, I've never had one." Lorelei plugged the sink and filled it with hot, soapy water.

"Do you want a drink while we clean this mess up? It's going to take a while," Jameson asked her, being careful not to get too close.

She knew what he was doing. Lorelei was not stupid. He'd been careful all day, careful not to touch her too much or push her too hard. Careful not to say the wrong thing and try to give her space. She appreciated it, she did, but the bond in her chest did not. She needed him. Every part of her ached to reach out to him and ease the need she felt soul-deep.

The bond knew they were at odds and fought her to soothe him. As an Omega, it was her job to calm his anger, ease his pain, and slake his lust. She fucking hated it. But she needed him, too. Her nerves had been frayed all day that she was away from him, and she was on edge.

"I need you, Jameson," she said, watching when his hands stilled on the glass of whiskey he had poured for himself. Walking to him, she took the glass, downing it in one gulp. It was her favorite whiskey and Jameson's namesake. She wondered if his mother had a thing for Irish whiskey as well.

"I don't want to need you. I fucking hate it. God, don't think this means I'm staying. Don't think this means anything, but I can't take another minute of this pain; I can't." Lorelei reached up, touching the strong lines of Jameson's face. Her breath shuddered in her chest, and the ache eased now that she was touching him.

Frozen under her hand, Jameson met her gaze. He looked ready to bolt. She'd known there was some plan in place; she'd seen him and Annabelle scheming, and she didn't care. Southern mamas fixed their boys' problems, and Lorelei knew she was a problem.

Maybe she wanted to be fixed. Maybe deep down, she didn't want to run off and die alone in the woods. She could barely stand a few hours without the touch of her Alpha; how was she supposed to survive leaving him? She wasn't; she wouldn't. That was the choice, and her only one left. Stay and live or leave and die; it had been reduced to that.

Refusing to think any more about it, Lorelei pulled Jameson to her, placing her greedy lips on his. She needed to stop hurting, and she definitely needed to stop thinking. She kissed him for the first time, making the biggest mistake of her life thus far.

His lips tasted like whiskey and peanut butter pie. Jameson tasted like a future she would have loved living in, a path that might not be hers anymore. She delved her tongue into his mouth and licked along the lines of his lips as she chased what might have been. His growl came, and she let it roll through her. The pain was gone now, but she needed him to fill the empty places inside her.

"Lorelei," he groaned. "I'm not going to able to stop. Please don't," Jameson begged, and she knew he'd been hurting too. She'd felt it all day; his need to comfort her was as great as her pain and anguish, and she kissed him harder, willing it away by untucking his shirt from his jeans.

"Lorelei," he growled once more.

"It's fine, Jameson. Just for tonight, it's okay. Let's just pretend everything is okay," she said, pulling away from his lips long enough to meet his eyes.

Gripping her hips, Jameson dragged her to him. Wrapping strong arms under her ass, he plunged into her mouth with his long-denied tongue. She kissed him back, loving the slide of it and the feel of his massive hands on her ass. She ground her hips on his rigid cock, teasing herself with the friction. Slick seeped from her core, soaking her jeans, and the scent of it filled the air. She thrilled at the feel of having her Alpha under her hands. He was her mate; there was nothing to be done about it. Dignity is overrated.

He purred for her, making her go limp in his arms. She didn't care; she wanted his comfort and needed him to make her forget that none of this was her choice. He purred as he sat her on the countertop, bringing her almost to eye level with him. His fingers skimmed her core through her jeans,

and she sank deeper into him.

"Please, Jameson, don't taunt me, don't tease me; not tonight." Lorelei looked at him, asking him with her eyes to strip her layers and just make her feel.

She slipped his shirt into her hands and slid it over his shoulders. He gripped her by the back of her head and brought her lips to his again, starved for her kiss.

Bracing herself against him, Lorelei pulled her mouth away, fixing her eyes on the sharp contours of her Alpha's chest. She'd never really looked at him, never seen him in this light. She'd ignored his magnificence every chance she could.

Her head lolled into his grip as her fingers slid lower, dipping through the lines of his body. He was glorious, and he was hers to keep or throw away. Her pussy clenched around nothing, begging her to get on with it.

She was empty without him, but hadn't she always been empty? Meaningless ruts with nameless Alphas to serve her estrous had never fulfilled her. They had satisfied an immediate need but never made her want them. Not like Jameson did.

Was it the bond forced on her? Maybe, but maybe not. He was right; she had liked him. That night on the edge of the dancefloor, before another Alpha took away her choice, she had liked him.

"Jameson," she cried, afraid of the thoughts running through her head. "Please."

He took her shirt in his hands, ripping it over her head. Her bra dropped next, and she didn't know how he got it off so fast. His mouth closed over her nipple, and he slid his tongue over the stiff peak. All thought fled when he grazed it with his teeth, causing her slick to pool on the counter. Her jeans were next; Jameson stepped away from her long enough to send them flying. Naked before him, Lorelei worked his jeans, pushing them down his hips to grip his cock in both hands.

He pulled away from her breast, gripped her head in one palm, and ravaged her mouth with his. Using her thumb, she spread the bead of pre-cum across his throbbing head. Jameson groaned, making her slick flow faster. He slid his fingers between them, using three to bring her honeyed wetness to his lips. His eyes rolled back when he sucked them dry. He repeated the process, tasting her desire, and filling himself with it.

Every time he reached down, Jameson flicked her clit. She was writhing in his arms, unable to stop herself when he placed his hand on his cock and angled it in. It took her breath.

Lorelei was no virgin, but she struggled to take his size without the help of estrous, real or not. She dipped her head to his chest, breathing hard until he was seated deep within her.

"Look at me, Lorelei," he demanded, his tone harsh.

Her eyes snapped to his just as the last inch of him sank home.

"I can be what you need," he said, stilling her mind. "I can be what you want," he added, stilling her hands. "Fast or slow, hard or gentle; tell me. I can be that," he pulled out, and she felt every inch of him leave her; it stilled her heart. "Tell me, Lorel. Tell. Me. Let me be what you need."

The orgasm ripped through Lorelei. His words, touch, and cock sent her over the edge, and she cried out into his hard chest. When he pushed inside her again, she came undone, clutching and scratching at his arms to bring him closer. He pumped between her thighs, his breath coming hard and fast. He gripped her ass hard, changing the angle until she came again, her slick joining his fluids to ease his way.

Jameson fucked her slowly, watching her face and thrumming her clit. Her body gave in to his, and he pushed behind her cervix into the place made for an Alpha's cock. She cried out when he hit that spot, uncaring that his parents were somewhere in the house and could walk in at any time.

His lips found her neck, her shoulders, her ears, and her breasts. There was no place he did not kiss or touch, he owned her body, and she let him take it. Between them, the bond sang, its voice steady and beautiful, tempting her with what was and what could be.

Spreading her legs wider, she asked him in. He lost it then, the restraint he showed all day falling away. His thrusts came faster, and his grip harder. He licked over the claiming mark and dug his teeth into it again, making it bleed freely. Lorelei didn't notice; she was too lost in the thrust of his hips to care. He growled, calling forth more sticky wetness.

Jameson drove into her until the slap of his balls on her ass filled the silence of the kitchen. Her moans turned to grunts, and she came again, her body milking his, asking for his seed. He didn't give it. Instead, he gave kisses and touches, leaving her body with no secrets.

His tongue licked the blood from her shoulder and the sweat from her face. His hips never slowed as he took what he needed and gave what she asked for.

When the next orgasm took her, making her whimper with relief as her body clenched his, Jameson wrapped his arms around Lorelei. Pulling her tight against him, he picked her up, angled his cock, and gave her his knot. It lodged deep behind her pubic bone, making her cry out with the pleasure of feeling it.

He stood holding her, sharing her shaking breaths. He held her so that their foreheads rested together, eyes closed, and fighting for air. Lorelei felt his heart pounding against hers and knew she was royally fucked. She shouldn't have gone to him. She shouldn't have kissed him like that. The bond was tighter now; content and sated, it hummed like a hummingbird's wings in her chest. She was sated too, more so than she ever had been.

Her body was limp, and only his strong arms held her legs around him. His knot held them together, and he spurted cum into her randomly, shivering when his balls released. She was stretched pleasantly full of his essence. She didn't hate it, but she should. Laying her head on Jameson's shoulder, she vowed to fight biology tomorrow and went to sleep in his arms.

A yip and sharp bark stirred her from sleep. Suddenly awake, she sat up and scrambled for awareness. She wasn't in her room. Jameson was wrapped around her, the rise and fall of his chest silent.

The room was dark, but she could make out pinup posters of pretty Omegas in various forms of undress by the light of the moon. Women from another decade watched her mate in the dark, causing Lorelei to growl quietly at them.

She sat up, realizing she was in Jameson's room. Not just his room, but his childhood room. Baseball gloves and football trophies lined the walls, making her shake her head. She laughed lightly for just a moment until she remembered why she was here, and her smile fell away.

The yip from below the window pushed Lorelei to action, and she was on her feet and moving out the door in moments.

Chapter 10

Jameson rolled over as the early morning sun teased him awake. He hadn't slept so hard in ages. His body sang with happiness, and the bond in his chest wasn't screaming for action.

Lorelei had been fantastic, and her surrender to him sheer perfection. He'd carried her to bed and licked her clean of their combined fluids, kissing her in between mouthfuls so she could taste how well they went together.

Her lazy, hooded eyes had watched as he devoured her, unable to stop himself. He'd known she was tired and needed sleep, but he couldn't stop himself from entering her again. He could smell the faint taint of her rawness in the air, had done it, anyway. Jameson had warned her he would be unable to stop, and he hadn't lied. Once he'd knotted her a second time, he let her collapse onto him. With his knot buried deep inside her, they'd both slept peacefully.

His eyes snapped open. The kitchen. His mother was going to smack him into next week. God only knows what he had left behind for his mother to find. He hurried to rise, finally noticing the Omega shaped empty spot beside him. Looking around, his brows narrowing in confusion, Jameson grabbed his jeans and pulled them on. He went to the other wing of the house, looking for Lorelei in the damned pink room that had been his until he declared as an Alpha. Slamming the door open, he rushed in, noting that the bed had not been slept in.

Worried now, he jogged down the stairs, hoping to find his wife in the kitchen. His mother stood in an apron with a dark glower on her face.

"Lorelei's gone," Jameson said, his words ending in a sob.

Worry flitted across Annabelle's face. It quickly changed to anger, and she grabbed a wooden spoon from the caddy by the stove. "I told you to stop trying to ride that girl every five minutes and let her come to you, Jameson. But no, you're too big for your britches. Jameson knows it all." She came down on him artfully with the wooden spoon, breaking it. She grabbed another and beat Jameson about his legs, rump, and arms as he tried to block her blows.

"Ma, stop. She came to me. She asked me, ma. Quit. She was hurting; we both were." Jameson used his dance lessons to try to evade his mother's wicked wooden spoon. She was a master with it though; she wielded a wooden spoon the way a sniper wielded a rifle, and she nailed him with every strike.

"And where is she now, Jameson? I could strangle you." With a sigh, Annabelle dropped her dishtowel and removed her apron. "Come on, let's go see if we can find her before that pack of coyotes does."

Jameson's heart stilled. Lorelei didn't weigh more than ninety pounds and wasn't five feet tall. She was half the size of a colt. He rushed for the door, grabbing the .22-gauge critter rifle as he went.

Halfway through the front yard, his mother slowed, putting up her hand to stay her son's frantic steps. Annabelle brought her finger to her lips to silence Jameson's exclamation, and his eyes followed her pointed finger.

Lorelei lay in the cradle of the sleeping red mare's neck and limbs. One small hand wrapped around the mare's red hair, and the other gripped a long wooden handle that had once belonged on a broom head. Around the sleeping pair, dog tracks covered the dirt in the mare's pen. Not dog tracks, coyote tracks. Enough tracks that the lone mare probably wouldn't have withstood the attack. One of her back legs was bloodied, and blood streaked Lorelei's arms. Jameson rushed to get to her.

The mare was on her feet, Lorelei beside her in an instant, her makeshift staff at the ready.

"It's okay," Annabelle said, easing Jameson to a stop. "Are you all right, Lorelei?"

"Yes, ma'am," Lorelei said, moving from the mare's side with a fond pat. The mare limped forward, mirroring her steps.

"Lorelei, what the fuck?" Jameson asked. His mother was on him in a heartbeat, wailing on him for all she was worth.

"Jameson Beauregard Battle, nullifying your birth certificate is too good for you. Hush your mouth and apologize. How dare you use such language in front of your mother, let alone your wife," her dainty hands rained blows on every part of him she could reach.

"Ma, I'm sorry. I'm just scared," Jameson said, covering his delicate parts in case she accidentally hit them.

Annabelle ceased her wild blows, patting her son on the arm. "I understand, son, and I know you were scared. Just watch your mouth."

"Yes, ma'am," Jameson answered, noting the glint of humor on Lorelei's face as she walked forward.

"She had no protection," Lorelei said, looking up at the mare's face. "The coyotes woke me up, yipping and hounding her. There were too many for her to handle," she finished, giving her makeshift staff an absent-minded twirl. He noted the bloodied ends of the thing and guessed she'd given better than she got.

But the fact remained that his little Omega had gone to the horse's aid alone, instead of waking Jameson up. Fury coiled in his gut; he forced it down.

"You looked tired, Jameson. I wanted you to sleep," she added, sensing his anger.

"Lorelei," he groaned, "I would have rather helped you," he tried to keep the tightness from his voice, failing miserably.

With a shrug of her shoulders, Lorelei slipped through the fence. "Is there anywhere else she can go?" she asked, not looking at her mate.

"We've tried to get her into the barn, but she won't let us lead her," Annabelle answered.

"Show me," Lorelei asked, opening the gate to the mare's small pen.

Annabelle's eyebrows hit her hairline, but she stepped aside and walked away. Jameson watched his battered mate follow her to the barn, dogged by the limping mare. Lorelei kept a reassuring hand on the horse, speaking softly while they went. The mare didn't look left and right, and she didn't offer to run; she just followed Lorelei into the cool darkness and out of the sun. He wondered how she did it and wished he could inspire trust in Lorelei the way she'd inspired it in that wild mare.

Annabelle opened a large broodmare stall, and Lorelei led the sorrel mare in, closing the door behind them. Stunning Jameson and Annabelle both, Lorelei took a drink from the water bucket in the stall corner and shook the fresh flakes of hay loose. Annabelle poured a scoop of grain into the feeder, and his wife went to that too, showing the mare there was nothing to fear.

Jameson turned on the box fan that would keep the mare cooler. Despite it being fall, the days could still be hot, even in the foothills. When Lorelei was satisfied the mare was comfortable, she left her, following Annabelle and Jameson to the house.

"Wash up, child," Annabelle said, looking thoughtfully at Lorelei.

Jameson moved to follow his mate up the stairs, needing desperately to check her wounds.

"Leave her alone, son. She's fine. Get the bacon so I can make breakfast; we need to talk." His mother opened the oven, pulling out a number twelve cast-iron skillet that had been in their family since the original Civil War. Strong as she was, Annabelle struggled with the pan's weight, finally using two hands to heft it onto the stovetop.

"Mom," He started.

"Don't mom me, boy." Annabelle sighed, placing her small hand on her forehead. "I'm not getting any younger, and neither is your dad. This place will come to you someday, as your brothers' lives are elsewhere. They don't want to farm, but you don't mind it, and that girl would love it. I underestimated the situation, very much so. That girl isn't right, but she's got a gift.

"Maybe she was raised by wolves, or maybe she was just left to run wild. She's just a hair above uncivilized, but I like her. You love her already; I can see it on your face, Jameson. She's something rare and unique, don't run her off. For God's sake, back up a little. Let her settle in. Like that mare, show her you can keep her safe; show her you know what's best, and show her you're a good Alpha. Lead. Then she'll follow, got it?"

"Yes, ma'am," Jameson said, handing his mother slices of bacon for the skillet.

"You two are going to help me get ready for this cookout. I'm not sure who's coming, but my guess is everybody. You can make your sweet potato casserole."

"Okay, ma." Jameson peeled sweet potatoes while his mother cooked dippy eggs. He buttered toast, fighting the urge to run upstairs and run his fingers over Lorelei. He needed to be sure she was okay, and it was killing him not to go to her.

She came downstairs in jeans and a loose gray tee. She carried her new boots in her hands. She washed and blow-dried her hair, leaving it in a waterfall down her back. Her lips were stained red, and her lashes black. She'd put on makeup, and he took it as a good sign. She hadn't bothered to wear any since the mixer, and he was glad to see her return to normal, even though didn't need war paint.

Claw marks marred the outside of her left arm, and there was a tiny scratch on her face. Jameson bristled when he saw them, but said nothing.

"Eat up, Lorelei. We've got a heap of cooking to do for the cookout tonight," Annabelle handed Lorelei a plate piled high with eggs, bacon, toast, and grits drowning in butter.

Jameson smiled when Lorelei ate the grits first, asking for more before touching anything else on her plate. She tore into her food, devouring everything he handed her. He smothered biscuits in apple butter and handed them over. When the bottom of her plate showed, he added more food, barely eating anything himself. He wondered when her real estrous was and if she'd be ready. She drank water and orange juice like she were dying of thirst.

His mother watched her with a soft smile, and Jameson knew the woman was as lost as he was to the sweet Omega at the table. They ate in relative silence, the clank of silverware on china the only noise.

Through the open windows, Jameson could hear the tractor running. It wouldn't take his dad long to bale the thin second cutting they'd raked yesterday. His mom was right; he loved this place. But he loved his house in the city too and couldn't bear the thought of letting it go. Time would tell where he and Lorelei landed. If he were honest, he didn't care as long as she stayed with him.

With breakfast over, they talked about old times. Lorelei washed dishes silently, casting glances between Jameson and his mother. He wondered what she was like in her hometown and hoped to take her there someday.

"Lorelei," he asked. "Do you want to visit your family? I can take you back to the Seventh anytime you like," Jameson said offhandedly as he dried a plate.

Her face shuttered, closing down. "Thank you, Jameson, that's very kind, but with Eve in the Sixth district, I have no desire to go back to the Seventh."

"All right, dove," he said, pretending he didn't see the hollow look in her eyes.

"Are you making this famous sweet potato casserole you were telling me about?" she tried.

"Why, yes, ma'am; yes, I am," Jameson laughed.

"Miss Annabelle, do you have any pepperoni?" his mate asked quietly.

Annabelle cut her eyes at Lorelei. "Yes, I do," she answered.

The three worked in the kitchen all morning and into the afternoon. Jameson didn't know what Lorelei was making, but she was always making something. His mother had given her a few tasks, such as shredding slaw and slicing vegetables. In between her assigned tasks, Lorelei boiled macaroni, measured cheddar cheese, and whipped eggs. He hadn't pictured her as being domestic and was surprised at the ease with which she moved around the kitchen.

He saw his mother notice, too, and noted her widened smile. Maybe Lorelei wasn't as feral as they thought; he knew nothing about her history. Music played on the radio, and Lorelei bobbed her head as she slid yet another pan into one of his mother's wall ovens.

As the afternoon faded, Earl came in. "Now, doesn't this place smell wonderful? Amazing what three Omegas in a kitchen can accomplish," he joked, getting a towel thrown at him in return.

"Your son is no Omega, Earl, now stop teasing the boy and get out; go wash up," Annabelle swatted at Earl's rump, chasing him from the kitchen with a laugh.

Jameson watched Lorelei watch his parents. The confused slant of her eyebrows did not reveal her thoughts, and he could only guess at them. Food was placed in warmers, and Lorelei walked upstairs without saying a word. She went to her wing, not his, and he didn't follow her.

"Go shower, son. Your brothers will be here soon." His mother brushed flour from her face, tossed her apron into a drawer, and looked around with satisfaction.

Jameson went upstairs, ignoring the draw of Lorelei to the other side of the house. He showered and changed, putting on a dark T-shirt and heavy socks. His father had all but promised to take Lorelei coyote hunting, and after last night's battle with that pack, he knew she would bite at the bit to go.

His room smelled like her, like them. She would eventually see that they were perfect together. He palmed his heavy cock in the shower until his balls eased from release. An Alpha usually claimed his mate during her estrous, and those days spent serving her needs slaked his own. Lorelei's estrous had been fake, and her need short-lived. He wasn't in a rut; if he were, Jameson didn't think he could control himself. But he was pushed damn close by her nearness and his inability to have her when he needed her.

He was trying to be patient and give her space to accept their bond, but he was walking a tightrope. He just hoped he could keep putting one foot in front of the other without falling off the side.

Jameson padded down the stairs, finding Lorelei already at the bottom. She had replaced her makeup and smoothed her long, nearly white hair. Lorelei looked up at him, smiling when she caught his eye.

She'd put on a long-sleeved tee-shirt that matched his; there was just enough of a cowl in the neck to expose his claiming mark. It had been covered by design or fluke these last few days, but tonight it was bare for his family to see. Maybe that was her point.

Large families were rare anymore. His mother is a happy enough Omega to have birthed eight healthy boys. It was even rarer to give birth to all Alphas; he knew that, too. Usually, there would be a smattering of dynamics, but his mother had disobeyed that statistic. It was also common for the oldest male to be the strongest Alpha, but his brothers knew that was false.

Whether it had something to do with how late he declared or not, Jameson could take all seven of his brothers in a fight. They'd beaten on him enough when the world still thought he was an Omega to earn their comeuppance, and he'd been happy to give it. If his mother knew about the fights they'd had, she'd jerk a knot in their tails so fast, but she didn't know. That woman was fierce.

Jameson's eye drifted to the bite mark on the curve of Lorelei's delicate shoulder, right above the protrusion of her collarbone. Given a choice, he would have placed it higher, right at the base of her neck, but that fucking animal had bitten her from behind, marking that spot. Jameson had needed to obliterate it with his own bite. If he had his way, he'd cover her in claiming marks, but he knew that was socially unacceptable and that she'd likely never forgive him if he did.

"You look great," she said, making his chest puff up with her attention. Her cheeks blushed red when his eyes refused to leave his mark. Despite rubbing one out in the shower, his cock hardened in his pants. He was struggling today; maybe her real estrous was coming. He had zero experience with this.

"That's my line, dove," he laughed, giving her a light squeeze on the arm. "Are you ready to meet my crazy brothers?"

"I'm nervous," she answered, her eyes dropping from his.

"Nothing to be nervous about. They're giant assholes but will be perfect gentlemen. Some of their girlfriends aren't the best, so we'll see how that goes together. My oldest brother, Darrian, dates an Alpha female who can be a real bitch. Mom can't stand her. Not because she's an alpha, just because her personality sucks. A couple of the others have Beta girlfriends or wives, and the ones closest to me are single. It'll be okay, I promise.

She nodded her head, falling into step beside him. At the door, she leaned down and slipped on the cowgirl boots he had bought her. They weren't fancy, but they were utilitarian and would get the job done tonight. That's when he realized she'd dressed for hunting and not a cookout.

Most of his family was scattered on the lawn. A cornhole game raged on one side and horseshoes on the other. Nearly twenty people mixed on the manicured grass, laughing and sipping drinks. All heads turned when the door opened, and Jameson and Lorelei slipped out. He reached for her hand, and she let him take it. Feeling her hesitation through their bond, he squeezed it once before going to meet them.

His oldest brother barreled toward him, setting his teeth on edge. When the other man didn't slow down and got too close to Lorelei, instinct took over. Jameson bent his knees, picking his brother up and body-slamming him to the ground with a feral growl as he pushed his mate behind his back.

"Oof. Get off me, you oversized Omega," Darrian laughed, swatting at his brother's arm.

"Darrian Jordan Battle," Annabelle yelled. "Now, you know better than that; I'm fixin' to take a spoon to your hide." The older Omega pulled at her baby's shirt, trying to haul him off her firstborn.

Jameson caught the hint of laughter in Lorelei's eyes but did not miss the wide stance of her legs and the looseness of her arms; she'd been ready to fight. She was always ready to fight.

"Get on up now, both of you, acting like toddlers. I declare." Annabelle swiped at Jameson again, making no headway in moving him.

Jameson hopped up, grabbing his brother by the forearm and pulling him to his feet.

"Hello, sister," Darrian said, reaching out a hand to Lorelei despite Jameson's warning growl. "Can't believe my little brother finally landed a female. I'd always imagined him settling down with a nice, curvy sheep." He threw his head back, laughing, causing a smile to crawl up Lorelei's face.

"Come here." He gripped Lorelei in a bear hug, giving her a noogie for emphasis.

"Darrian," Earl said, stepping forward.

"It's okay," Lorelei laughed, swatting the Darrian away and stepping back into Jameson.

Immediately calmed by her actions, he wrapped his arm around her shoulders, pulling her closer.

He loved his brothers. With barely a year between each one, they had grown up close. Darrian, being the oldest, had helped a lot when Jameson was born, and their relationship was tight.

His other brothers would never approach his mate the way Darrian did and get away with it. There had been too much competition for resources growing up. They were all close, but Darrian and Jameson were the closest.

"You did good, kid." Darrian reached up, ruffling the tangle of dark curls on top of Jameson's head.

"Bruh, next time you think to rush toward Lorelei, don't. If I don't kill you, she might." Jameson let the pride he felt bleed into his voice.

"Yeah, I heard all about your mad skills, sis. I also hear we are hunting coyotes tonight."

"Yes," Lorelei said simply, all but ignoring the other man's enthusiasm.

"Did you grow up hunting?" Darrian's brother asked.

Lorelei tilted her face up to Jameson, and he watched it fall. His back stiffened with the need to see her smile again.

"In West Virginia, everyone hunts. It keeps disease from spreading among the animals and the freezers full for the winter. For some, it's a hobby; for others, it's survival," her voice was steady as she answered, not giving away which it meant for her.

Jameson knew Lorelei and Eve were close and had basically grown up together, but he knew little more than that.

"West Virginia?" Jameson watched his brother's girlfriend, Meghan, step into view.

The woman was a foot shorter than him and all lean muscle. Where Lorelei's muscular body had soft curves, Meghan's did not. The predatory glint in her eye screamed at Jameson to intervene before she could speak again. A low growl sounded from his core, warning her to tread lightly.

"Yes, West Virginia," Lorelei stepped from the protection of his arms, moving into Meghan's personal space. She extended her hand and narrowed her eyes. "Lorelei Nash," she said, her voice dropping an octave.

Megan accepted the handshake. Jameson watched surprise flit across her face as Lorelei's steel grip equaled her own. Meghan inhaled deeply, scenting his mate. Jameson watched as Meghan eyed his claiming mark and took a deeper breath. Her eyes widened at Lorelei's sweet scent, threatening to roll back, but the Omega forced them to stay on hers by squeezing her hand harder.

"Back off, Meghan," Darrian warned.

Jameson stepped forward, gripping the back of Lorelei's hair and pulling the tips gently to calm the sudden intensity flowing through their bond.

"I just wanted to introduce myself, Darrian," she said, taking a step back and dropping eye contact before Lorelei did. "You bounded over here like an oaf and hogged Jamie's new mate the second they stepped out the door," she finished with a laugh, turning away and heading back to the others.

Jameson caught the thundercloud of his mother's face and knew the night was going to be a disaster. Anxiety crept higher as he stalked behind Lorelei. His brothers and their various guests hung back, instinctively knowing he was on edge.

Introductions were made, and the tension in the air dissipated, but his anxiety continued to increase. Heart pounding at twice its normal rate, Jameson laughed with the others but refused to let Lorelei get any farther away than an arm's length.

The way Meghan tracked her movements set his teeth on edge. He'd never fought a woman for dominance, but if she didn't back off, he would. She was pushing his buttons, and she knew it.

Lorelei knew it too. The way she fingered her claiming mark let him know she felt the tension pouring off of him. It also helped draw Meghan's, and every other Alpha present, eyes to the delicate curve of her shoulder. Jameson was barely hanging on.

"How did you lovebirds meet?" Remington asked during a lull in a wicked game of cornhole.

Remington, Jameson's brother nearest in age, had always been a peacemaker. He had a way of de-escalating tense situations.

Jameson appreciated the effort but hated the question because there was no right answer. His mother knew the truth, but she would never tell his siblings.

"We met at a party," Lorelei said, looking up and catching his eye. She was doing her best to calm him. She even reached around to grab his hand, offering him a small smile. "It was one of those stupid mixers they have in the capital to get Alphas and Omegas together. He asked me to dance, and the rest is history," Lorelei finished, sipping from her glass of sweet tea.

"Supper's on," Annabelle yelled from the tables set up on the grass.

His brothers whooped and hollered as they raced like puppies for the food. They jostled for position, fighting over plates and silverware. Then they fought over spoons and tongs like idiots.

Jameson watched the smile spread across Lorelei's face as she watched them. She gave a small shake of her head at their exuberance.

Funny how a grown man can go back to his mama's house and act like a teenager again. Out in the real world, Alphas must show their strength. To show weakness is to invite a stronger male to take what's yours. But on your mama's lawn, you could act a fool all you wanted because she would never judge you.

"Darrian is the head of a large investment firm," Jameson started. "Remi is the CEO of the largest chain of luxury hotels in

Atlanta. Gauge and his wife run a non-profit in Savannah and drove up for the day," Jameson said, laying a hand on Lorelei's shoulder. She let him, and some of his anxiety slipped away. Families were complicated, but he loved his. He'd known his brothers would test and pull at his relationship, expected it even.

He hadn't anticipated how it would gird him to battle, though, and he blamed the newness of his claim on Lorelei, hoping it would settle down because he really didn't want to strangle one of them to death, but he would.

"You have a successful family," she said, watching the antics of full-grown men.

"I just wanted to put their actions into perspective," he answered.

"They're acting like fools," she laughed, nodding her head in understanding.

"Exactly." Jameson urged Lorelei toward the food tables; he could hear her stomach growling.

"It must be nice to have a safe place to fall," she sighed, walking forward.

Jameson couldn't stop himself from gripping her arm and pulling her around to face him. "I am your safe place, Lorelei," he growled, letting some of his pent-up aggression bleed into it.

"I see that," she tried to laugh it off, but he watched her pulse pound in the hollow of her throat. Her eyes were wide as she inhaled the scent of anger and pheromones oozing from him. "I'm trying," she said, dropping her eyes.

Jameson let her arm go with a sigh. "I am too."

"Stop being a volatile Alpha asshole and come eat, you dumb fuck," one of his brothers shouted, earning a beating with a spatula from Annabelle. "This is why I never want an Omega mate. They turn your brain to jelly."

"Language," she yelled, nailing the dodging man as hard as she could. "He'll calm down if you idiots back off." Annabelle dissolved into laughter as her son expertly evaded her flailing swats.

"Ma! I'm too big for a spatula and old enough to say the F word."

"You don't say?" Annabelle chased the man away from the food with a spatula. "Too big for your britches is what you are; you can eat last."

Roars of laughter rippled around the table, causing Jameson to roll his shoulders and relax.

He piled a plate high with food, handing it to Lorelei, who was behind him.

"You don't need to," she started.

"I need to; I need to, okay?" he interrupted, emphasizing the word so she got the point.

"Thank you," she said, waiting for him to make his plate.

Jameson sandwiched Lorelei between himself and his mother. He watched her wary eyes scan around her like she didn't trust the situation, and the claim in his chest screamed. She was killing him. She was absolutely killing him.

Chapter 11

"Who made the mac and cheese?" One of the cookie-cutter brothers asked. Lorelei had never seen so many men look alike. They could have been octuplets. Jameson was bigger and more muscular, but they all favored one another closely. Dark, tousled hair fell in different cuts, and their clothes nodded to their various styles. Still, their looks were eerily similar.

"I did," she answered.

"It's fucking amazing."

"Bruh."

"That's enough, boys, you're giving your mother palpitations," Earl said, shutting the good-natured teasing down.

"Thank you," Lorelei answered.

"What's your secret?" Thalia, Gauge's Beta wife, asked. There were so many people that it was easy to forget who was who and who went with who.

"Family secret, if I told you, I'd have to kill you," Lorelei chuckled.

Thalia looked around nervously, her eyes popping to Gauge.

"I'm kidding," Lorelei said, taking a bite of Jameson's mouth-watering sweet potato casserole. He hadn't lied; the man could cook. She laughed at her plate. He'd covered it with all the dishes he, himself, had prepared. He was feeling the Alpha thing today. She almost felt bad for him. Almost.

"Omegas are known for their vicious streak," Meghan added, not bothering to hide the challenge in her voice.

"Meghan," Earl said, silencing the Alpha female. "Enough from you."

"I'd love the recipe," Thalia continued undeterred. She was a cute thing, medium in height and build, neither too tall nor too short. Her unruly dark blonde curls had been braided back but fought to escape.

Lorelei had spent little time around Betas, but she liked this one.

"I'll write it down for you, then," she answered, fighting to contain the purr in her throat over Jameson's casserole. Unfortunately, he noticed, and his eyes dilated. Shaking her head, she shoved another bite in.

"That'd be great, thanks. Jameson says you're a CPA with an MBA," she continued. "What is this bread thing with the pepperoni in it?" Her eyes rolled back in her head as she tasted the warm concoction.

"It's a pepperoni roll," Lorelei said with a smile. "It's a West Virginia thing," she added, shooting Meghan a pointed glare. Fuck her, she thought, not daring to say it aloud and risk Annabelle's ire.

"I need the recipe for this, too," she moaned, drawing Gauge's eye. His eyes grew predatory as he watched her enraptured face.

"Yeah, we, uh, need that recipe, too," he stated with a growl.

Lorelei couldn't help but laugh out loud at them. "Then you'll have it," she chuckled. "Yes, I have an MBA and am a CPA. I'm not working much currently," she said, shooting a look at Jameson. "But I do some work for the Seventh District."

"It's about time you got it right," Meghan mumbled under her breath.

"I also do some per diem work for a couple of businesses in Morgantown and own a few rental properties there," Lorelei added, ignoring the Alpha female for now. They were going to have a come-to-Jesus moment, but Lorelei wasn't there yet. She wanted to enjoy her meal and the nearness of Jameson. The way he smelled calmed her, and she let it.

"Interesting," Thalia offered. "Gauge and I run a non-profit in Savannah. We've been having issues with our books; maybe you could look at them." Thalia's face was open, showing no trace of malice.

Most Omegas were uneducated. Omegas spent their lives breeding the next generation of Alphas and Omegas, and many thought educating them was a waste. Eve's parents had paid for both of the girls to get whatever degrees they wanted. They'd encouraged their independence and put them to work for the Seventh's government upon graduation. Not everyone had agreed with their choice, but the Seventh was a different place with different people.

There'd always been Alphas and Omegas in West Virginia; the bombs had just solidified it. There, Omega women gutted deer, and Alpha men changed diapers. It was a way of life; sometimes it was harsh and unpredictable, and it was always wild. But it took everyone to survive in those isolated mountains and valleys.

"I would love to," she answered, smiling back at Thalia.

From across the table, Meghan scoffed, huffing out a breath.

Jameson slammed his fork down and rose. "I'll get you another plate, dove," he said, glaring across the table at his brother's girlfriend.

"Thanks, babe," Lorelei said, sliding over enough to allow Jameson's large frame to unfold.

She didn't want these people to see the discord between them. Didn't want to show weakness. Yes, they were his family, but families were tricky. She knew that firsthand.

He came back with a plate covered in sliced ham, fried chicken, sweet potatoes, and collards. She didn't have the heart to tell him she didn't like collards.

She could feel his need to care for her and let him do so. He cut her ham, sliding a bite into her mouth with his fingers. She bristled on the inside but allowed it, knowing he was close to losing control. He slid in another piece, rubbing his thumb along her lower lip.

With a disgusted grunt, Meghan rose to the table and went to grab a beer. Lorelei watched the Alpha female from the corner of her eye while devouring the food Jameson brought. The others, choosing to ignore the situation, followed Lorelei's lead.

She leaned back with a groan, placing her hand over her rounded food baby. "I can't eat another bite," she said.

"Not even banana pudding?" Annabelle said, throwing down the gauntlet with her eyebrow.

"Miss Annabelle, oh," Lorelei said with a groan. "I could probably slide some of that into the cracks."

Jameson moved to rise, but his mother shushed him. "I'll get it, son," she said, glancing at him and Lorelei.

By default, Lorelei had leaned on him, her full belly weighing her down. A small dish of banana pudding slid in front of her, and she started scooping it up despite Jameson's laugh.

Someone had dragged out an ancient game of lawn darts. Music played in the background; drinks were mixed, and a small firepit glowed. With a sigh, Lorelei rose, using Jameson as a springboard to get on her feet. His chest rumbled with pleasure.

"You want a beer?" she asked, moving toward the drink table.

"I'll take a whiskey," he answered, watching her movements.

"I'll make it two then." At the drinks table, she added ice to two glasses, pouring three fingers each. She downed her first glass in two gulps and poured another.

"You smell amazing, Omega," A low female voice said from behind her.

Lorelei turned to find Meghan blocking her view of Jameson.

"But you smell like another man. Are you confused, Omega? Not sure who you belong to? Walking around the city streets smelling confused will get you and Jameson killed, you know. Perhaps I can help you clear the confusion." Meghan stepped closer, reaching for Lorelei's arm.

Lorelei set her drinks down with a heavy sigh.

Stepping into the much larger female, she twisted under her grip, rotated out, and flipped the tall woman onto her back with a fierce growl. Lorelei landed on her chest, pinning the other woman's arms with her legs. The switchblade she had stolen from Jameson's nightstand was in her hand and at Meghan's throat in a flash. Meghan bucked under her, trying to dislodge the smaller woman.

"Don't fuck with me, Meghan," Lorelei threatened. "I don't know you, and you don't know me." The knife gleamed in the sun's light. "Don't presume to understand something you can't, Alpha," Lorelei said with a sneer. "I won't tell you again."

It happened before anyone could react. Lorelei was on her feet, and Meghan gasping for breath on the ground before Jameson could unfold himself from the picnic table with a loud roar. He caught the movement of the switchblade as she slid it back into her pocket. Darrian yelled and went toward Meghan; Earl and Annabelle were on their feet, heading toward Lorelei.

Jameson stepped between his family and his mate, and they stopped advancing; his eyes had blackened, and no iris showed. In the moment's chaos, Lorelei disappeared.

In the barn, she walked to the sorrel mare, opened the door, and slipped into her stall. The mare's head whipped up and her ears pinned, but when she saw who it was, her head dipped back down into the pile of hay. With a sigh, Lorelei slunk forward, slipping her hands into the mare's mane.

She heard Jameson roar again and knew he'd be on her trail in a minute. Lying her head on the mare's soft neck, she breathed in the horse's scent, letting it calm her. Faced with what she knew was coming, she took deep, cleansing breaths before rolling her head and leaving the safety of the mare's stall.

She'd just needed a second to get herself together. Meghan was a bitch, an Alpha female testing the boundaries and pushing buttons; Lorelei knew that.

Still, she wasn't wrong; not even a little. Sometimes it is easier to accept pretty lies than hard truths; they also tend to be more welcome.

Meghan had told her a hard truth she'd known but hadn't wanted to acknowledge, and Lorelei had put a knife to her throat because of it.

The barn door banged open, slamming closed again of its own accord. Jameson stood in the shadows, chest heaving and eyes unfocused. His head swiveled her way, and his nostrils flared; he scented the air with a snarl. She had known running from him would make it worse, but at the moment, she hadn't cared. She'd understood he would lose it and didn't want to be on the lawn when it happened.

He stalked toward her, gripping her throat in his large hand and bringing Lorelei to her toes. Jameson buried his nose in her neck, inhaling her scent like he needed it for survival. He did not speak, just breathed in her scent as he growled low in warning. She went limp in his grip, knowing it was not the time to fight him.

Alphas were dangerous, and this one had been on edge all day. Lorelei knew he wouldn't hurt her; she trusted him that much, but he was beyond reasoning with. One hand wrapped around her throat, and the other gripped her hip, pulling her into him; Jameson growled at her. She gave him her throat in submission, and the angry growl changed.

Chest heaving against hers, he pushed her away from him, hooking his leg behind hers until she fell back. Strong arms kept her from hitting the ground, cradling her against the fall.

His hands roamed everywhere: her face, her neck, her breasts. He ripped the shirt over her head, and she let out a whimper. His growl changed back to angry as he freed his cock from his jeans, forcing her hand to stroke it while he opened her pants. Two thick fingers sank into her flesh, coaxing her slick to flow.

Jameson removed his fingers, brought them to his nose, and inhaled deeply. Licking her slick off of them, he dipped them into her again. She stroked him languidly as his eyes held hers.

He pushed her bra up, exposing her breasts. She didn't fight; she'd known this was coming all day, and she couldn't help what could not be changed.

They'd left the safety of his home before he was ready, and he saw challenges to his dominance everywhere. Yes, he loved his family, but the dissonant bond in his chest demanded he act, and here they were.

Eve had a degree in Dynamics, not Lorelei, but she was no fool. She hadn't asked to be claimed, hadn't wanted it, but it was done. Ripping her jeans off so that they turned inside out, he crushed her with his weight, prying her legs open with his own.

She couldn't help but cry out when he sheathed himself inside her with one stroke. He pulled at her scalp in the way an Alpha does to calm a difficult Omega, but did not pause the sharp snapping of his hips. All she could feel was him. The size and weight of him inside of her prevented any other thoughts from entering her mind.

Lorelei kept her head turned, and Jameson buried his face in it, his low growl demanding she remain still. He didn't want her to fuck him; he wanted her surrender, and she gave it. Maybe when he was calmer, they could talk; maybe not. Maybe they would never talk about this.

It didn't matter that she didn't want to feel anything; she did. Jameson's body in hers ignited a fire she hated to enjoy, his long, sharp thrusts hitting that deep spot.

She burned for him as he pummeled her, bruising her cervix and making her grunt with each invasion. Wrapping her arms around Jameson's shoulders, Lorelei came apart with a cry. Her body clenching around his, begging for his knot. Jameson tipped his shoulder to her, inviting her to claim him with her teeth as her core spasmed around his cock, but she refused.

With a yell, he pulled his cock free, covering her in thick streams of cum. It rolled down her sides and splashed across her face. Jameson jerked on his knot, encouraging more to spurt over her flesh. He rubbed it from her head to her toes, bathing her in the scent of his seed. "You. Are. Mine. There is no confusion. Do you understand?" he said, pinning her with a dark glare.

"Yes," she answered, dropping her eyes.

Jameson rose with a frustrated roar, grabbing his pants and shoving his legs into them before leaving her alone in the barn. She'd never felt more empty in her life, and the dissonance between them was worse than it ever had been.

Rising slowly on sore legs, she went to the frost-free hydrant in the barn and washed most of Jameson's cooling cum off. She found a roll of paper towels in the feed room and dried herself before slipping on her clothes. Her pussy hurt, throbbing in time to her heartbeat as she buttoned her pants.

How could she face all those people? They were Alphas, most of them anyway. Their sense of smell was so acute that they would have a play-by-play of what had happened. Gingerly, Lorelei sank onto a hay bale, placing her head in her hands.

The barn door opened, shutting abruptly again. Lorelei looked up to see Annabelle leaning against it. Heat rushed to her cheeks, and she choked out a sob.

"Are you okay?" the older Omega asked.

"Does it matter?" Lorelei answered.

"To me? Yes. To the world, probably not," she started. "When Jameson comes down from his pheromone high, he will be crushed by his actions. He was practically raised as an Omega; he wants to fight his instincts, but that's the problem with instincts, they're intrinsic and hard to fight." Annabelle sank down next to Lorelei on the hay bale, releasing a long sigh.

"The better question is, are you hurt?" she asked.

"I'll heal," Lorelei answered before breaking down into sobs. "I never wanted this; I can't do it," her sobs strengthened, and Annabelle pulled her into the safety of her bosom. "I don't want to live like this," Lorelei finished, the tears coming hot and fast.

"There, there, sugar. Let it out." Annabelle rocked Lorelei from side to side, crooning as she sobbed. "It will be okay if you let it. I promise, but only if you want it to be. No, you didn't have a choice then, but you have one now. You do," she said when Lorelei chuckled ruefully. "My son's life is yours to take. I understand your sadness and respect your pain. But you need to understand your power. You think you've lost it, but you've only just found it, Lorelei. Jameson can't be happy unless you are happy; his emotions feed off yours. That's the way it goes.

"All of his thoughts are for you. Your well-being, joy, and sorrow are his to carry and understand; that is the Alpha's burden. He would give you anything to ease your pain.

"Can it be undone? No, it can't. But you can choose to move forward. You can choose to find a path to, if not happiness, comfort. That's where your choice lies now." She stopped, taking a deep breath.

"Earl bought me from my father when I was fourteen," Annabelle continued, "He's years older than I am, and both of our families were influential and affluent. He paid a large bride price in money, land, and investment holdings to secure my hand in marriage. I didn't want that. To my fourteen-year-old eyes, he was ancient. The thought of him made my skin crawl. Omegas fifty years ago had even less choice than they did before NS304. My father sold me. It was legal. The end."

"My mother cried and tried to talk him out of it, but no Alpha male wants an Omega daughter around for her first estrous." Annabelle stopped, wringing her hands for a moment. "When it was apparent it was coming, Earl came for me. I said goodbye to my mother and my siblings and was taken to his farm in the hills. He was kind enough to wait until it hit before he took me, but I was only seventeen, and he was ten years older. I didn't understand. I hated him for it; God, did I hate him. Even under the haze of estrous, I hated him." She paused, taking a deep breath. Lorelei lay still in her arms, considering her words.

"You know what he did? He served me through it in the way an Alpha does. He claimed me with the first knotting and felt my hatred for him during the rest that followed. My age didn't matter; my desires didn't matter; nothing mattered. All that mattered was that he had claimed me, and I was his. To myself, I was nothing, but to him, I was everything.

"Darrian was born nine months later, and I had a baby every year after for eight years, Lorelei. Most Omegas don't catch that often, but I was blessed, I suppose. With Jameson, my uterus gave out. Women aren't deer, meant to have a fawn every year until they die. I became too weak from carrying eight Alpha males and almost died from blood loss. That is an Omega's burden," she paused with a faint smile on her face.

"My mother never explained it to me; it wasn't polite to do so back then," she went on. "Not the sex, or the knotting; none of it. I was scared, hurt, and confused. That first year? I'm not sure my feet touched the floor of our bedroom. He was always, you know, there." A soft blush crept up her cheeks. "It was hard, to say the least. But you know who taught me about myself? Earl. He knew. I learned of my power through him, and believe you me, you have more power than you think."

"Do you love him?" Lorelei asked, her voice shaky.

"Now? Absolutely. We forged a bond in those first years that turned to love. There's no taking the claim back. I understand what happened and why Jameson did it. But you're right, he didn't have to.

"Jameson could have left you with that other Alpha's claim on your skin. What kind of man was he? If he hadn't been killed, who would you have been tied to? My son loves you already; it's hard not to. You're fierce and loyal, yet kind and sweet, smart and

118

multi-talented, and you're beautiful on top of it. You could have been tied to a man who used drugs to claim you for the rest of your life. Is what Jameson did worse than that, or better? He challenged another Alpha's claim, so you weren't forced to suffer. You can move on if you choose." She looked down at me, her face questioning.

"Women always carry the burden, Lorelei. Alphas do what they need to do, and Omegas do what must be done; the distinction between those things is important.

"We carry the future within us, giving up everything of ourselves to nurture it to adulthood. We carry the brunt of a man's desires, both good and bad. We are overlooked and undervalued by most, if not all. The weight of the world lies on our shoulders because of who and what an Alpha is. Without us, there would be only violence and strife. You are necessary.

"Jameson will come to you and do things you never asked for, and you will give him yourself to calm that savageness he carries. That is your burden, but you can love him too, Lorelei. You can; he's a good man. I raised him well. Honestly, he's the best of the lot. I understand right now it's hard for you to give him a chance, but I don't want him to wither away and die if you don't choose him; he's worth more than that. But make no mistake, so are you." Anabelle disentangled the hot, sweaty Omega from her arms and rose.

"They're getting ready for the hunt. Darrian asked Meghan to leave. She did what she did on purpose, knowing the outcome. Even if she were an Omega, she would be a cunt."

Lorelei's eyes flew open in surprise, and her hand went to her mouth in shock.

"Don't tell the boys I used that word; that's just between us girls," Annabelle winked, laughing at Lorelei's shock. "A proper Southern lady knows the things to say, but more importantly, she knows where she can say them." She winked.

A genuine smile crossed Lorelei's face as she looked up at her mother-in-law. Taking her proffered hand, Lorelei rose to her feet with a wince. She limped through the barnyard and toward the house.

The backyard was empty, and the tables were cleared. A low fire burned in the firepit, and she stopped, adding more wood to it to delay the inevitable.

The foyer and great room were also empty when they walked into the house, and she was glad. She didn't think she could face anyone but Annabelle right now.

Maybe that's why she'd come. She knew what Lorelei felt and wanted to share with her. It had eased her pain, lessened it just a little. Lorelei knew she was going through what most, if not all, Omegas went through before NS304. Her case was a fluke, she hoped, something that wouldn't be repeated.

Over the years, Omegas have gained more rights and freedoms. Her situation was a setback, but life was getting better for them in the grand scheme of things.

"I'm sorry for what Meghan did," Darrian said, startling her and causing Lorelei to whip the switchblade from her pocket and turn on a dime.

Darrian stared at the knife, understanding something before she did. She gave the blade a long look before easing it closed and sliding it into her pocket. Lorelei had known it was there; she'd not forgotten about it. Had she wanted to hurt Jameson or stop him, she could have. She hadn't wanted to, not really.

Covering herself with her arms, Lorelei responded, "You can't apologize for someone else; you aren't responsible for what she did." Her eyebrows scrunched together, and she couldn't quite bring herself to meet his eyes.

"Then I apologize for bringing her today; I should have known better. Meghan was raised in the traditional Alpha way; these new laws are foreign to her. I'm not making excuses, not at all," he added when Lorelei's eyes narrowed on him. "I'm saying that I knew that about her and should've put two and two together. What she did, she did on purpose."

"It's not your fault, Darrian," Lorelei responded, stepping back when he reached out to hug her.

"Look, Lorelei," he said, dropping his arms to his side and slumping. "I broke up with Meghan; I'm done with her. I've been done for a long time, but she pushed my last button. Family is everything, and you are family. She hurt you and my brother, and that is unforgivable."

Lorelei nodded her head once, finally bringing her eyes to Darrian's.

"My brother is a decent enough man; please don't hold Meghan against him." He stepped away, letting her pass. His face blanched a shade when he noticed her wince and cradle herself as she walked up the stairs.

She opened the door to her bedroom and stepped back when she saw Jameson on her bed. He sat with his shoulders slumped and his head in his hands. He raised his red-rimmed eyes to hers, scrubbing his face with his hands as he took her in.

"Lorelei," he started.

"Don't. Just don't; not yet." Stepping sideways, she closed the door behind her and rested her head back against it. "I need some Tylenol and a shower, James," she said, using the name he told her to call him by and not the one she liked.

His shoulders dropped lower, and he rose with a sigh. "I'll go," he said.

"You don't have to go; just give me a few minutes. Okay?"

"Okay," he said.

She limped past him, and he put his head in his hands and sobbed, his shoulders shaking when he saw it. "Goddamnit, Lorelei. I fucking hurt you,"

"It's what I'm made for, Right?" she whispered. "I can handle it."

"No. Fuck. No, it's not. Goddamnit. It's not what you're made for." He pounded his fists on the mattress and sank to his knees. Wrapping his arms around her legs and burying his face in her stomach, he whispered, "You shouldn't have to handle it."

Lorelei sighed, massaging her hands in Jameson's mop of dark hair, soothing the Alpha. She wouldn't tell him it was okay; it wasn't. But she offered what comfort she could, and doing it made her feel a little better.

When his shoulders relaxed and his ragged sobs stopped, she pulled away. "I need to shower and change. I still want to hunt those coyotes, and your family is waiting."

Nodding his head wordlessly, he wiped his nose on his sleeve and pulled back from her. Gingerly, she walked to the bathroom, shutting the door behind her. She leaned heavily against the wall, tilting her head back with a sigh. After her heartbeat slowed and her ragged breaths calmed, she started the shower, stripped out of her wrecked clothes, and thought hard about what Jameson's mother had said.

Chapter 12

Jameson rose on shaky legs, listening to the sound of Lorelei moving in the shower. He took a minute to get himself together before heading downstairs to get Lorelei a bottle of water and some Tylenol. His mother was in the kitchen, putting the last of the dishes away.

"You can take a spoon to me if you want," he said as he walked to the fridge.

"I know I can, son. I think you've probably punished yourself enough," she said, wiping her hands on her apron before taking it off. "Lorelei is tougher than you know; she'll be all right."

"She shouldn't have to be, ma," he sighed, scrubbing his hands down his face.

"You're right; she shouldn't. But it is what it is, JB. Your relationship will smooth out. Your brothers love her, even though there is some concern about her quickness with her knife." His mother came forward and gave him a hug.

"She stole it from me," he said with a wry laugh.

"Even better. Don't leave her for too long, dear." Patting his arm one more time, she turned and walked away.

Jameson took the stairs slowly, giving Lorelei a few minutes to herself.

In her room, he could still hear the shower running. Easing the bathroom door open, he was engulfed immediately in heavy steam.

"I'm leaving some water and Tylenol on the counter. Your robe is on the hook," he said.

"Thanks," she said, sounding small behind the shower curtain. "I'll be right out."

She came from the bathroom with a towel on her head and a thick robe wrapped around her. He noted she was moving more easily, and the iron clamp around his heart eased.

He hated what he'd done. God, Meghan had pushed all the right buttons, but he'd been on edge all day. He didn't think he could forgive himself and doubted she ever would. Fuck biology.

He understood the pros and cons of being Alpha better than most; he refused to blame biology. Except he'd seen it through a haze of red and had had zero ability to stop himself.

It was one thing to knot her to solidify their bond and another to take her out of anger on the barn floor like an animal. He hadn't even tried to make it easy for her; he'd just pounded away like a rutting dog. Fuck.

He had brought her here too soon. Hoping his mama could fix his mess, he had made a bigger one. There was no fixing this.

His heart stilled when she dropped her robe, exposing her back to him. Angry bruises dotted the backs of her arms and the small of her back where he'd gripped her.

She shook her hair free of the towel, easing a dark shirt over her head. "Is everyone going hunting?" she asked softly, keeping her back to him while she pulled on underwear and jeans.

"Just us, Dad, Darrian, and Hunter," Jameson answered, keeping his ass firmly on the edge of her bed instead of going to her like he wanted to.

He watched the slight nod of her head in acknowledgment.

"I'm sorry, Lorelei," he said, watching her carefully.

She nodded her head up and down, turning to meet his eyes when he spoke. Her dark eyes were fathomless, seeming to soak up the light in the room.

"Forgive me. Please," he added, trying to keep his voice even. His mama raised him better, and he felt he owed her an apology, too.

"The list of things I'm required to forgive keeps growing," she said.

"You could beat me with a wooden spoon. Better yet, ma has an extra spatula or two," he said, a tight smile pulling on his lips.

"You do make a mean sweet potato casserole," she tried. "It's hard to let go of that kind of cooking."

"There's that, too," he said. "I'll cook every day for a week." Rising, he took her hand, bringing it to his lips. "I'm sorry, dove. Let me make it up to you."

"I don't think a week is long enough, Jameson," she said, and his soul calmed at the use of his given name. He hated the sound of James on her tongue.

"A month then. All meals for a month, you pick the menu," he tried.

"Why do you call me dove?" she asked, slanting her eyes his way.

"If I answer that, there will be another thing on the list, and I'll owe you two months of cooking," he said, opening the door for her.

Pushing it shut again, she asked, "Why?"

Sighing, he moved back to the edge of the bed. "Do you know anything about mourning doves?" he asked.

"No," she answered.

"Doves are unique in the bird world, one of a kind actually," he started, dipping his head down. "They are strong fliers, fast, and agile with maneuvers. They're very hard to catch unless they want to be caught, but they are hunted widely. And they do things no other bird does, and they mate for life. Doves are the only species of bird to kiss one another," he paused with a heavy sigh. "Dove also rhymes with love, and I knew if I called you 'love,' you would jerk a knot in my ass."

"You think you love me?" she asked, pinning him with her eyes.

"I know I do, Lorelei. I love you and have from the minute I saw you."

"At the party," she said, disbelief plain in her voice.

"I first saw you way before that goddamn party. When you were fighting for freedom in the woods of the Seventh, I caught glimpses. I saw you standing on that fucking rock when Eve was shot. You were at her bedside in the hospital and walking with her through Greenville. It was fate. Everywhere I went, I saw you. We're good together, Lorelei. We are," he said, going back on his promise to himself not to beg her.

"I never saw you," she said simply, meeting his eyes.

"It doesn't matter because I saw you." Jameson rose heavily. He didn't want to go coyote hunting; he wanted to take Lorelei to bed and hold her, purring until she fell asleep in his arms.

They were going home tomorrow, come what may. He loved his family, but he hadn't been ready to share his mate and shouldn't have tried.

She turned away, opening the door and walking down the stairs on bare feet. He waited a breath before closing the door and following.

"What weapons you want, girl?" Jameson heard his father ask Lorelei as soon as her feet touched the bottom step.

"What'cha got?" she answered with a shy smile.

"I've got just about everything," he added, his voice gruff. Jameson caught the hint of a smile, though, and knew Earl liked Lorelei.

"Everything?" she laughed, her smile finally reaching her eyes. "In that case, I'll take a compound bow with a twenty-three-inch, left-hand draw, an antique Glock 19, and a Marlin .45-70."

"Well, damn," he drawled, making the word two syllables like a true southerner should, making his son laugh too.

"All right, How about a kid's recurve that is ambidextrous. I've got the rest. You sure you want a .45-70? It kicks like a mule," he added, giving Jameson a wary eye.

"I've been kicked by a mule, and the .45-70 kicks harder. Yes, I want it."

"Okay, little lady. It's your shoulder." His father moved into the great room and opened a gun safe, pulling out firearm after firearm until he had the ones he wanted. Then he popped into the garage and came back with the bow. It had a shoulder strap and an old quiver of arrows.

"I didn't know you were a lefty," Jameson said, pulling a Remington .243 from his dad's stash. Personally, he thought the .45-70 was overkill for coyotes and better suited for big game.

"I'm not really; I can use either hand, but I'm left eye dominant, so I shoot lefty.

"Good to know. If your plan is to shoot me, shoot straight," he said with a rueful laugh.

"I always shoot straight, Jameson. And I never miss." She gave him a wink and walked to the door, not bothering with shoes. Then he remembered that none of the Omega Force had worn them while they fought, making them silent and deadly in the woods. He really hoped she didn't plan on taking him out, but if she did, he guessed he deserved it.

Afternoon had turned to dusk, and the scent of pine was heavy in the light, misty rain that fell. Coyote hunting wasn't easy. They were predators and knew a setup when they saw it. Coyotes were smart and cagey, often able to tell the difference between real prey and even the best prey calls.

The five of us stalked forward through the yard and out into the field beyond. His father's round bales made for excellent cover, and they slipped in behind them to get ready. Lorelei chose the bale farthest from him, on the very edge of the field.

She'd slipped the Glock into the waistband of her pants and laid the .45-70 against the hay. Her movements were smooth and efficient, and he couldn't take his eyes off her. He caught the others watching, too. It wasn't unusual for a Southern woman to know how to hunt, but Lorelei's dynamic made her a rarity. Until you met the Omegas from the Seventh, then you came to understand that there was more out there than you realized. The citizens of

130

Greenville had learned a lot since their arrival. The Omegas traveled in packs through the city streets, bringing their brand of culture to the area.

Lorelei sank to a crouch and called once the others were settled. He'd heard nothing like it. The rabbit's scream she mimicked made gooseflesh rise on his arms, and his hair stood on end. His brothers cast a nervous glance his way.

Lorelei changed the pitch and the pace of her cries until Jameson's hands shook. It was unnerving and unnatural how accurate they were. Knowing those noises came from his mate triggered something in him. Clenching and unclenching his hands, he forced himself to remain calm.

It didn't take long. The pack of coyotes descended from nowhere, and Jameson realized her wisdom in choosing the place furthest away. Crazed for blood, the coyotes barreled right past them, darting and weaving toward the cries, right toward Lorelei.

The first shot sounded like a cannon, shaking Jameson from his reverie. Lifting his shotgun, he fired shot after shot, pumping the action and reloading as fast as possible. Screeches and cries filled the air along with the scent of gunpowder. It cast an eerie haze over the ground, turning everything faintly yellow.

When the haze cleared, eight coyotes lay dead with arrows through their lungs, and six more from various firearm rounds.

He wished he had simply thought to watch. The skill it took to nock an arrow, draw, aim, and fire a bow at a quickly moving target blew his mind. To do it eight times in a few seconds was unbelievable. Lorelei was a predator, too, and he let that sink in.

Hunter whooped, throwing his fists in the air. Running, he flew to Lorelei, picked her up, and swung her around before setting her back on her feet and coming to shake Jameson's hand.

Lorelei giggled, and the sound was so foreign that it took his breath away. Her face was all smiles, and her eyes were bright.

"Best. Sister-in-law. Ever," Hunter shouted, his glee contagious.

Darrian and Earl laughed as they looked at the surrounding carnage. Typically, they would have left the pack alone, but once coy dogs had a taste for livestock, there'd been no other choice.

"Get the truck, Hunter, and we'll throw them over the hillside," Jameson's dad said, his own smile wider than Jameson had seen it in a while.

With another whoop, Hunter turned and ran to the house.

Jameson turned to Lorelei, reaching for her hand. She stepped neatly away from him, looking into the woods beyond. "There's a little time until full dark, Jameson. I'll be back before the moon rises," Lorelei said, looking over her shoulder at him.

Picking up the .45-70, she dissipated into the growing night. One breath she was there, and the next not. Jameson stepped forward, reaching into the mist and finding nothing in his grasp. There was no snapping of twigs or movement in the brush; she was simply gone.

Turning in a slow circle, he called her name until Darrian came to him and put a large hand on his shoulder.

"She'll come back, JB," Darrian said, ruffling his baby brother's hair.

"I don't...I don't think so, Darrian," Jameson said, his words coming out in a rush. "And I don't deserve it if she does." Head hanging low, Jameson turned, walking back to the house. "I," he started, needing his big brother's advice. "Things between us are...complicated," he said.

"I know that," Darrian started. "I think we all sense that there's something off." He pulled Jameson into a side-armed bro hug, and Jameson told him everything.

When he was done, Jameson felt better, but Darrian felt worse. He'd secretly dreamed about courting an Omega, but he wasn't sure he had the fortitude for it. He'd seen his father lose it over the years, and Earl was not a man to lose it, but then neither was Jameson. With Omegas, all bets were off, even for strong men.

Clapping his baby brother on the shoulder, he said the only thing he knew to be true. "Southern women are built on a platform of indelible grace. Their capacity to forgive is limitless. But that grace should not be mistaken for weakness, because they will light you up for your indiscretions, even though they forgive you while they do it. She'll come around, buddy; the bond will see to it."

"I didn't want it that way, and neither did she," Jameson said, looking hopefully into his brother's face.

"Well, brother, you gotta ride the horse you have and not the one you hoped for." Darrian moved away, leaving Jameson alone.

Full dark had settled over the farm, and the moon's tip was visible on the horizon. Jameson sank into a chair by the firepit, a highball glass of whiskey hanging from his fingers. His brothers echoed around him, their voices low in the dark. Sparks snapped and popped off the fire when another log was thrown in, mesmerizing him. His heart was heavy, but the bond was calm in his chest, and he didn't know what that meant.

Gauge and Hunter laughed, and someone turned on a country station, playing the music low. Jameson had never felt emptier in his life. The Alpha-Omega bond was designed to make them both happy. That was the purpose of the thing.

Once the bond was in place, there should be no more emptiness. Whether it was breaking another Alpha's claim, trying to claim Lorelei during a false estrous, or something else, their bond was fucked up.

Around him, the voices of his family skittered out, and an odd silence settled over them. Lifting his eyes, Jameson saw why.

Lorelei appeared from the darkness, her light blonde hair luminous in the firelight. Her large eyes absorbed the darkness and spat out stars.

Silently, she pulled the massive ten-point buck along by its antlers. With a huff, she dropped the field-dressed deer at the edge of the firelight. He never even heard the .45-70 discharge, but the large hole through the deer's left lung told the tale. It weighed more than twice what she did, and her powerful muscles strained with the effort.

"Whew," she said, unloading the rifle like a professional and pocketing the round. "Something for Miss Annabelle's freezers. You got a place to hang this up?" she said, looking at the deer.

Jameson and his brothers sat frozen, watching as the Omega finished materializing from the darkness. She sank into the empty chair next to Jameson, taking his whiskey and drinking it in one gulp, and handing him back his empty glass. Lorelei pulled the Glock from her waistband, dropped the magazine, and cleared the chamber before handing it to Jameson by the grip. "Thanks for the loan," she said, leaning back into her chair and closing her eyes. "That's the most fun I've had in ages."

Jameson looked around the fire to see that everyone was as speechless as he; their stunned faces matched his. Sensing the pause, Lorelei opened her eyes back up and said, "What?"

"Nothing," multiple voices said before silence reigned again.

With a shrug of her shoulders, Lorelei gestured to Jameson's empty glass, "Where's the bottle?"

"Uh, I'll get the buck," Gauge jumped up, walking to the discarded deer. Grabbing it, he dragged it toward a small building, glancing at Lorelei over his shoulder.

"I'll get the whiskey," Darrian walked toward the house, meeting his brother's eyes and holding them.

"Next time, I'm bringing moonshine," Lorelei said, not catching the odd looks Jameson's family gave.

Jameson's heart stilled at her words, and he took a moment to glance over at his little Omega. She'd said next time, and his heart lifted. The bond between them felt calm, and he wondered if roaming the woods was the key to her happiness.

Darian came back with a bottle of Palmetto Whiskey and a grin. He handed the bottle to Lorelei, and she took a swig from its mouth before passing it to Jameson.

"That's smooth," she sighed.

"It's distilled locally, but watch out, it has a bite," he warned.

Lorelei tipped her head back and laughed loudly. "I'm definitely bringing moonshine next time," she said, her eyes dancing in the firelight.

Jameson sipped from the bottle before handing it back to Lorelei, meeting her eyes with a grin. She answered his grin, taking another drink.

"Anyone?" Lorelei offered the bottle, holding it out from her.

The bottle was passed around until it was empty. Conversation and laughter flowed, and the scent of wood smoke blanketed the air. One by one, people excused themselves, heading to the house for bed until it was just Lorelei and Jameson.

"Dance with me," Jameson asked when they were alone, and he was more than a little tipsy.

"James," she sighed.

"Please. And call me Jameson. James doesn't sound right anymore," he said, interrupting her before she could refuse him.

Sliding her small hand into his large one, Lorelei allowed him to pull her close. Moving to the subtle notes of a country song, they slow danced by the fire as the smell of smoke and whiskey filled their noses. After the third song, she relaxed, and after the fourth, she leaned into him, causing his heart to stutter and almost stop.

When the fall, southern night grew chilly, Lorelei pulled away, walking into the house with Jameson trailing behind.

Chapter 13

Goosebumps trailed up Lorelei's arms as she headed up the wide, curving staircase. It had been a long day, and weariness hit her as suddenly as twice-distilled moonshine. With a small shiver, she stepped inside, waiting for Jameson to follow so she could close the door.

"I had a good time tonight," she said, glancing up the stairs leading to her side of the house.

"Me too," Jameson said, trying to find a place to put his hands. "Can I come up?" he asked. "Just for a minute," he added when it became clear she would say no; his dark eyes were so sad that she didn't have the heart to turn him down.

"Okay," she answered with a sigh. Her feet padded lightly on the stairs as she turned and headed to her room. "I need another shower," she said, glancing over her shoulder at her mate. "I've deer's blood under my nails."

"My mom will appreciate the meat; things get lean out here sometimes, and these whitetails are pretty cagey. How did you find him?" Jameson asked, sitting on the edge of the frilly pink bed.

"Eh," Lorelei started, knowing what she was about to say would sound crazy to anyone that hadn't grown up in the woods. "I could smell where he was bedded down. He must have used that spot enough that the scent was heavy. I caught it before the coyotes came in and followed it afterward, hoping I could catch him when he got up for the night.

"He was a few hundred yards to the north of us. He waited until the shooting stopped, I guess, and figured he was safe." She finished with a little shrug of her shoulders. She and Eve had spent years tracking deer and were pretty good at it.

"That's nuts," Jameson said, shaking his head. The smile on his face was full of pride.

She gave another shrug and walked to the bathroom, shutting the door behind her. Taking her time, she washed until she was clean, taking time to condition her hair. Jameson's family was great, in that large family, Southern way. She'd had nothing like that in her life, and she didn't hate it, despite the circumstances.

She loved Miss Annabelle and wondered if she could be happy with Jameson for that reason alone. Maybe Annabelle was right, and things could get better if she let them; it was hard to say. It was harder to do. Deciding that the decision could be made tomorrow, Lorelei turned the water off, dried, threw a long shirt over her head, and went to find Jameson.

He sat on the bed like he hadn't moved an inch while she'd been gone.

"Hey," he said, scrubbing his hands over his face, then bringing his eyes to hers.

"Hey," she answered, leaning against the door.

"I, uh, God." He leaned forward, inching his way closer to where she stood. "I need you. Not like… fuck." Jameson stood pacing in front of the door.

"Jameson," Lorelei started.

"No," he interrupted, his pacing becoming faster. "I need."

"What do you need?" she asked, her voice growing sharper. She was tired, she was sore in her core, and she was just about over what Jameson needed.

"Can I just hold you?" he asked, slowing his pacing and meeting her eyes. "That's all, I swear." He stopped, sighing heavily. "I swear."

Lorelei stood, saying nothing. Maybe Annabelle was right that Omegas carried the lion's share of the burden. Watching Jameson stalk around a pink room with ribbons everywhere, she doubted that was entirely accurate. He was the head of the Marine's Cyberwarfare branch and didn't strike her as the kind of guy to actually need anything.

The bond went both ways; she knew that. Jameson suffered when she suffered, and his need to soothe her was so great that he remained in a constant state of upheaval.

"Okay, Jameson," she said with a sigh, not quite meeting his eyes. "Okay." Her eyes darted to him, catching the relieved slump of his shoulders.

Lorelei watched as he stripped out of his jeans, slipping his shirt over his head. He certainly was a beautiful specimen. He didn't look like he sat behind a computer screen all day. His muscles rippled with each movement made, and his skin slid over their hardness like silk.

The tousled dark curls on the top of his head were damn near unruly and softened his appearance's overall hardness. On top of being beautiful, he was cute. Shaking her head at herself, she slid under the covers he held open for her, letting the scent of spice drift to her nose.

Immediately, Jameson pulled her close, making her feel small against him. Purring loudly, he massaged the back of her neck, easing the tension she held there. Powerful hands moved across her trapezius muscles and down her spine, but stayed in safe territory. She relaxed despite herself. His purr grew louder, sounding more sure.

"I've never purred before, and now I can't stop. It's weird," he said, his tone half-serious and half-joking. "Everything is so weird."

She could feel him shaking his head behind her. "You're okay at it," Lorelei deadpanned, letting the humor she intended bleed through. He rewarded her with a light chuckle that she liked the sound of. "What do you do for The Alpha? She asked, her words slurring. But she wanted to change the subject. She wasn't ready to talk about their relationship when she knew nothing about the man himself.

"Well, I'm in charge of gathering intel on the New North and the Middle West. You know, finding out what they're up to and the state of affairs behind their walls. I also keep tabs on individuals or groups that may be against the ideals of the New South. If needed, I place, uh, stories here and there to steer public opinion. Oh," he stopped, taking a long pause, "And I pilot drones when needed."

"Drones?" she asked.

"Yeah, we keep a fleet of drones at the ready," he said, never stopping the rumble in his chest.

"Interesting," Lorelei said, smiling to herself. "Did you assist The Alpha during the recent troubles?" she asked with a chuckle.

"Uh, yeah," he said cautiously.

"Drones tried to keep eyes on us," she said, smiling to herself. They'd seen the drones during their ride to the battlefield; they knew they'd been watched.

"You're, uh, beautiful when you sleep," he said, sounding contrite. "That's about the only full glimpse of The Omega Force we ever got. Y'all bedded down under some trees that first night."

Lorelei belly laughed, feeling his chest move with laughter, too.

"Your friend, Eve, is a good shot." Jameson went back to massaging Lorelei's scalp and tugging at her damp hair.

"I'm better," Lorelei answered, her voice serious. "Now, with a bo staff or hand to hand, EJ's your girl, but I'm better with anything that shoots."

"I saw that in action tonight. I wouldn't want to be on the wrong end of that." Jameson sounded concerned, making the bond in them uneasy.

"I wouldn't hurt you, Jameson. I wouldn't do that, and I do understand what you did and why you did it. Just because I disagree doesn't mean I don't understand," Lorelei said, feeling their bond settle.

"Are you going to leave me?" he asked, his voice low.

"I haven't decided, Jameson." She thought about adding more, like about how she wanted to talk to Eve first. Or how she wanted to weigh her options, but she didn't.

"That's fair, Lorelei," he said, increasing the depth of his purr. "I understand. All I ask is that you give us a chance. If, after you get to know me as a person and an Alpha, you still want to leave, I won't stop you; I will try to let you go," he said. She felt the chuckle start in his chest and bubble outward.

"You'll try?" she said, feeling a smile form on her face.

Typical Alpha, thinking he actually had a say in whether she stayed or went. Their bond hummed with humor, and she knew he was trying to joke with her.

"I mean," he said, fighting to keep the chuckle from becoming a full-on laugh. "If you can get out of the restraints, past the locks, and not get eaten by the alligators in the moat, you might make it."

"That's fair, Jameson," she replied, unable to stop her own laugh. "Jerk," she finished.

"Hey, I saw you fight; I feel like your chances are pretty good." Jameson did laugh then, hard and loud.

Lorelei thought he might be laughing more to relieve pent-up stress than because what he said was funny. Though it was kind of funny.

"I mean- Alligators," she let herself give a small laugh. "The Seventh doesn't have those, so their chances are better than average."

Jameson flipped Lorelei around so that she faced him, then tucked her into the hollow of his arm, resting his chin on her head. He never stopped purring, and the rumble in his chest thrummed through her, making her eyes heavy. His hands moved through her hair, pulling and rubbing until there was no way she could stay awake another minute.

"I want to take you home tomorrow. Are you okay with that?" he asked, surprising her.

"That's fine," she answered simply. She'd felt that Jameson was restless and wanted to leave. She'd known it was coming; the surprise was that he asked her instead of telling. He really was trying; she gave him credit for that. "I just wish things weren't so complicated."

"Are they really?" Jameson asked. "They don't have to be. Yes, there are cracks, but nothing is broken. We can fix this. I believe that." Jameson nestled Lorelei closer in his arms.

"But I didn't have a choice in this, and that's the problem," Lorelei answered, not fighting his need to be close to her.

"I understand that, and I don't want to minimize what you feel, but I want you to think about this, Lorelei. I didn't have a choice either, not really. Xander was going to die regardless. He broke NS304, and Lukas isn't kidding when he says the penalty for that is death.

"My choice was to let his claim settle and the chips fall where they may when he died, or try to break it. I couldn't let that be your fate because that wasn't fair to you either.

"I didn't break his claim out of selfishness; I wasn't exactly ready to take a mate. Hell, I can't even purr right. Maybe in a few weeks it would have been easier for us. I wanted to get to know you and see where things went.

"But I couldn't stand to see you break, and my only other choice was to walk away and let you suffer. I couldn't do that." He sighed against her, choosing to say nothing else.

Lorelei stilled in Jameson's arms. She'd never thought about it like that. It hadn't been an entirely selfless act, but Jameson hadn't been entirely selfish either. Just because he'd liked her from a distance didn't mean he would've chosen to claim her after they got to know one another.

Had he saved her? What had he saved her from? She honestly didn't know, which made the conversation that much more confusing.

"I said that your purr is okay," she said, trying again for levity. "It's almost good," she let her smile rise against the hard skin of his chest, hoping he felt it. "I'm sure it'll, you know, get better."

"Okay, now you're just being a jerk," Jameson said, stopping his steady purr.

"Don't stop," Lorelei asked. She felt her body stiffen and hated it.

Jameson's purr restarted, and she relaxed into him again. He pulled at the strands of her hair softly, and if she was honest, it felt good; all of it. The purr was perfect, not that she'd ever heard one before, but this one satisfied her on a fundamental level. No way she admitted that, though.

"Who's your favorite brother?" she asked.

146

"I have no favorite," he laughed, kneading her shoulders.

"Now, that's not true. Everyone has favorites."

"Darrian, I guess because he's the oldest, and he's always been there. He helped a lot when my dynamic declared, and he's a good listener. And Remi; Remington is so steady it's hard not to love him. In a house full of hair-trigger Alphas, consistency is nice." Jameson snorted, then rubbed his cheek along the top of Lorelei's head. "Yeah, consistency is really nice." Jameson's southern accent thickened as he finished talking.

"I bet that was tough, thinking you were an Omega then turning into an Alpha," Lorelei said, inhaling Jameson's whiskey and spicy campfire scent.

"It was, and it wasn't," Jameson answered quickly. "I think I always knew I wasn't an Omega, but mom was so excited about the prospect that I went along. In my heart, I knew it didn't fit." He smoothed his hands along the blonde lengths of Lorelei's hair, causing her eyes to close. "What about you?" he asked.

"What about me?"

"Favorite sibling, growing up in the Seventh. All of it," he asked.

Lorelei sighed, feeling the weight of so many answers. Jameson's arms tightened around her. "Well, EJ is my favorite sister. I have an older brother somewhere, but we were never close. There's a lot of money in Morgantown, but we didn't have it. My parents weren't involved in my life, and Eve's pretty much adopted me from the day we met. They paid for my college and everything. With them gone, EJ is the only family I have," she finished.

"You have me now. And Lukas. As Eve's mate, he's your family now too." Jameson deepened his purr, and Lorelei hoped he couldn't feel the sadness she felt.

"I suppose you're right; The Alpha acts like an overbearing big brother." She smiled because he actually did. He made a big deal about the fact that she wasn't going to any of the Alpha-Omega mixers last week, saying he just wanted to see her 'settled.' The only reason Eve and The Alpha had been there was so Lorelei would go.

"My family loves you," he continued. "They're your family now, too.

"Meghan doesn't love me," Lorelei said.

"Meghan's a jealous tramp who doesn't care about anything but herself. Trust me, she isn't family."

"What does Darrian see in her?" she asked.

"Nothing anymore; they are definitely over," Jameson pulled tighter on Lorelei's drying hair, rubbing lazy circles on her scalp.

"If that's because of me," Lorelei started.

"No. It isn't because of you. It's been coming for a long time; this weekend was just the last straw for him. Alphas aren't good together. She's never faithful. Darrian has been, but Meghan has not Meghan. They've been over for a while; she's a strong Alpha, and she's continuously driven to stray. She'd be better off finding an Omega to bond with. That would be the only thing that might settle her. Seeing how she acted with you was just the last thing in a long line, I assure you."

Lorelei nodded her head but said nothing. Most of her believed what Jameson said. Darrian hadn't been at all upset after Meghan left; if anything, he seemed happier, but still.

"Let us be your family too, Lorelei. My mother adores you. My dad told me if I make you unhappy that I have to answer to him. Let us love you," Jameson said, stifling a yawn. His purr faltered for a minute before he picked it back up again, making Lorelei smile.

His yawn was contagious, causing her to yawn against his chest. She didn't answer him; she said nothing at all. She'd listened to what he said, though. More than that, she'd heard him. She'd sleep on it and save the hard decisions for tomorrow.

Chapter 14

Jameson's left shoulder was asleep, and his throat hurt from purring all night. But he couldn't complain. Lorelei had her face smashed against his chest. A line of cooling drool dried on his chest, and she hadn't moved a muscle after her eyes closed.

The sound of her deep, even breathing soothed him like nothing ever had, and he felt something he hadn't since this all started. Peace. It was like he let out the breath he'd been holding. She was still with him. She could've run. At any point over the last few days, she could've ghosted him. He knew that. Lorelei had proven her ability to disappear over and over. Yet, here she was.

He bent his nose to her hair, dragging the scent of her into his lungs. She smelled like the white-flowered honeysuckle that grew wild in the mountains they'd trekked through in the Seventh. She smelled like sunshine and campfire smoke with a little bit of soap mixed in.

Jameson let her smell roll through him, cementing her in his mind and heart as his mate. His cock hardened, but he shifted his hips so that she wouldn't notice. He fought every instinct he had to bury himself in her and add the scent of his cum to her floral layers.

Yesterday, he'd held her down, pinned her like an animal, and rutted her without mercy. He'd lost control and hurt her. The way she flinched when she moved afterward gutted him, and he couldn't let that happen again.

Until her next estrous, he needed to lay off. Whether that meant he took ten cold showers a day or rubbed one out morning, noon, and night, he needed to get his shit together. That she spoke to him at all was one miracle.

That she hadn't ghosted him in the woods was another.

Instead, she'd let him hold her while she slept.

Omegas- what the actual fuck? He was grateful for whatever it was that made an Omega pliant and forgiving. He was even more grateful she was a southern Omega because Darrian wasn't wrong when he talked about a southern woman's grace. There is something special about them. Lorelei might make him pay, but he hoped she wouldn't abandon their bond entirely.

She stirred against his chest, licking her full lips lightly, and he tilted his head back so that he could see her face. Her lips weren't pink but cinnamon-colored like his freckles. The coloration was unusual, that white-blonde hair against naturally tanned skin. Her dark brown eyes opened, and she caught him looking at her.

"Hey," she said, blinking her eyes slowly against the mid-morning sun.

"Hey, you're beautiful," Jameson said, mentally slapping himself for not turning on his filter before he spoke. She was beautiful, though. It wasn't a lie.

Shaking her head against him, she yawned, pulling her head back and stretching her back out. "Man, I slept hard," she said, bringing a smile to his face. "I drooled on you."

"Yeah, well, what's a little drool between friends?" he laughed, giving Lorelei a little wink. If anyone asked him, he would say he liked the drool. "Ma probably has breakfast and coffee on if you're ready," Jameson said, carefully pulling his hard-on further away from her. It would go away. Eventually.

"I could use some coffee," she answered, her voice muzzy from sleep.

Jameson disentangled from his mate and the sheets, tucking himself into his boxers and turning away as Lorelei rose. He tugged his jeans on, catching Lorelei checking out his ass. He grinned, straightening slowly to button them, then flexed the muscles in his arms and back as he pulled his shirt back on, hoping she'd like that view too.

As an Alpha, he was naturally cut. But he spent time in the gym to counteract the effects of long days behind a control panel or computer screen. That appreciative glance from his mate made those hours at the gym worthwhile.

From the corner of his eye, he watched her slow perusal of his body as she walked to the closet. "I'm going to run and brush my teeth," Jameson said, catching the brief look of surprise that crossed Lorelei's face. "I'll meet you downstairs when you're ready."

Jameson slipped out of the bedroom, shutting the door behind him, then tiptoed down the stairs to his side of the house. He didn't want his ma to catch him with last night's clothes and a hard-on.

In his room, he turned the shower on, stripped, and dove under the hot water. His hand found his cock immediately, seeking to relieve the pressure in his balls. Fuck, but Lorelei twisted him up inside. Her mouth, face, hair, smell, and everything about her was perfect, and his body reacted to it.

He gripped his shaft tight, stroking the length of it as hot water pelted his skin. Feeling like a naughty teenaged boy, he pumped his fist harder, pounding into the base of his cock to speed his release. With a groan, he came against the wall of the shower, tightening his fist around his knot so that it wouldn't form.

Hot cum streaked down the wall, and he clamped down tighter on the flesh at the base of his cock, causing another hard spurt to shoot out of him. Breathing hard, he held on. If the knot formed, it would be uncomfortable until it abated unless Lorelei's sweet pussy were there to milk it for him. Every teenage Alpha eventually learned the trick. Fortunately for Jameson, Darrian had caught him walking around with a noticeable knot and told him about it early on.

With a shaky breath, Jameson braced against the shower wall as his heart slowed. It wasn't what he wanted, but it might keep his impulses in check a while longer.

Washing quickly, he left the shower, dried, and dressed before hurrying to find Lorelei.

"Sorry, I'm late, ma," he said when he entered the kitchen and found his girls already at the table. "I didn't shower last night and stunk to high heaven."

Lorelei cocked an eyebrow at him, but he hurried to the stove to fill a plate. Grabbing a cup of coffee first, he dropped a kiss on his mother's and Lorelei's heads before taking the spot at the table.

"How did you sleep?" his mother asked.

"I slept really well. How about you, Lorelei?" Jameson rushed to answer.

"Uh? Good?" Lorelei said, a slow smile spreading across her face as she caught on.

Annabelle's eyes narrowed, and she turned to Jameson with a glare.

"Miss Annabelle, I slept like a baby. Very well rested, thank you for asking. Jameson, glad you slept well," Lorelei said, smearing homemade apple butter on a hot biscuit. "I imagine it will be a long day."

"Yeah, exactly. Nothing like a good night's sleep," Jameson answered, grabbing a biscuit for himself.

"Interesting," Annabelle said, swatting Jameson on the shoulders with his father's newspaper.

"Mom! What?" Jameson asked, dodging her strikes and knowing the answer. Although Lorelei and Jameson were legally married, his mother wouldn't accept the claiming mark as proof of that. Nothing but a church wedding would allow Jameson to sleep in Lorelei's bed without getting beaten by his mother with something...anything.

"I know what you're about, young man. Mind your manners," she said, sitting back down.

"Yes, ma'am," he answered, noting the contrite way Lorelei hung her head, which would only confirm his mother's suspicions.

"He was a perfect gentleman, Miss Annabelle, I promise. This is new for him, and he struggles with control, but I promise he behaved." Lorelei said, popping another biscuit into her mouth. Her eyes closed in pleasure, and Jameson had to look away or risk needing another shower.

"Well, if you say so, dear. You two need to plan a church wedding soon; this needs to be set to rights." His mother gave him the sweetest smile edged with steel, and he knew there was no choice here. Short of Lorelei running for the hills, this was happening.

"Yes, ma'am," he said, filling his mouth with eggs so that he wouldn't be forced to say anything else. Lorelei said nothing and kept her head lowered.

Mollified, Annabelle looked at her son, fixing him with her stare. "What time are you leaving?" she asked.

"After breakfast. The Alpha wants to come by with his mate tonight and bring Lorel's things," he answered.

Lorelei's head popped up, and a fast smile graced her lips.

"Really?" she asked.

"Yes, really. I was kidding about the locks and the moat. Mostly, anyway. It'll be fun. We'll cookout," Jameson intentionally did not look at her. He buttered another biscuit and added another spoonful of grits to his plate. Her smile grew, and Lorelei practically bounced in her seat. He hoped his nonchalant approach would ease her fears.

"Thank you, Jameson," she said, squeezing his arm.

"You're not a prisoner, Lorelei," he added.

"She'd better not be, son, or you'll answer to your dad and me," his mother watched the exchange with a pleased expression.

"Yes, ma'am," he answered. Let her come to you, his mother had said. His way hadn't worked; he was hoping hers would.

After breakfast, they packed up, said their goodbyes at the door, and headed home. Jameson, very familiar with southern

156

goodbyes, stood patiently by while everyone hugged, hugged again, and promised to talk soon.

Then it started over again until each person had gone through the routine multiple times. A proper southern farewell takes time, hours even. He'd known this and planned accordingly. He'd told his parents and Lorelei that The Alpha was coming at three. The Alpha was actually coming at five. The only way to get out of his parents' house was to fib a little.

No one wanted to piss off Lukas Alexander Jennings, so they were almost on their way in time to make a three o'clock appointment with him. As Lorelei slid across the bench seat of his old truck next to him, his relief at having her alone again was overwhelming.

She buckled up, not hesitating to slide into the seat next to him. He smiled as they drove away. She fit so perfectly at his side that he couldn't imagine her not being there. The last thing Lorelei said to his mother was that she would see her later or talk over the ComLink. A weight lifted from his shoulders as they sped toward home.

Chapter 15

They walked into Jameson's house, the smell of oiled wood and ancient walls comforting. Warm, late-afternoon sun streamed through the back of the house, casting shafts of light onto the dark wood floor, adding to the place's homey feel.

She'd been so worried about being late that Jameson had told her the truth of his deception. She'd laughed so hard that her sides hurt. It was funny that a military man would lie to his mama to ensure he was meeting another military man on time.

Jameson carted her things upstairs, leaving her to walk around the main floor opening windows. She was relaxed- maybe even happy. Lorelei couldn't understand it and maybe didn't want to. Whether it was the bond or something else, she felt settled and was no longer anxious to run.

Lying to herself, she maintained she still might, that she still could. But Jameson had made her think. Her mind might still want her to go, but the rest of her did not. It wasn't so bad.

Here was an Alpha that used his brain as much as his muscle. But God was there a lot of muscle. Jameson was smart, funny, handsome, and well established, and regardless of why- he cared for her.

In the kitchen, she set about making hamburger patties for him to grill. They'd stopped at the grocery on the way home and picked up things to fill their fridge, for she guessed that was what it was. Theirs.

A frisson of anxiety went through her that was immediately calmed by Jameson through their bond. You're okay, it said. You're with me, and I've got you, it reassured.

Her breathing slowed, and she went back to peeling potatoes to fry in onions and a pound of butter. Jameson joined her in the kitchen, both hands behind his back.

"My dad sent you this," he said, pulling out the antique Glock 19 that had been her favorite. "He would have sent the .45-70, but this was more practical." He handed the pistol to Lorelei, grip first. "It's loaded, but there isn't one in the chamber.

Lorelei's hand flew to her mouth, and her eyes shot to Jameson's. "Why?" she asked, voice shaking with emotion.

Jameson's smile was soft when he said, "He wanted you to have it; wouldn't take no for an answer. Don't shoot me with it, please." He finished with a wry grin.

"I'll try not to," she said with a wink.

"There's more," he said. His face closed, and Lorelei couldn't help but notice the look of terror that briefly crossed his face before he shut it down. "My mom gave me this to give to you when I was ready. But what she meant was that I had better give it to you because I am ready. And she's right. I am."

Jameson sank to one knee and bent his head, keeping his eyes on hers. "Lorelei Nash, will you do me the honor of being my wife? Please don't say no. Just don't say anything. If you change your mind, I'll keep my word and try to let you go except for the alligators, moats, and restraints. We're already bound, Lorelei, but I will accept your decision. Will you please wear this ring while you consider me?" he stopped, taking a deep breath.

"Like this house, it was my grandmother's ring. She'd be honored if you would accept both along with her grandson. I will always do my best, Lorelei. I will put you first; no one will come before you. Will you please accept this ring as a promise to think about marrying me?" He stopped talking, his shoulders slumping as he waited.

"You want me to wear that ring as a promise to promise to think about marrying you?" Lorelei asked, her shock bleeding into her words.

"Um, yes," he answered.

Lorelei looked at the ring in the box in Jameson's outstretched hand. It was more beautiful than anything she'd ever seen. Even Eve's mother's ring hadn't been as lovely as this one. The diamond in the center of the setting was massive and surrounded by smaller diamonds in a square. Diamonds went all the way around the band; the entire ring sparkled in the sun.

Diamonds were beyond rare, most having been destroyed when the bombs went off. Mines no longer existed, and the only diamonds were in museums or heirloom pieces like this one. This ring alone would set their family up financially for generations.

"I can't, Jameson. My God, it's priceless. I can't take it, let alone wear it."

"You're priceless, Lorelei. To me, to my family, you are priceless. Rings are meant to be worn, and this one is no exception." Jameson's eyes stayed locked on hers. "Please. Uh, no pressure," he laughed.

Smiling down at him, she said, "Right, no pressure. Just a promise to promise to think about it? You're sure?"

"I've never been surer of anything in my entire life, Lorelei. I walked up to you at that mixer with this as my end game," he paused, taking her left hand. He slid the diamond over her ring finger, his heart beating so hard she could see it. "You and I are like smoke and fire; we would have gotten here. I know that. We go together; I just want you to promise to consider that."

"No pressure," she said.

"Exactly," he answered, giving her his widest smile.

"Okay," she started, and she could feel his relief through their bond. "I promise to think about marrying you at an undetermined time and place in the future."

"Thank you, Lorelei. You've made me the happiest man in the New South. No pressure. I mean, if you break my heart, you break my mama's heart too, but that's cool. I can accept that if you can." He gave a sly grin, dodging her fist as it came close to connecting with his jaw. Using his mother against her was low, but one hundred percent within a southern boy's arsenal.

"You need to start that casserole, Casanova. The Alpha and my best friend will be here soon," Lorelei said, chasing Jameson with a wooden spoon around the counter.

"Got it," he said, whirling away and heading to the pantry.

They worked in comfortable silence to make dinner. Jameson stepped away to light the firepit in the backyard and dim the lights throughout the house. Lorelei had to admit it was nice. Everything was nice; what more could she ask for? Things could be so much worse for her as an Omega, but she couldn't see how they could actually be better. How far could she have gotten using random Alphas and screaming for a better choice?

The ring sat heavily on her finger, and she couldn't help but stare at it. It caught the light, her clothes, and her attention every time she moved her hand. It was so big and shiny that no one would ever believe it was real and cut off her hand to try to take it. But she knew. The weight of generations sat heavily on her heart, far more weighty than the ring on her finger.

For better or worse? Could she do that? Who was she kidding? It was done. Marriage or no marriage, the bond was as solid as the scarred mark on her shoulder. It would go as well or as horribly as she allowed.

Sharp knocking at the door pulled Lorelei from her thoughts. She heard Jameson move to answer it and hung up the dishtowel she'd used to wipe her hands. Everything around her felt so…domestic.

"Where is she? You better not have hurt her, or I'll gut you." Pregnancy hadn't made her sister any less fierce; if anything, she was more so.

"In here, EJ," Lorelei said, rushing to get between her sister and the Alpha she had just threatened.

She rounded the corner in time to see The Alpha of the New South sigh so deeply his body seemed to swell with it.

"Babe, I've mentioned before that you shouldn't threaten other Alphas. It can lead to misunderstandings." The Alpha said.

"And I told you I will threaten anyone I want, and if that lunkhead friend of yours hurts Lorelei, I will gut him. There is no room for misunderstanding," she repeated, like he might not have understood her the first time.

He understood all right. His face twisted with a snarl at Jameson, "I will not allow her to gut you, Jameson. I can't say she won't ding you up a bit, though, but I'll stop her from gutting."

"Yes, sir," Jameson said, laughing deeply, which probably wasn't the smartest thing he could've done in the face of Eve's anger.

Eve growled, then Lukas growled, and then Jameson started growling. "Stop it!" Lorelei said. "Calm down, damn. I'm fine, you're fine, we're all fine," she finished with a laugh.

Eve let out a chuckle, leaning into Lukas. "Right," she said. "Hormones." She rubbed the swell of her belly and smiled up at the scariest Alpha in the New South without apology. The smile he gave back was panty-melting, and for a split second, Lorelei saw what Eve saw in the giant brute and was happy for her friend.

"Dinner's ready when you are, Sir," Jameson added.

"Stop with the 'Sir' business; we're here as friends," Lukas said, stepping back toward the front door. "Help me grab your mate's things and show me where you want them," he finished without preamble.

Eve hugged Lorelei hard, pulling her into the steel grip of her arms. "Are you okay?" she asked when the Alphas had gone.

"I'm okay. Sometimes confused and sometimes angry, but okay," Lorelei answered, going silent when the men came back, carrying large boxes filled with her things.

"Where do you want them, James?" Lukas asked.

"In our room, I'll show you," Jameson said, slipping sideways so the oversized box would fit on the stairs.

164

"Our room?" Eve asked when they were gone again. Her red eyebrow arched as she gave Lorelei a long look.

Lorelei answered with a shrug of one shoulder.

"If you want to go, know I will help you," Eve whispered, her voice low and fierce.

"I know, sister. We'll talk. Let's eat first; I'm starved," Lorelei answered.

"Me too, sister. Me, too. I could eat a whole deer." Eve laughed, tossing her head back and sending her curtain of red hair flying.

"Speaking of deer," started Lorelei. "I need to tell you a story."

"Just one?" Eve said, raising an eyebrow.

"Uh, well. No. More than one, but food first."

With the French doors open to the backyard, fall slipped inside the house, cooling the air perfectly. They sat at the large table, eating as the sun faded.

When the dishes were cleared and drinks poured, Lukas followed Jameson into the backyard to add more wood to the fire. Lorelei poured herself a glass of moonshine over ice, handing Eve a bottle of water.

Walking to the camp chairs around the firepit, Lorelei sank down, letting the fire chase the chill away. Eve sat next to her, watching as the Alphas lit citronella torches against the ever-present southern mosquitoes.

"So, tell me really," her best friend said, squeezing Lorelei's hand in hers.

"I'm angry," Lorelei said, her voice colored with bitterness. "I'm furious. I feel betrayed to my core- by everyone. It's not that I don't understand; I do. It doesn't change how I feel," Lorelei cast a glance at Jameson, her eyes filled with emotion. "Maybe it's irrational."

"No," Eve interrupted. "It isn't irrational, not at all. You have every right to your feelings," she finished, her brow furrowing as she dropped Lorelei's eyes.

Lorelei nodded her head, the pit of anxiety in her stomach easing. "I don't think you're to blame, EJ. You know that."

"I tried. I wanted them to give you to me," Eve said, her voice dropping low.

"I know. That night is fuzzy, but I remember. Are you happy?" Lorelei asked, abruptly changing the subject.

"Yes," Eve answered without hesitation.

"I complain about not having a choice, but you didn't have one either, EJ. You picked Lukas Jennings on paper because he was the alpha best suited to your endgame, to our endgame. That isn't a choice," Lorelei's voice sharpened, causing the two alphas to look up from their own conversation.

Eve sighed, scrubbing her hands over her face and casting a glance at her husband. "I love him, Lorel. He and this baby are my

166

life, but not all of it. I still work and earn a paycheck. I train daily and go on lunch dates. Yes, I picked Luke out after researching other Alphas. No, I didn't ask to be claimed by him when he did it, but I wouldn't trade it for anything.

"God, Lorelei, I used to chain myself to cave walls and nearly starve during estrous. I was ready to die, committed to the idea, even. And now?" she stopped, her eyes going soft and distant. "I wouldn't change anything. None of it. Being mated doesn't mean your life is over.

"NS304 gives us more than a choice; it gives us rights too. Your situation sucks; it does." Eve stopped talking when the Alphas moved behind them, finishing lighting the torches. Feeling the seriousness in the discussion between the two Omegas, they moved away to give them space.

"Lorelei, I have a lot to say, and I can't be sure how patient they will be with this conversation, but listen to me. You were born to parents who didn't care; you grew into a child who went unnoticed. Then a beautiful woman bloomed from the bones of that child, and here we are. I love you; you are my family, and I care for you more than anyone, but you have a chance for something you never had: a family of your very own.

"Luke says Jameson is a powerful alpha, and I believe him. He never would've handed his little sister to an unworthy man,

Lorelei. Like him or not, he would never see me unhappy, and he knows that my happiness is tied to yours.

"Neither of us had a choice, not really. And yes, that sucks, but we have a choice now. Be happy, Lorelei. Jameson is gorgeous. He's sexy and kind; choose that," Eve said, drawing a low growl from her best friend at her words.

Laughing at her jealousy, Eve continued, "Move forward, not back, Lorelei. If he is ever unkind, we will kill him together, but give him a chance. A chance of having a life with him is much better than chaining yourself to emptiness while your estrous rages without a mate. Trust me on that one," she added with a dark chuckle. "Zero stars, do not recommend."

Lorelei watched Eve's smile play out, marveling at the change in her friend. She noticed how bright Eve's rounded cheeks were and how the edge of starvation was finally gone from her. She looked relaxed and happy, no less dangerous if you knew the woman, but different too. "I hear you," Lorelei said.

"Does he have a nice dick?" Eve asked with a wide grin.

"EJ, hush!" Lorelei whisper-yelled. "You know he does. All Alphas do, and that knot...I never knew. God, the knot," Lorelei groaned at the thought, glancing at Jameson and catching his worried eyes.

"Is he kind?" Lorelei asked, her smile growing sly.

"Mostly, he hasn't been unkind. He's tried, that's for sure," Lorelei answered, not yet seeing where this line of questioning by her friend was going.

"Has he cared for and provided for you?" Eve pinned her friend with her eyes, demanding the truth.

"Yes," Lorelei sighed. "He's given me everything that I asked for, but my freedom."

"And that is the one thing biology will never allow him to give, Lorel. Move on and be happy. I rest my case," she said, squeezing her friend's hand in hers.

"It's easy to forget you are a fucking lawyer, EJ, God," Lorelei said, scowling at her friend by the light of the fire.

"I know; it's cute. I sat for the bar exam and passed, Lorelei. I'm really a lawyer now. That wouldn't have been possible before NS304," Eve said, her eyes shining with unshed tears.

"Holy shit, EJ. That's huge. Congratulations," Lorelei said, pulling the smaller Omega into a hug. "But no, NS304 wouldn't have been possible without you. You are behind that, not Lukas. It never would've happened without your sacrifice." Tears fell as Lorelei spoke, and she didn't move to wipe them away.

Her friend had been through so much. She'd suffered through being claimed against her will, being forced to leave that angry mate bond, and fight her own people. She'd almost died. "I've never been prouder of anyone in all my life, EJ. Never. You're amazing."

"And so are you. Claim your future; it's there. I swear it."

Lorelei nodded her head, thinking of everything her friend said.

"Speaking of lawyer stuff," Eve started. "I want to sue the New South on your behalf," Eve finished.

Lorelei spewed her drink everywhere, choking as it came out of her nose. Her eyes and throat burned as the alcohol came back up the wrong way. "You want to what?"

"I want to sue for the violations of your newly gained civil rights." Eve looked so calm sitting there that all Lorelei could do was stare at her.

"It was a violation, Lorel. That asshole Xander's estate owes you, and so does the capital." Eve's face hardened, and Lorelei saw the dangerous edge of her friend she recognized so well. Eve hadn't let this go; she had let nothing go.

"No, EJ. Just no. It's in the past, and I want it to stay there. I don't want to dwell on it while it's dragged through court."

"You could sue Jameson, too, and Lukas. They also violated NS304 as it is written."

The glint in Eve's eyes was so sharp that Lorelei had to smile. "Wouldn't that be a conflict of interest?"

"Eh, I'm willing to argue that in front of a judge," Eve chuckled.

"Oh my God, EJ. The New South is in trouble," Lorelei laughed. "I don't want to sue the capital, Lukas, or my mate," she started.

"So, he's your mate now?" Eve interrupted, quirking one red eyebrow to her hairline.

"Turn it off, Solicitor," Lorelei said, shaking her head. "He's claimed me; ergo, I am his mate."

"Have you claimed him back?" Eve asked, leaning forward. The second eyebrow joined the first, amusing Lorelei.

"What? God, no. I'm not ready." She spoke so loudly that both Alphas once again turned her way.

"Cowgirl up, sister. It'll change everything. Nice ring." With a wink, Eve rose, walking to refill her water and grab another dessert.

The rest of the night passed too quickly. Eventually, the Alphas joined their Omegas, and Lorelei enjoyed the warm flow of conversation around the fire. It felt good, but above good, it felt right.

Eve wasn't wrong. Lorelei had grown up with nothing, and now her life was full. She hadn't wanted an Alpha, but she had one. Jameson was everything an Alpha should be, but more than that, he was everything most Alphas weren't.

Reaching between them, she took his hand and was immediately rewarded by the biggest smile she'd ever seen. Jameson rubbed lazy circles on her palm, making their bond sing. Her heart hurt, but not in a bad way. More like it was so full, it might burst.

The Alpha moved to leave with his mate, and the Southern Goodbye started. An hour later, Jameson shut the door behind them, flipping the deadbolts and sighing.

"That was good," he said. "Your stuff is upstairs, but maybe we can unpack tomorrow?" he asked, watching Lorelei from the corner of his eye.

Heart pounding, Lorelei closed the distance between them. Before she could change her mind, she stood on her tiptoes and claimed Jameson's lips. She kissed him, and his startled grunt struck a chord in her heart.

Slowly, he gave in, placing his hands lightly on her hips. Lorelei explored Jameson's mouth, loving how he tasted with a hint of whiskey on his tongue. Before Eve, she'd had no past, and before Jameson, she'd had no future. She raised her hand, unbuttoning his shirt slowly.

Deepening the kiss, Lorelei felt Jameson's restraint break; he hauled her up and rested her on his hips. Taking the stairs two at a time, he walked with her down the hall.

Kicking the door to their room open, as asked, "Are you sure?" he asked, looking at her with such intensity that she was caught in the dark depths of his eyes.

"Yes," she said, her voice so muted she could barely hear it.

Jameson deposited her on the bed, bending between her knees to work her clothes off. Heart pounding in her chest, Lorelei let him take care of her. She finished with the buttons of his shirt, running her hands over the sharp contours of his muscles, loving the way they felt.

Lorelei eased her hips up to allow Jameson to remove her jeans, his face disappearing between her thighs the moment they were bare.

Anticipation and need slammed through her at the first soft swipe of his tongue, and her slick flowed as she came immediately for him. Back arching and nipples taut, she let go. Her body quaked as the first orgasm faded. Her breath hitched; she'd never come so fast or hard. Not even in estrous had she felt like that. It was like falling through darkness and landing in a field of stars.

Jameson sucked and swallowed everything she offered before starting again, eliciting a small whine from his mate at the lack of refractory period he gave her. He sucked her clit hard, slipping his tongue inside of her until her hips bucked off the bed, and the next orgasm spiraled closer.

"What do you want, Lorelei?" he asked, his voice husky and muffled by his position between her thighs.

"Everything, Jameson. I want it all." Her breathy words were all it took, and Jameson pulled himself up Lorelei's body, stopping to suck her tight nipples. Using the flat of his tongue, Jameson swirled and lapped at the sensitive peaks. Lorelei felt like she was going to burst.

Jameson palmed her clit, and she bucked against him, seeking the friction she needed. With his mouth on her breast, his palm on her core, and her hands buried in his hair, she came screaming against him.

"Jameson!" she cried, clutching him to her desperately, her need growing stronger.

"Fuck, Lorelei. My name from your lips. I'm going to cum before I slide into you. You do want me to slide into you, right?" he asked, half laughing and half groaning.

"Jameson," Lorelei found she couldn't say anything but his name. Words eluded her as her heart pounded harder, and her need spiked higher. Her pupils were blown, and her nostrils flared over and over at his scent.

"Please," she croaked out.

She felt him line his cock up and push balls deep in one thrust. Her slick made it easy, but there was some residual soreness from his rough fucking in the barn, and she cried out.

174

"Sh, sh, sh, baby. I've got you. Fuck, I've got you," he said, pausing long enough to allow her body to accept his size.

Lorelei felt his body thrum like a live wire. The bond between them begged for satisfaction, but she ignored it. This wasn't about the bond; it was about her. And it was about him.

Crashing her lips against his, she tasted him, groaning at his magnificence. The words came then; she gushed about his size and his strength. She praised everything about him, encouraging him to stroke her deeper, and he did. She praised each stroke of his hips, telling him he was perfect. Lorelei could feel the tightness of his balls against her flesh. Like a fist, they hit her in the soft spot in between. Spiraling higher and higher, she clawed his back and sang in the Omega way as he fucked her. She'd said yes, but it was all Jameson now. He was a good Alpha, the best Alpha.

"Stop!" she cried, fighting to get away from him.

"Fuck, Lorelei. Fuck!" he said, pushing himself off of her and grabbing his slick-soaked cock. He stood at the side of the bed, preparing to walk out the door. His chest heaved as he stared at her.

Lorelei growled at him, swiping her little claws across his chest, drawing blood. She rose in a frenzy, grabbing the soft sheets, furs, and blankets from the baskets and arranging them.

She mumbled under her breath, growling and purring. But Lorelei was past understanding what she was doing; she just knew what she needed. Beside the bed, Jameson stilled.

She caught the look of wonder on his face, and it spurred her to complete the nest faster. It was her first one. She'd never practiced like most Omegas do. She'd never had a safe place to do so. Eve's home had not been hers, not really. But Jameson's was.

She built the nest quickly, needing him in it immediately. Grabbing his spice and whiskey-scented shirt from the floor, she added it to the final braided layer.

Lorelei looked up at Jameson before crawling over the lip of her nest and inviting him in with a purr. Jameson wasted no time. He buried his cock in her again, and this time, there was no pain. His lips found hers, and she kissed him, mixing her purrs and growls into an age-old song. It was a song sung from a genetic memory, not from experience, but it was beautiful. Lorelei hadn't known it could be like this.

This wasn't estrous, she knew that. This was something else, something she didn't understand. And she didn't care. Eve's words had filled her mind with possibilities. This was her choice, and she was making it.

She howled as his lips found her nipple again. His hips worked against her expertly, and she snarled at the thought that they had

176

ever moved against another's body. Her walls fluttered, and he groaned.

Something about that infuriated her. Another woman had known the touch of those lips. Another woman had known the silken feel of his cock; she knew it. She just fucking knew it. She tried to calm herself, but couldn't. Her growl deepened, and Jameson pulled back, not understanding the fury that flowed through their bond.

Lorelei swiped at Jameson again, pleased at the bloody marks she left on his chest. Gripping his hips, she arched her back so that his cock slipped past her cervix into that space only an Omega has. She rode him hard. His body went rigid as her walls gripped tighter. Crashing his mouth into hers, she rose to him and came, pulling his body with hers and forcing him deeper.

And then she chose to live.

Jameson may have chosen her, but until that moment, she hadn't chosen him. She felt his knot form and his movements falter. As her orgasm hit, Lorelei bit onto the flesh at the base of his neck, ripping it away. Lapping at his blood, she came hard. Those women were history now, never again.

With a roar worthy of a lion, Jameson came. Pushing his knot deeper before it flared, his body knotted hers as his hot cum bathed her. She begged for it all, milking and claiming him as hers. She may have been his before, but he was hers now too.

Chapter 16

A smile broke across his face as he woke up. His Omega was draped over him like a hot blanket. Holy. Fucking. Fuck. Jameson thought as he cracked his eyes open.

Lorelei lay peacefully in sleep. Her face slack and unworried. He didn't understand what had happened, and he didn't care. His body ached deliciously, and he'd never felt this way. This was happiness. The feeling? This was everything.

The bond hummed between them. Complete now, he felt her everywhere. Few Omegas bit their mates. He'd read a lot on the subject, and the working theory was that only invested Omegas claimed their Alphas. Something had come over her last night that he didn't want to question too closely. She'd been so angry with him. Marking and claiming him had been a side effect of that anger that he hoped she wouldn't regret come the morning light.

Tilting his head back so he could see her face more clearly, his smile grew. Her full lips were smeared with his blood, and strands of her blonde hair had dried to it. Gently, he swept her hair from her face, tucking it behind her ear. Her muted growl made his smile grow and his cock twitch. Lorelei ground against him with a purr. Her purr was unlike anything he'd heard before, and he knew that not all Omegas did that either.

He was one lucky bastard.

He didn't know what happened, but he wasn't fucking questioning it.

She angled her face, rubbing her cheek against his chest, first one side and then the other, marking him with her scent.

She wasn't in estrous; he knew that. Her scent was sweet, for sure, but her need had been satisfied, and she'd slept for much longer than an Omega in heat would. Lorelei and Eve had talked for an hour while he and Lukas had walked the yard, pretending not to notice.

Jameson felt he owed Eve. Whatever the Omega had said to Lorelei changed the dynamic of his relationship.

Interesting.

Lorelei heaved a sigh, grinding on his cock again. She spread her legs wider, and the hot feel of her slick coated his balls as it flowed. He lay quietly. As much as he wanted to flip her over and bury himself in her pussy, he wanted to see what she had in mind first. As much as he wanted to push her, he didn't want to push her.

Her slick left a slippery trail over his cock, and she angled her hips so that his head was at her entrance. Teasing herself, she worked her hips until he was at the end of his control. The sweet smell of his Omega's pussy filled his nose, making his heart slam into his chest.

Slowly, she pushed herself up his body, bracing her arms against him. Eyes closed, she reached between them and angled his cock into her. God, she was hot. Jameson let out a long groan at the feel of her tight pussy clenching him. Fuck. She was going to make him cum with one thrust. He was a terrible Alpha.

She rocked her hips, eyes still closed. Her mouth dropped open, and her head tilted back, long blonde hair touching the curve of his thigh. He couldn't take his eyes off of her; never had he seen anything more beautiful.

And then she opened her eyes.

His breath caught in his throat, and his heart hammered. She was going to kill him. Lorelei was going to kill him. The intensity of his feelings was not normal. None of this was normal. Her dark eyes were so expressive that he fell into them.

She ground against him again, and he felt himself slip past her cervix into that tight spot made for his cock. Fuck. He was dying.

She rolled her hips, and praise for him started falling from her lips; he hadn't moved a muscle. Eyes glued to her face, Jameson watched as she pleased herself on his body. Her pussy gripped him like a vise, and he ground his teeth, willing himself to last. Then the orgasm rippled over her. Like a tsunami, it built, and she held none of it back. Her face changed, emotion and sensation sliding over it as the wave crested, then crashed around him.

Slick flowed, coating his cock and dripping down his balls; the feel of it was too much. He gripped her hips, slamming into her once.

"No," she whispered. "Not yet." Her eyes met his and held them.

He felt the aftershocks of her orgasm cascade through her and bit his tongue so that blood flowed, but he did as she asked. When the last of the orgasm faded, she breathed deep. Sliding off his cock with a shudder. Her hot mouth found his nipple, and he thought he was done.

The feel of her tongue on that flesh was surely going to end him. Then she found his other nipple, nipping it with her little teeth. Unable to stop it, his hips bucked.

"Sh, sh, sh, I've got you," she said, mirroring his words from last night.

Then she kissed a line straight to his straining cock. His knot was already forming, and she grabbed it before slipping his cock between her lips and as far as it would reach down her throat. In one deft move, her lips touched his base.

He forced his eyes to stay open and watch her throat work to take him. He wasn't small. No Alpha was, but he was bigger than most he'd seen in high school locker rooms. Yet her throat took him. She slid her mouth up, pulling him almost all the way out before putting him balls deep in her throat again. And then she fucking purred.

Cum exploded out of him, and his surprised roar echoed through the house. Her small hand found his hard knot and worked it like an instrument, and he fucking sang for her. Unable to control his movements, he bucked and writhed in her grip, but she held fast, her face smashed against him. He gripped the sheets and rode out the ecstasy of the most mind-blowing orgasm he'd ever had.

She kept his cock in her mouth, milking his knot of everything he had until he trembled in her hands. Jameson Beauregard Battle doesn't tremble, except when he does. In her hands, he was nothing. Jelly. A shivering mass of nerve bundles. She'd killed him all right.

She purred as his soft cock dropped from her mouth, then licked him clean like a cat. His balls, his thighs, his shaft, all of it was spotless when she finished. All the time she licked, she purred and sang his praises. With one more rub of her cheek against his thigh, she plopped across him with a deep sigh.

He guessed that when Lorelei was in, she was all in. Fuck, he hoped he deserved her.

"You are mine," she said. High on Alpha cum, her eyes were glassy and satisfied.

"Yes," he answered.

"Coffee, please," she added with a sigh before rolling off him and walking naked to the shower.

He heard the shower turn on, unable to move. She'd made him immobile. How the fuck had she paralyzed him? He wondered if there was such a thing as Omega venom. If so, he was a goner. He lay there a few moments, willing himself to move until slowly, twitch by twitch, his muscles responded.

This wasn't even an estrous, he thought, almost laughing out loud at his lack of prowess. Despite what Lorelei said in the throes of an orgasm, he doubted he was any good at this shit. He was a fucking dead man, but what a hell of a way to go.

He stood in the kitchen naked, confused as to how to work his coffee pot. He'd made coffee a billion times, but today? Nope. He was a fucking computer programmer, the best one in the land, but he couldn't work his kitchen appliances.

Lorelei had sucked the brains right out of him.

Fuck.

Somehow, he managed to get the coffee going and the stove on with bacon frying. He wanted to join Lorelei in the shower but knew she'd be starving. Part of caring for an Omega was making sure they ate enough. She had a high caloric need, and he intended to fill it.

"Wow, Jameson. That's a good look," Lorelei laughed from behind him. "Don't let that bacon grease get you," she finished.

The twinkle in her eyes was adorable, and he turned to her, crocheted pot holder in hand.

Damn, if she wasn't the most beautiful thing he'd ever seen. She'd dressed in soft jeans and a red, long-sleeved tee that made her eyes pop. It made everything pop.

"Coffee?" he said, offering her a cup.

"Thanks," she said, closing her eyes at the first sip. "I can finish that if you want to shower."

"I'm not showering. Ever," Jameson said, his voice low and serious.

Lorelei tilted her head back and laughed hard. "Jameson Beauregard Battle, you had better take a shower if you want a repeat performance.

"I want to smell you on me. I want others to smell you on me, Lorelei," his voice dropped to a growl, and she realized he was serious.

"Me and bacon?" she asked him, her face serious now.

"You, bacon, and coffee, there's nothing better in life," he added, breaking the serious mood with a smile.

"Okay," she said, her face looking thoughtful. "I like it." She came to him, running her hands up his chest and letting her fingers dance across her claiming mark.

"I, uh,"

"Don't, Lorelei. Don't apologize. I love it. I'm honored to wear your mark." He ignored the hot pops of bacon grease that hit his back.

She nodded once, stepping away from him and bringing her coffee to her lips. "You might want to flip that before it burns," she said, heat burning in her eyes.

Jameson turned, smiling to himself at her sharp inhalation of breath when he turned his backside to her.

"Lorelei," he said. "I don't want to break the mood or anything, but are you okay? Do I need to stock up for an estrous in the next few days? If so, I want to prepare." Jameson's confusion bled into his voice, making him sound unsure. He didn't know the cause of her change of heart, but he needed to make sure that he was ready if it was estrous related.

There was a long pause. Jameson kept his back to his mate, flipping bacon.

"No," she said after careful consideration. "I'm past due, but no telling what that drug did to me. It's not that close, though; I can tell that much."

"Okay," he said simply. "I'll stock up anyway, just in case, but good to know."

She touched his back, and he didn't turn to her. Cracking eggs one-handed, he continued to cook for his wife as she traced the myriad claw marks she'd made.

"Are you mad at me?" she asked, her soft voice firm.

"No. God, no. No, Lorelei. I'm overwhelmed and a little confused but not mad. Fuck, no. I've never been happier in my life." He turned to her then, wrapping his arms around her. Burying his nose in her hair, he bent to hold her close.

"That's reasonable. You just," she started, stopping before her thought came out.

"I just what, dove?"

"You offered me that ring," she started again. "Then Eve and I talked. She said things that made sense and a lot of things that made me think." Lorelei paused again, looking over his shoulder.

Jameson took the hint and turned around to flip the eggs; he was too good of a chef to let them burn.

With his back turned, her words seemed to come more freely. "Last night, I knew I wanted you. I chose that. I saw what it could be like if there was no anger between us, and it was so good. God, you are so good. I've never," she paused again, and he waited, watching the eggs to give her space.

"I've never felt like that. I meant what I said, you are amazing, and you do make me feel things I've never felt. You are fantastic in bed," she added, making Jameson choke on his spit.

"You are, stop it. You know you are, Jameson. And then," Lorelei stopped, sighing. "And then, I wondered how you got that way, and I started getting mad. I know I had no right to be, I wasn't a virgin, not by a long shot, but it pissed me right the fuck off that there were women out there who had experienced what I experienced with you. I don't know what came over me."

Jameson turned off the burner and pushed the pan aside, turning to grab Lorelei in his hands.

"Don't apologize, Lorelei. No one, and I mean it, no other woman has experienced what we experience together. I'd never knotted a woman until you. Yes, I had sex. Just sex. I used women to get by, the same as you used men. None of that matters anymore.

"I knew you were out there somewhere. I had no desire to give to a woman what I want to give to you. You can have it all, Lorelei. All of me, everything; it's yours. I love you. I've loved you from the second I saw you. I feel things for you I think aren't normal and might be fatal. Fuck, you're everything to me. No other woman has been anything; It's you, dove. Only you."

Jameson crushed her mouth with his, his kiss wild and harsh. He needed to punish her for thinking that there could ever be anyone but her. Need came over him again, and he saw red. Like in the barn, he needed her to understand.

She kissed him just as wildly, but it wasn't enough. Turning her from him, he unbuttoned her jeans and slid them over her hips before shoving her shirt to her shoulders.

Glorying in her soft groan, he stripped her ass bare and cracked it with his palm three sharp times before dipping his fingers to her soaking pussy, making her cry out. Holding nothing back, he swatted her again, loving the way the globe of her ass pinked up from his hand. Circling her clit until she arched her back, he said. "You're mine now, dove. This is mine," he growled, going knuckle deep in her tight pussy. "Do you hear me, mate?" his voice dropped, demanding an answer.

"Yes," she said without hesitation.

Grabbing her hip for support, he slapped her ass again, loving the way she leaned into him. Fuck, his wife was responsive.

"Mine."

"Yes," she moaned. "Please."

Angling his cock, he pushed in to the hilt. Despite her sucking him off this morning, his balls were already tight to his body.

"Lorelei," he growled, causing slick to pour from her.

She whimpered but said nothing.

Taking his thumb, he strummed her clit until she fell apart, and he had to hold her up. She weighed nothing, so it was easy.

"Lorelei," he demanded.

"Yes," she groaned, her walls begging him to cum for her.

"Say it. Fucking say it," Jameson growled.

"I'm yours."

"Only mine," he said, slamming his hips into her at a punishing pace.

"Only yours," she cried out, coming on his cock again. Her body pulled him so deep, and at this angle, it was divine torture waiting for her to get shit straight in her mind.

"That's right, dove. You. Are. Fucking. Mine." With each word, he slammed his hips to her, accentuating his point. "And I am yours, say it. Fucking say it."

"You're mine, only mine, Jameson. All mine. Just me." Her breathing was ragged, and she sagged in his arms.

"That's right, love. That's right. That's fucking right, I'm yours. Pulling from her, he came in hot, heavy streams across her back. As much as he wanted to knot her, Jameson needed to feed her more. His girl was hungry. He could hear her belly growling. Maybe he was a good Alpha after all.

Using one hand, he rubbed his seed into her skin, loving the way it made her smell. There would be no more showers for her today; she needed to understand. She needed to smell him on her and her on him; they were one thing now, not two; this was how it was supposed to be.

Scooping her up, he carried her to the table, sitting her on his lap. He purred for her until her heartbeat slowed and breathing evened. His cum was dry when he redressed her. Tucking her mussed hair behind her ear, he kissed her nose. "I love you," he said. "Stay here and let me finish breakfast."

Jameson warmed her coffee and brought it over, her dazed expression thoughtful as she watched him. He felt light as he fried potatoes in bacon grease and plated their food. She had said nothing, just sat sipping coffee and watching him. And she had watched him. Everything he did, her eyes followed.

When breakfast was ready, he sat her on his lap once again, feeding her from his fingers. He needed to do it, felt it deep in his soul.

Their bond had been unusual. Had she been in true estrous, he'd have fed them both their joined fluids. It's how Alphas and Omegas survived the long days of a rut. He and Lorelei hadn't had that. They were starting in the middle instead of the beginning, but they would be okay. Jameson would see to that.

Lorelei pinned her eyes to his as he fed her, taking nothing for himself. The eggs were overcooked but easier for him to pick up that way. Eventually, her confusion turned to calm acceptance, and her belly filled.

When she was full, she tucked her head under his arm like a bird, and Jameson shifted her on his lap. He ate, letting the peace of the morning wash over him.

"I want to take you shopping today, Lorelei. We didn't get nearly enough things for you," he said, pushing his plate away but not moving to rise.

"I have enough. Lukas brought my things," she said, her voice muffled by his skin.

Jameson laughed, feeling his smile go wide. "He brought three boxes. One is full of moonshine. One is full of weapons and equipment to make moonshine. And one is full of old clothes and makeup. You're mine now. You will have more," he said, his voice stern and uncompromising.

"More doesn't always mean better," she argued.

"In this case, it does. We're going. I have to make an appearance at work tomorrow and start back on a regular schedule the day after. I'll see you settled first."

She nodded against his chest, making no effort to remove her head from the crook of his arm.

Kissing it, Jameson rose, shifting her position so that she was cradled against his side. Her legs curled around his waist and her head stayed tucked under his arm. She was quiet, and he hoped he hadn't hurt her, but she needed to learn. She needed to understand that what they had couldn't ever be duplicated, repeated, or felt with any other.

He'd meant what he said, all of it. Jameson rinsed the dishes, stacking them in the dishwasher. He'd wipe out the cast iron pan later; they didn't need much cleaning anyway.

Sitting Lorelei on the counter, he smoothed her hair away from her face and wiped stray mascara from under her eyes. "There," he said. "Let's go." He gave her a smile, loving the way her eyes watched his.

She nodded once, and he picked her up, settling her on his hips. If he had a choice, he would carry her everywhere. Closing and locking the door, he opened the driver's side of his truck, stepping up into it with her in his arms. As it was illegal to drive with a pliant Omega on your lap, Jameson shifted her into the seat next to him, buckling her up.

He drove the few short blocks to Main street. Yes, they could've walked, but he didn't want to. Shopping was a necessary evil, but he didn't want to drag her through the streets of Greenville just yet. Soon, he would calm down enough to give her the freedom she wanted, just as Lukas had done with Eve. But Jameson and Lorelei's relationship was too new for him to be comfortable with her walking all over town.

Hand in hand, they went. Lorelei perked up and began talking again, but her manner was still subdued. She smiled up at him as they went, though, and through their bond, he felt her serenity.

From store to store, he took her, buying clothes of all kinds and toiletries. He also had her pick out things for their home, like towels and throw pillows. Women needed throw pillows, Omegas especially. He didn't understand why, but so many stores sold them they must be essential.

Anything she looked at for more than a few seconds, he bought. She seemed to like plants, and as he had none, she picked out a few. His job paid well, and he's saved his whole life, but there was old money too, old family money. If she wanted it, she'd have it.

They stopped at a nesting store. Jameson had never seen the like, but there were piles of furs, fleece, and blanketed finery everywhere. Lorelei lost her shit, and Jameson loved it. Everything she rubbed her face on, he bought. They left with bags and bags of the softest, fluffiest things an Omega could ever want. Jameson couldn't wait to see the nest she built with them.

The smile on Lorelei's face was more repayment than he ever needed, and the soft looks the aging Omega shopkeeper had given them were encouraging. He was doing something right.

After packing away their purchases, he took her to lunch at the Italian restaurant on the river. It was their first actual date, and that made him sad. This is how it should've started. Shopping, lunch, and light conversation should have eased them into what came next, but fate is a fucked up bitch and does what she wants.

He held her hand while they waited for their meal. Lorelei had ordered two plates, and the waiter just smiled. This was one of EJ's favorite restaurants, and the staff had quickly gotten used to a bossy Omega. They had adjusted faster than Lukas, or so the story went. That thought made him laugh.

"What's so funny?" Lorelei asked him, narrowing her eyes.

"Everything. God, look how Greenville has changed. You ordered food for yourself, and me too, actually. The wait staff doesn't treat you like a pariah. There's a fucking nesting store on Main street, Lorelei. I know it's small changes for now, but you did this. You, EJ, and all of the other crazy ass Seventh district Omegas. Before, Omegas couldn't be shopkeepers; now, you can own property and hold a job. EJ is a fucking lawyer for real. I'm so fucking proud of you," he said, the truth pouring out of him. "And I'm proud that you're mine. I'm honored." He grabbed her hand, holding the tiny thing firmly in his large one.

"Oh," Lorelei said, her mouth open in shock.

"I mean it."

The smile she gave him was beautiful. He'd never seen anything like her before. She was an angel sent from a long-gone God, and he felt so lucky to have her.

"I don't know what to say," she murmured, her cheeks blushing slightly.

The sight of it made Jameson's cock harden, and he wondered if he would ever get enough of being buried inside her. "You don't have to say anything," he said, giving her his brightest smile.

They ate, enjoying their meal and the fall sun glinting off the water. Climate change had made the weather unpredictable, but today felt like actual fall. The breeze blowing off the river ruffled

Lorelei's hair, obscuring the details of her face. She shoved it behind her ears before finishing her lunch, and all he could do was watch her. Maybe he was an Omega deep down. He wasn't sure if all Alphas felt these emotions, but it seemed incongruous with the Alpha way. He didn't know.

But he knew he was crazy about her.

After lunch, they strolled along the path by the river. It was crowded due to the lovely weather. Hand in hand, they walked, watching ducks swim. Lorelei fed the large, brightly colored fish that swam close to the surface, begging for pellets.

As Lorelei bent down to toss another handful in, an Alpha jostled too close, bumping her with his knee and sending her sprawling.

Jameson grabbed the other man's shirt and hauled him up with a growl.

"Sorry, bro. I wasn't paying attention," the other man said, holding his hands out in supplication.

"Then pay more attention, *bro*," Jameson said, tucking Lorelei behind him. His growl deepened, and he wanted to flatten the other man for touching his mate.

"I'm fine, Jameson; no damage done." Lorelei sighed, placing her hand on his arm. Maybe he was an Alpha after all, he thought.

Jameson didn't stop growling until the other man was out of sight. Then he turned to Lorelei, inspecting her from head to toe. "Are you okay?" he asked.

"Of course, I'm okay, Jameson. It was an accident; the walkway is crowded." She scoffed at him but added a soft purr to help calm his nerves.

"I smell your blood," he growled, sniffing her neck and along her collarbone."

"Jameson, stop." She purred louder, attracting the attention of anyone within earshot, which was the exact wrong thing he wanted. "I scraped my knee; it's nothing. Come on, I saw an ice cream shop I want to try."

Tilting his head back, Jameson took several calming breaths, then scooped his mate up, settling her on his hips.

"Jameson," she yelped, slapping his chest like he was a caveman, which he understood he was.

He purred softly, and the deep rumble in his chest quieted her. "I'm glad you mentioned the ice cream shop, Lorelei. There's something near there that I want to show you."

With her in his arms, he could take normal strides, and they arrived at the ice-cream shop within minutes. His rage had lessened, and his heart slowed by the time they got there. Lorelei had tucked her face under his arm again, and even though they had gotten weird looks that bordered on ugly, he loved it. Fuck them; God doesn't like ugly.

"What kind of ice cream do you want, dove?" he asked, setting Lorelei on her feet in front of the long glass case filled with paper containers of ice cream.

Jameson watched as she perused the line, her face crinkled in thought. "Two scoops of mint chocolate chip with chocolate syrup on top, please," she said, smiling brightly at the young Beta female shopkeeper.

Jameson hid a shudder at her order. "I'll take peach on a sugar cone," he said.

"Ugh," Lorelei complained. "Fruit doesn't belong in ice cream," she said, giving him some serious side-eye.

"Neither does toothpaste," he grumbled, pulling his card out to pay for their treats.

"But," Lorelei said, eyeing him again. "When I kiss you later, my breath will be sweet *and* fresh." She gave him the sweetest smile as she took her cup from the Beta.

Jameson froze, hand in midair. She had a point. She was killing him, but she wasn't wrong. There was nothing wrong with sweet and fresh. Fuck, now all he could do was think about kissing her. He was so screwed.

Taking their ice cream, they strolled down the sidewalk. Jameson passed several benches before choosing one on a quieter end of the street.

They sat in silence, enjoying the fall air and sunshine. He watched Lorelei from the corner of his eyes, marveling that she was his. She ate her ice cream, letting her eyes roam the empty street beyond. She was always alert; she always seemed to be scanning for danger, and he wondered what her life was like before they met. Something made her vigilant, and he hated that she'd been so scarred.

Someday, he'd take her to her hometown and face her demons down with her, showing her they no longer held sway. She wore his diamond, and it shimmered in the sunlight. Catching the sun's rays, it turned them into a clash of white lights on the sidewalk.

When their ice cream was done, he took her cup, depositing it in the trashcan near their bench. "Turn around," he said, watching her face carefully.

She turned, taking in the light gray building façade behind them. White shutters and cornice boxes made the front of the building look fresh and clean. Black wrought iron fencing with an ornate design gave the building a high end, professional look.

"What is this?" she asked, her brow wrinkling in confusion.

"It's an office building," Jameson said, his voice clogging with emotion he didn't understand.

"Uh. Okay? It's lovely," she said, still not understanding. How could she?

"It's yours," he said, unable to say more.

Thoughts flew over her face like a flock of birds. "Jameson, I don't understand."

"You're doing a lot of jobs, Lorelei. You need an office. Whether you believed it at the time or not, Gauge and Thalia will have you doing their books. Darrian has called as well, asking if he can get you to take over some of his firm's accounting work. You already do work for the Seventh, and Lukas is funneling New South business your way too. You were working out of a musty, rat-infested room in the basement of the capitol. This is better."

"Jameson," she started, her voice dropping enough that he heard her denial in it.

"No, Lorelei. You are my wife. You are a Battle now, and that means something. Not only does it mean something to me, it means something to my parents. The name Battle is well known in these parts, and I am honor-bound to uphold the prestige the name carries." He took a step toward her, dwarfing her shoulder with his large hand.

"You want to work, and I'm," he took a deep breath, pausing to get the next words out. "I'm okay with you working outside of our home, but you will do it here and not in a dingy basement next to the Alpha gym. Eve needs an office too, and there's more than enough room to house all the Omega entrepreneurs you want."

In a moment, she was on him, her arms and legs wrapped around him like a spider monkey. "Thank you, Jameson," she said, her sweet lips buried in his neck.

Chuckling, he supported her hips with one arm and opened the gate with the other. Adjusting her slightly, he pulled the keys out of his pocket, letting her in.

"There are six large rooms downstairs and four up. It is an ancient residential building converted to offices in the early two-thousands, making this place almost as old as ours." Setting her down, he took her hand, leading her through the rooms.

The front two rooms were smaller. One used to be a formal living room and the other a small library. He watched Lorelei take it all in, her eye turning critical.

"These would make great reception areas," she said. "Maybe have an administrative assistant here."

He smiled when she said that. She could see it now, and she was hooked. "That's a great idea," he said, smiling at her eagerness.

They passed the sweeping pecan stairs so that he could take her deeper into the building. "There are two large offices back here. Both have French doors that open to a small green space."

Lorelei's shoes clicked on the shining hardwood floors, her mouth opening in a soft O as she took in the office he thought she'd look the best in. Sunlight filtered through the many windows, illuminating the brilliance of the newly refinished hardwood. "Oh, I like this room," she said, running her hand over the pecan chair rail along the wall. The top half of the wall was painted white, and the lower half done in pecan wainscotting that matched the floor."

Nodding his head but saying nothing else, he guided her through the other rooms. The other large office was across the hall, and behind them was a bathroom and small kitchen area.

She had stopped talking, taking in everything around her. Jameson took her upstairs, where there were more, smaller offices set up. A smaller bathroom and waiting area stood at the top of the stairs, but the many windows and open feel of the second floor made the rooms feel much bigger than they were.

"I don't know what to say, Jameson. This place is fantastic. It's too much. I can't accept it," she said, rounding on him with her hands on her hips.

"You can, and you will. This isn't something we are negotiating. The Capitol building is a few blocks away, and I can walk it in under two minutes. This is a prime location but set back as to not draw attention to the occupants. It also has off-street parking for two vehicles. It's perfect for you, Lorelei."

"Jameson."

"No," he said, fixing her with his best angry glare.

Sighing, she closed her eyes and said, "Thank you." Before opening her eyes in time to see the smile bloom on his face.

"You are most welcome, dove." Taking her hand, he tucked it under his bicep and walked her down the stairs and to the door. "The only thing I ask is that you wait a few days. I realize I am, uh, volatile. I'm trying. For now, please humor me and stay out of the public eye unless I'm with you. I'll calm down, I swear." He stepped outside, locking the door behind them.

Lorelei gave a loud laugh at his expense. "I know you're trying; I appreciate that. But I'm not sure you'll calm down anytime soon, although I'll give you the time you ask for."

"See? Compromise," Jameson growled, walking Lorelei back the way they came, loving the sound of her laughter.

It was late when they got home. Warm light greeted them through the windows of their house, and the stained glass glimmered invitingly. Jameson carried their purchases inside, refusing to allow Lorelei to do anything. With a sigh, she lay on the couch, growling about bossy alphas and lunkheads.

They had picked up a pizza so that neither of them had to cook. Jameson carried that in, too, setting it on the counter. Lorelei's eyes had drifted closed, and her breathing deepened. Hating to wake her, he ate pizza and watched her sleep. He couldn't believe the turn of events that made her accept him, but he wasn't going to question it. The bond between them hummed happily, leaving no doubt that she had indeed settled into it.

"Babe," he said, shaking her shoulder lightly. "I can hear your stomach growling from the kitchen." Jameson had let Lorelei sleep as long as he could stand the noises her hunger made.

With a growl in his direction, Lorelei cracked her eyes open. She pulled her luscious lips back, baring her teeth and deepening her growl.

Chuckling, Jameson hauled Lorelei to her feet. "Eat, bed," he said, swatting her on the ass and laughing when her growl changed pitch. "Come, little dove, none of that. You'll get me riled up and posturing."

"Fine," she said. "Eat, shower, bed," she finished.

Then it was his turn to growl; he wanted her to smell like him.

"See? Compromise." Lorelei deadpanned, causing Jameson to shake his head.

"I should know better than to spar with you," he said, as he placed their dishes down.

"Yes, you should," she said with a conciliatory smile.

Jameson insisted on washing Lorelei himself, unable to quell his need to care for her. He soaped her hair, enjoying the soft moans his fingers on her scalp brought.

While the conditioner soaked in, he washed the rest of her. He explored every inch of her body until he knew where her freckles were and where her dimples hid.

Lorelei indulged his need with tired sighs and soft smiles. When she was clean, he patted himself on the back for not fucking her. He wanted to, but need didn't ride him, so he guided her into their nest. It smelled so strongly of them that he was calmed further. Holding her naked body to his, he held her lightly until they fell asleep.

Chapter 17

Lorelei awoke alone. The morning sun shone through the windows of their bedroom, warming the slightly chilled air. She stretched in her nest, loving the way it felt on her skin. Jameson's scent was so strong that she purred involuntarily for him, despite his absence.

Glancing around the room, she knew what her plans for the day were. It was a mess. They'd been busy yesterday, and her boxes were still strewn haphazardly around the room. Empty glasses and Jameson's father's Glock lay on the bedside table, and the floor was littered with dirty clothes. She was a horrible Omega.

She had one job, she laughed at herself. No, really, she had many more than one job, but she should've taken a second over the last few days to straighten the mess being out of town made. Not to mention the mess of her moving in. Sighing, she stretched again, stopping her purr with the sheer force of effort. Happiness rolled through her, and despite her earlier reluctance, she let it. How could she complain about the way she felt?

She'd known Jameson had to work today, but hadn't known she'd miss him. What the fuck? His side was still warm, and she thought maybe she could catch him. Lorelei rose, grabbing a robe but not brushing her teeth.

The smell of coffee wafted up the stairs, and she hoped he'd left her some. Maybe she would call his mother and set up another visit, or perhaps invite them here. Her day would be full, and he would be home before she knew it, she thought as she opened the door to the hallway.

The peace of the house filled her, as did the silence. Her bare feet made no noise as she walked down the warm wooden stairs. Jameson was not in the kitchen, and the pot was off, but a quick glance showed that his truck was in the drive. Grabbing a cup of coffee, she waited for him.

A soft click down the hallway made her smile. Likely he had used the bathroom downstairs to get ready so that he wouldn't disturb her rest. He was a good Alpha. As much as Lorelei loved her sleep, she appreciated that he had let her have it.

Turning her back to the hall, she pressed the button on the remote to cue up the weather. She hoped to open the windows and doors while she cleaned; it would make the process better. Maybe she would even put on loud music and dance around while she did. The bond hummed happily in her chest, and she rubbed it. It wasn't a physical link, not something she could actually touch, but its metaphysical presence was no less real.

Smiling, she turned, hoping Jameson was done down the hall. A sizeable icy hand covered her mouth, cutting off her scream, and another ripped open her robe, cupping her breast hard. She knew it was not her mate who held her. More hands touched her, and her screams came louder then.

A loud growl sounded, but she was mated now, and no other Alpha could ever make her sing.

"Doesn't matter, bitch. You're ours, wet or not." The voice was deeply accented, like Jameson's, but unrefined.

From behind, her legs were kicked open, and fingers jammed deep inside her. More fingers pinched her nipples, and another hand gripped her hair.

Trying to stay calm and read the situation, Lorelei took a breath.

"That's it, bitch, relax into it," another voice said. "Fucking Omega slut."

She knew there was more than one, but she needed to know how many, and glanced at the reflection in the television as one man fucked her roughly with his fingers. She would cry later; now was the time for threat assessment.

Three Alphas stood behind her. They weren't as large as Jameson, but there were three of them, and she was in deep trouble. She stopped screaming behind the hand.

"That's right, bitch. You should be ours. Without the interference of The Fucking Alpha and his computer geek, you would've been. As Xander's brothers, his property came to us when those fuckers killed him. Guess what, sunshine? You're his property." She felt a cock threaten her entrance, and the bond in her chest tightened with fury over it.

She belonged to Jameson, not these men. Her body was his, not theirs; she started fighting. Bucking and railing against the hands that held her, she surprised them at first, and their grips loosened. She shot away from them only to be grabbed by her ankle and jerked to the floor.

"Fuck that, bitch. You run, and you'll regret it. By law, you're ours. Those fuckers had no right, and the three of us will break that bond James used to steal you from Xander." One man pinned her arms above her head, and another sank between her thighs. The third stood, spreading her legs wide with his feet.

She could find no purchase for fighting them; stretched tight, she could only wriggle her body. Fingers jammed into her again, and she cried out in pain.

"Fuck, you're dry," the taller one said.

Lorelei could see it now. They looked a little alike and a little like Xander. More importantly, one of them was the man who bumped into her on the walkway yesterday. He kept her legs painfully spread while he stroked his engorged cock over her.

"Move, Russel," that man said.

"Fuck you, Tim. I'm going first," the man between her legs said.

Lorelei's core fought to keep his fingers out, clamping down and not allowing moisture to flow, but it didn't stop him. He was hurting her to get past her defenses. When the man didn't move, he was rewarded with a shot of cum over his shoulder.

Lorelei screamed as it splattered on her chest and abdomen. All three laughed at her. Through their bond, she felt Jameson startle. And then she felt his roar.

But the man kneeling between her legs used his brother's cum as a lubricant and forced his cock into her opening, groaning as he pumped twice. His eyes closed as he pumped again, and Lorelei's rage-filled scream became more shrill.

She felt Jameson and knew he was coming, but it was a five-minute sprint from the capital, and in five minutes, this man would cum inside her, and that wasn't fucking happening. The other man's grip on her arms lessened. He tried holding her with one hand as he reached for his cock and aimed it at her mouth as he jacked himself off. The man between her thighs thrust into her again.

"I'm going to enjoy fucking you until you're loose, bitch. I'm going to breed you like a dog," he said, swiping his fingers over Jameson's bite mark., "That shit is getting cut out of your flesh, whore."

He pushed into her again and hung his head with a long groan. Lorelei took the opportunity and whipped her head up, crushing his nose with the force of the blow. His cock left her body, and Lorelei twisted away, ripping herself from the three men.

Omegas might not be stronger than Alphas, but they are faster. On shaky legs, Lorelei sprinted to the stairs. She was followed by laughter as they slowly came for her.

"That's it, bitch, go to a bedroom and hide. We can smell your cunt, and when we find you, we'll fuck you on a nice soft bed. All of us. Tim's gonna take your ass first, but don't worry, I'll get it second."

Forcing herself to calm down, Lorelei raced up the landing and to the second floor. Heavy footsteps and chuckles echoed as the men followed her. In her bedroom, she looked around frantically.

Jumping out the window was an option, but then she might not be able to run. She could hide, but they would find her. She knew that. Jameson was coming, but she didn't know when. She felt his rage through their bond, but couldn't be sure he would arrive in time.

She heard the men round the landing and took a calming breath. Then her eyes found the Glock. Sidestepping to the nightstand, she picked it up. As quietly as she could, she racked the slide and put a round in the chamber.

"I think Russel is going to fuck your ass first, now that I think of it. He deserves it for the broken nose. We're going to make you suffer, bitch. You're going to suffer for years and years for what you did,"

The footsteps paused outside her door, and Lorelei took a breath in, closing her right eye and extending her arms in a two-handed pistol grip. Inhale one, exhale two, inhale one, exhale two, she repeated in her head. She was trained for this; she'd killed many men. But she'd never done it with her bond howling and her body aching; she'd never done it naked and violated, but she'd done it.

She widened her stance. The door burst open. Inhale one, exhale two. She sighted down the first man, the one who had come on her, and pulled the trigger in a quick double-tap. Inhale, heart, exhale, head. She shifted her stance toward the man who had put his dick into her. He had put his fucking dick into her. Inhale, heart, exhale, head.

The front door crashed open, and Jameson's roar shook the foundation of the house. In less than four seconds, it was over. Two men lay dead at her feet. The third man screamed, ran for the window, and dove out.

Lorelei stood still, the gun in her hand, and trained on the door. Jameson came to a sliding stop in front of her, taking in the scene.

"Baby," he said, "Put the gun down." Lorelei's eyes snapped to his, but she couldn't see him. All she saw was an Alpha. Another fucking Alpha.

"Dove, please. I've got you," he said.

Inhale one; exhale two.

"Lorelei, it's me. See me; I am yours!" Jameson pounded on his chest, ripping his shirt aside so Lorelei could see her claiming mark on his flesh.

Inhale one. Exhale two.

Her hands shook from the strain of holding the Glock extended. Adrenaline waned, leaving her shaking all over.

"I've got you, dove. I've got you." Jameson came forward, taking the Glock and sliding it across the floor.

Lorelei felt the tears fall hot and fast down her face. Her eyes were wide open, and she couldn't seem to blink. The tears fell anyway.

Jameson sniffed her neck before taking Lorelei into his arms, and cradling her to his chest. He purred for her, the jagged purr from their beginnings, but it calmed her anyway. He didn't think about going after the escaped man. No, he'd seen only her; she knew that.

"Jameson," she croaked, her voice raw from screaming.

"Shhh, dove. I've got you." Jameson walked her to the chair in the room's corner, sitting so that he could rock her.

His purr strengthened and evened out, and he poured his love for her through their bond. Lorelei's eyes drifted closed at the sound. But she smelled like another man, and another man had cum on her. Had been inside her. How could Jameson love her now? Her tears fell harder.

"It changes nothing, Lorelei. Nothing," he said, murmuring into her hair, but she knew he lied. It changed everything.

She had told him she was only his, and now she was not.

Sinking deep into the dark headspace in her mind, she let go.

Angry voices dragged her from the darkness; she fought to go back, but she could hear her name. Men were arguing about her.

"We need to get her tested," The Alpha said.

"Fuck that," Jameson said.

"Jameson, listen to me. She's going to the hospital, and they are doing a rape exam. It's the only way. Jordan Hollins is claiming that they broke your bond. He is claiming that she killed two Alphas bonded to her, which is punishable by death. Jordan Hollins claims that NS10 and NS134 give him the right to take her from you. I cannot kill everyone involved in this to fix it, Jameson. Not this time," Lukas roared. "This is a legal matter now. Jordan has asked the high court to hear his case, and they agreed."

"Fuck that," Jameson said, "I shot those motherfuckers."

"We both know that you didn't, Jameson. I get it. Believe me when I say I would rip through all of them, consequences be damned, but this is the first challenge to NS304."

"I killed them," Lorelei interrupted, her voice so low she thought they wouldn't hear.

"And you did an amazing job, sweetie. That was sharpshooting in tight quarters. Excellent work, my sister. I'm proud of your courage," Lukas said.

Jameson said, "No, she didn't. I did."

His roar filled the room, making Lorelei's head spin. She whimpered softly, cringing into the soft blanket wrapped around her. "She's not going anywhere!" he shouted.

"Are you challenging me? Alpha to Alpha, Jameson, are you challenging me?" The Alpha's voice had dropped low and deadly.

"What do you want, Lukas?" Lorelei asked.

"I will fucking challenge you if that means no one else puts their hands on my mate!" Jameson stepped forward and began ripping the room to shreds. Furniture broke, and shards flew.

"Jameson!" The Alpha infused his voice with power; it rippled over Lorelei's skin, making her cringe again. "You are upsetting your mate. Stop and think of her; this is no longer about what you need or want."

The room became still; Lorelei couldn't hear her own breathing. Finally, she heard Jameson sigh.

"Lorelei, what do you want?" Jameson asked.

"A shower," she said without hesitation.

"Not yet, Lorelei. We need genetic samples from your skin," The Alpha said, his voice soft.

"Where's Eve?"

"She's coming, but we had to clear the scene first," he said.

"They didn't touch me," Lorelei lied.

"We can smell them, Lorel. It's not your fault. None of this is your fault, but we've already collected genetic material from the kitchen floor. You need an exam to see if there's damage, and I need samples to use as evidence. I'd much rather kill the entire bloodline, but they are claiming a violation of their rights. It's going to the high court, so there's nothing I can do.

"In the future, Lorelei, remember that dead men tell no tales. Don't leave witnesses behind. Understand, sister?" Lukas had stepped closer to where she lay, hiding in the blankets. His face was kind, but she saw the depth of his anger and knew that only the fact that he was the strongest Alpha in the land kept it at bay.

"I understand that where Alphas are concerned, there is always damage," Lorelei said, meeting The Alpha's eyes. "I'll go."

Jameson roared again, stepping toward her. Clutching the blanket tighter, she evaded his arms, following Lukas out the door.

"If you can't keep it together, Jameson, stay here," The Alpha said, stopping Jameson at the door.

"How many waiting rooms did you destroy in the Seventh when Eve was on life support, Lukas?" Jameson whispered, his voice lowering. He stepped into The Alpha's space, bumping him with his shoulder.

Lukas had the nerve to look sheepish. "A few," he answered.

216

"How many fucking doctors did you fire, rip apart, or put in the hospital when they told you to take Eve off life support and let her go?" Jameson asked, growling at the other man.

Lorelei shrank against the doorframe. "Jameson, stop," she begged. "Please, this isn't helping."

"I will give you leeway because of the situation, Jameson. But my patience is limited," The Alpha said, clapping the younger man on the shoulder. "You're not wrong, friend. You're not. But Lorelei needs you. Thankfully, Eve slept through my tantrums in the Seventh."

Lorelei turned away from them, not wanting to look any longer.

"I'll take you, dove," Jameson said, moving to open his truck door.

"No," she said, tears welling in her eyes at the big truck that had oddly come to mean so much to her. "I don't want to get it dirty," she said. Even to her, her voice sounded small, and she hated it. This wasn't her; she knew that. But knowing it and changing it were two different things.

"I'll take you," The Alpha offered, moving to his shiny black government vehicle.

"No." Lorelei moved to the back of an officer's cruiser, slipping into the seat and closing the door behind her.

The Beta officer looked at The Alpha, who nodded his head silently. "We'll meet you there. Get the fuck in, Jameson."

Lorelei met Jameson's eyes through the barred windows, and the look on his face crushed her. He was devastated. The bond urged her to go to him and let him care for her. Her brain needed time to catch up with what had happened. She raised her hand to him as the cruiser drove away.

The ride to the hospital was silent. Maybe the Beta officer spoke to her, and maybe not; Lorelei couldn't recall afterward. When the cruiser rolled to a stop outside Capital Memorial, Eve jerked her door open and pulled her from the car.

"Ma'am," the Beta officer said, trying to stop Eve. Lorelei watched as shock cascaded across the officer's face when he realized who he was talking to. "Nevermind, ma'am, carry on."

Eve huffed, gripping her friend by the arm. "I will not ask you what happened because I know the gist of it. Before we go in here, tell me one thing," her sister paused, causing Lorelei to raise her dark eyes to those bright blue ones. "Did you give them our double-tap?" she asked seriously.

"Yes," Lorelei answered.

"Good. The heart shot first means they saw the headshot coming. Excellent work," Eve gripped Lorelei's arm, and instantly she felt better.

Lorelei looked her friend over, noting the black pencil skirt and white shirt. The soft swell of her belly was covered by a tailored black jacket. "I'm sorry I pulled you from something; it looks like it was important," she said.

"Now, hush up right there, Lorelei. Nothing is as important as you, but I just came from court. I'm representing you in this. I went to your bail hearing," she added.

"Bail hearing?" Lorelei asked, confusion rippling through her, then she remembered she wasn't the victim. She'd killed two Alphas. It was illegal for an Omega to do so. "Oh," she said, wilting into the smaller Omega's arms.

"Let's get this done, Lorelei. The more ammunition I have in court, the better. I hate that this happened to you. Goddamn, Lorelei. I'm so glad you killed them. Too bad you missed the third fucker; he's the one making noise and bringing the case."

"I didn't miss, EJ. He jumped out of the window before I could get the shot off." A small smile broke on Lorelei's face, making it feel stiff.

"Okay, okay, Lorel. Let's get you checked in, and while we wait, we'll talk. Once the staff comes into the room to do the exam, keep quiet. I don't trust that they will keep anything confidential. Do you want Jameson with you?" Eve asked, her heels clicking on the tile as they walked to the triage desk.

"No." Lorelei nearly tripped as Eve stopped, gazing her.

219

Eve hugged her friend to her, being careful to keep the blanket between them. "Listen up, sister. It's going to be okay. I know it doesn't seem like it right now, but it will be. You are too strong to let another person's actions change your path. Do you hear me?" Eve said, shaking Lorelei a little. Her big blue eyes were so earnest that for a moment Lorelei forgot her pain.

Eve had been raped too. Stolen by a strong Beta male, EJ had been taken to a shithole in the middle of West Virginia, where God only knows how many men had raped her. Lorelei never asked, and EJ never said. Eve had killed the Beta and escaped. She had come back from that. Lorelei didn't know how, and in the darkest part of her brain, she didn't believe it was possible. But not only had EJ survived, but she thrived, and it gave Lorelei hope. If Eve could do it, Lorelei could do it.

Something passed between the sisters, and a hard knot eased in Lorelei's chest. "Those men couldn't take what you didn't give, Lorelei. You didn't give them anything except two bullets apiece. Understand? You're here, and they're not. Don't let them win in the end." Eve offered her a small smile, a glimpse of her own pain shining through. "I swear to you, it gets better."

Lorelei nodded, and Eve continued their walk down the hall. They checked in at the desk and were taken immediately to the back. They tried to keep Eve from entering the exam room with her, but EJ shut them down.

Lorelei was dressed in a paper gown, waiting for a healthcare provider with Eve across from her.

"I never had this part," Eve said, looking around the room uncomfortably.

"You can do it now if you feel you missed out," Lorelei said, laughing a little for the first time.

"I'm good, thanks. Tell me what happened," Eve said, and Lorelei did.

Leaving nothing out, Lorelei told her. Starting at the beginning of the story with Jameson and ending with the ride to the hospital, Lorelei let it all out. There were tears and a few laughs between them, and in the end, Lorelei felt better.

"Did any of the men break the bond?" Eve asked when the story was done.

"No, EJ. They never tried. I was never knotted or bitten. One of them jacked off on me, but the one that," she stopped, catching her breath in a ragged gasp. "The one that raped me didn't finish."

"That's good, Lorel. The surviving brother is claiming that Jameson's bond was broken, and that you killed your bonded mates," Eve said, observing Lorelei's face.

"God, no. Jameson's bond is strong. In fact," she added, looking aside. "I bit him too; I accepted him as mine."

Eve's face split into a cheerful grin. "I'm so glad, Lorelei. He can make you happy," she added. "Beyond that, though, those murders were committed in self-defense against alpha rapists trying to break a solid mate bond that was legally placed.

"NS304 gives an Alpha the right to claim another alpha's mate if the Alpha in question has died. Jordan Hollins is claiming that you were the property of his brother and, therefore, should have been handed over to him.

"This is where it gets tricky. NS10 states that an Omega is the property of the Alpha that claims her. NS134 states that if a bonded Alpha dies, his omega passes to the next strongest Alpha in his bloodline. Not all Omegas survive the death of a bonded mate, and this provision provided for them if they did.

"NS304 has a few flaws in the writing that will be changed. Believe you me, I will work to close the loopholes Lukas left when writing it. NS304 gives you rights as a person, guaranteeing that you are an individual in the eyes of the law and not another's property. I don't think Jordan Hollins has a leg to stand on. We have a good case, Lorelei. Jameson is your bonded Alpha. NS304 supersedes any other law in the land, and I will fight to help put this behind you." Eve reached out, placing her hand on Lorelei's knee.

"Thank you, sister. I know you'll do your best." Lorelei said, covering Eve's hand with her own.

"My best?" Eve scoffed. "This thing is in the bag," she added with a salty wink to make Lorelei laugh.

Eve was right. Her bond with Jameson was solid. Even as he raged on the other side of the building somewhere, it wasn't because he was angry at her. He wanted someone to break in half. He was in a red rage, but none of it was aimed at her. His anger was directed at the men who had violated the sanctity of their home. Through the bond, she felt Jameson calm himself.

During the exam's discomfort, when swabs were taken and clippings collected, he sent her strength. She could feel him purring to her through their bond, and she relaxed to get through it.

When the speculum went in, and Lorelei gasped from the pain, he purred louder, sending the calming rumbles through the cord connecting them. Somewhere he waited, not to judge her, but to comfort her. She felt better knowing that. Did it ease the pain she felt? Not really. It didn't make her feel clean or unviolated. His comfort made her feel hopeful that just as EJ had moved on, Lorelei could too.

When the long exam was over, and the nurse allowed her to shower in the adjoining bathroom, she thought more clearly. With the smell of the strange men off her, she realized Eve was right. Having a strange man's dick in her changed nothing. It was just a dick.

She was still Lorelei Nash. No, that's not true. She was Lorelei Battle, and that bitch is tough. That dick hadn't changed her DNA.

Her struggles and triumphs were the same, and she had killed the fuckers that dared touch her. Just like before. She wrapped up in a towel and went to find clothes.

The small smile curving her lips fell when she came from the bathroom to find the nurse waiting on the chair. The concerned look on her face alerted Lorelei that there was more, but when dealing with Alphas, wasn't there always?

"Here are some scrubs," the nurse started. "They've been sterilized with steam, so they have no scent that can trigger your mate. He's calmed down, but before The Alpha settled him, he was angry. The waiting room will need remodeling. Again." She finished with a small smile. "Listen, Mrs. Battle, we have one more thing to discuss before I release you." The nurse sat waiting for Lorelei to nod her head.

"Judging by what I saw on my exam, your next estrous is close. My concern is that your attacker's sperm will survive long enough to fertilize an egg," she stopped, letting the weight of her words sink in.

Lorelei gasped, "What? No. He didn't finish."

The nurse shook her head, her eyes growing sad. "I took the samples. There was semen in your vaginal vault. How it got there, I don't know, but it did. I've cleaned you as deeply as I can, but sperm swim. An Alpha's sperm can live for seven days, Lorelei. However, I can give you a pill. Technically, I need your Alpha's

224

permission, but I'm so sick of this bullshit. If I can speak freely, Lorelei, take the pill. I'm offering it based on NS304, and I will stand by that decision and let your friend represent me in court if necessary.

"You have the right to choose. The pill will keep a fertilized egg from implanting; it will flush with your estrous, but it also means that no fertilized egg will implant this cycle, regardless of who fertilized it. Do you understand?" The nurse finished, pinning Lorelei with her eyes.

"Give me the pill. Please," Lorelei said, her voice firm and unwavering.

With a solemn nod, the nurse handed the pill over. It was a small, white thing nestled in a plastic cup. Lorelei had never heard of a pill that would block the implantation of an egg. Omegas didn't catch on every estrous, but she couldn't take that chance.

She needed to heal, and so did Jameson. They both needed to be sure that when the day came, the child was theirs. Their child would be born out of their bond and would feel that. She couldn't stomach the thought of not being sure and doubted her body would accept another Alpha's sperm, but she couldn't risk it. She downed the pill.

"I'll leave you alone to dress while I go talk to your mate. Avoid penetration for as long as you can. There was damage, and you'll be sore. You'll need a few days to heal, or the damage could worsen," the nurse said, moving to leave.

"Thank you," Lorelei said. "You were kind, and I appreciate it."

The nurse gave a small smile. "NS304 has helped; it has. We see fewer cases now, but one case is one too many."

The nurse left, leaving Lorelei alone. The stretcher had been stripped and cleaned, and she sat on the edge to dress. Her thoughts raced again before settling. Taking the pill was the right thing to do. She didn't want children now, anyway; she wasn't ready. Taking another deep inhale, she held it before letting it go, repeating the process until she was calm. Then she got dressed.

Chapter 18

Jameson watched the steely-eyed nurse walk his way, rising to meet her. The Alpha sat with Eve a few chairs away, and the nurse's approach ended their quiet conversation.

"Mr. Battle," she started. "Lorelei is dressing, but there are a few things we need to discuss before she comes out; have a seat." Jameson didn't want to sit. He wanted to rip this bold woman's head off and scream down her throat, but he sat anyway.

He'd calmed some, but his need to see Lorelei was so strong he felt like a live wire touching the ground. Casting a glance at The Alpha, he sat.

"I'm going to get to the point, sir," she said, taking the seat one away from him so as not to be too close. "Physically, your mate will be okay. However, she sustained some damage during her attack that needs to heal.

"She has a concussion and a small laceration to the back of her head that required a few staples. There is bruising and tearing outside and inside her vagina, which could worsen if not given time. She fucking fought them," she paused, a small smile curving her lips, and Jameson knew Lorelei had another person in her corner. "But she injured herself in the process. None of the damage is permanent as long as it is allowed to heal. You'll need to let her

227

guide what comes next. Do you understand what I'm saying to you, Alpha?" The nurse's glare fixed on his face.

"Yes," he answered. Fury built in his chest as the nurse spoke, and he wanted to kill Jordan Hollins five times over. He wanted to bring the two men Lorelei shot back to life and stomp them into the ground, but Lukas was right. It wasn't about him right now. Trying to steady his shaking hands, he thanked the nurse and watched her leave.

Jameson glanced over at Eve, noting that there was no surprise on her face. She'd been in the room during the exam and had probably already briefed The Alpha.

Looking small in hospital scrubs meant for Betas, Lorelei padded down the hall in hospital socks. She looked like a lost child as she glanced around. Jameson had her in two steps, taking her in his arms and settling her on his hips.

The pounding in his heart slowed as he scented her. She smelled like herself, and her honeysuckle and sunshine scent calmed him. There was no trace of another on her, and he appreciated the effort that must have taken.

"I've got you," he said, feeling her chest heaving as she cried quietly into his neck.

Purring, he pulled at the long strands of her hair. "Take me home," she said, her lips against his neck.

He cast a glance at The Alpha, who nodded his head. Lukas had sent professional cleaners after the crime scene investigators were finished. They'd been instructed to eradicate any trace of what had happened and given Jameson's credit card to ensure it was done right.

She was asleep in his arms before they could get to The Alpha's transport vehicle. Eve said nothing, her face closed as they all piled in.

"I warned Lorelei about the court case," she whispered. "She understands what's coming, Jameson." Eve glanced at Lukas from the corner of her eye, and Jameson wondered if this would cause them problems.

He certainly didn't care. Lorelei had been through enough, and this bullshit with Hollins' relatives was ridiculous. He just wanted it to go away.

"Come to my office tomorrow, Jameson. We have issues to discuss. This case will go before the high court in two days, three at the most; she'll need to testify," The Alpha said when Jameson's house appeared.

"That's not long enough; it's too much for her. I won't allow it," Jameson hissed, startling the Omega sleeping in his arms. His soft purr sent her back to sleep. "With all due respect," he added as The Alpha arched a brow.

"She's stronger than you give her credit for, Jameson," Eve whispered. "This isn't her first rodeo. She'll be fine. She needs to do this to put it behind her, trust me." The look Eve gave him reminded him how tough she was.

It also reminded him that not only had Lorelei been in this situation before, so had Eve. God, he hated it. This was a horrible world; it would be better if Omegas ran it.

He slid out of the transport vehicle before it stopped, looking at Lukas and giving him a nod.

"Thank you for everything; I appreciate it," he said, manners getting the best of him.

Lukas and Eve drove away with a tight nod, leaving him alone with his limp Omega in his arms.

He unlocked the door, entering the house cautiously. He hadn't taken in all the damage before they left for the hospital, but had seen enough. Lorelei's attackers had entered through an unlocked first-floor bedroom window.

Supporting Lorelei with one forearm, he walked the lower level, checking doors and windows as he went. He hated they had gotten into his home, although Jameson understood that they would have gotten her eventually, no matter where she'd been. Their attack had been planned, and they meant to make her theirs. The surviving Hollins said it had been inevitable and still believed he held a claim to Jameson's wife.

The bond in his chest was quiet. It wasn't an uncomfortable silence; it was just silent. So many emotions had flowed between them today that exhaustion settled in. Mental exhaustion is no less draining than physical, and Jameson felt the weight of them both.

He glanced at the kitchen floor that had been covered in Lorelei's blood. It was clean now, and no trace of the other Alphas remained. The robe they'd ripped off her was gone, and any trace of her attack erased.

"She'll be all right, Jameson," his mother surprised him, and he turned on her. "Easy, son. Your father and I won't allow you to go through this alone." Anabelle placed her hand on Lorelei's back, giving it a small rub. "We're settled in the back bedroom. He's already asleep. I just wanted you to know we're here for you."

Jameson couldn't stop the hot tears that came to his eyes. "Mom," he said, trying to stifle the sob and not wake Lorelei. "I don't know, man. I don't know if I can do this; how can she do it? Fuck," he finished.

"I'm going to excuse your language this one time, Jameson, but mind your manners," she said, moving her delicate hand to his arm. "Do you know what my first impression of Lorelei was?" she asked.

"No, ma," he answered. "You and I really didn't talk much about it."

"My first impression of this girl is that she is wild, wild like the mountains and the weather. Wild, like the rivers that cut through the land, making their own way. She's untamed like waterfalls and thunderstorms.

"When we first met, she growled at me. She perceived me as a threat to you and rounded on me with wild eyes and ready hands. Jameson, she's going to be okay; you both will. She doesn't know it yet, but she loves you.

"Maybe you'll never tame her spirit or take the fight out of her, but you don't need to. She's accepted you, she said, glancing at the bite at the base of his neck; time and the bond will fix the rest. You're hers now, and there's no coming back from that.

"The history of Omegas is filled with things like this and worse, son. She survived; the rest will fix itself." Annabelle pulled her son into a hug, wrapping her small arms as far around his as she could.

"I just don't want her to be broken, ma. We rescued some captive Omegas in the Seventh, and they were shells, empty things with vacant eyes. What if I wake up in the morning, and that's Lorelei?" he asked, the tears finally falling. Alphas don't cry, but since it was okay in their mother's arms, he didn't stop.

"It won't be, baby. It won't be." Annabelle pulled away. The love and encouragement in her eyes settled his soul; he wanted to believe her.

"Thanks, mom. I'm going to take her and let her rest now." He walked to the stairs, noting that the tiny, bloody footprints that dotted them earlier were gone.

The lights were on in their room. The bloody area rug covering their hardwood floors had been replaced by another one. This one was a softer gray and white and looked more feminine. Lorelei's nest had been removed, and all their bed coverings were replaced. There had been blood spatter on everything. The room smelled of fresh paint, and it covered the scent of blood and gunpowder. Almost.

Sighing, Jameson shifted Lorelei in his arms. He needed a shower. The only thing left to remind him was himself. He'd changed his shirt and washed his hands, but the scent of blood and other alphas clung to him.

He laid Lorelei on their bed gently so as not to disturb her. When she stretched and rolled over, he purred for her, sending her back into a deep sleep. She had bruises on her face from where she'd been grabbed. Her tiny arms were dotted with finger marks, and her wrists were a solid band of purple from where she'd been restrained.

He left the door open while he showered so that he could see her. Lorelei's chest rose and fell steadily, and he hoped his mother was right. They'd gotten to a good place, and he hoped to get back there. They were stronger than this.

He slipped on boxers to cover himself before pulling out the bags of nesting material from the closet. He piled them in the baskets by their bed, glad they'd been protected from the earlier bloodbath. From the laundry, he pulled the shirt he'd worked out in a few days ago. It smelled so strongly of him it stunk, but he took it to the bed anyway.

As carefully as possible, he undressed his wife, noting every mark on her body before sliding his shirt over her head. She sighed, scenting him around her. A small smile carved her lips, causing him to sigh again. God, he loved her. Tucking her hair behind her ears, he rose to turn the lights off before pulling the blankets over them both and falling asleep with her.

The growl of an angry kitten woke him from a deep sleep. Hair and eyes wild, Lorelei stared at him with her teeth bared. The growl raised in pitch, and he grabbed her by the back of the neck on reflex, giving her a little shake. She swiped him with baby claws, drawing a line of blood on his chest.

"Dove? What the heck?" he asked, surprised by her attack.

No one was home behind her eyes, and he grew worried. She clawed him again, drawing four neat lines across him with her claws. She turned her nose up, scenting his blood before pouncing on his lap and sinking her teeth into her claiming mark, worrying the flesh at the base of his neck, alternating between rubbing her mark and biting it.

He groaned, lying still. Lorelei needed something, and he'd try to give it, but confusion rippled through their bond. She brought her nose to the hollow behind his ear, breathing him in. Rubbing her face along his cheek and neck, she growled low. Under other circumstances, it would have been cute, but now all he felt was worry. He purred for her, and she clawed his chest again, her angry eyes cloudy.

"I'm yours, Lorelei; you're okay." His words seemed to calm her, and her growl softened. She moved her face to his chest, marking him with her scent by rubbing both cheeks across it. Her growl changed to a purr as she worked lower, covering his torso with her scent.

"Lorelei, no," he hissed when she threatened to move lower still, and her purr turned into a vicious growl. His cock was soft, but it wouldn't stay that way if she continued.

She caught his chin with her claws and grabbed her by the back of the neck once more, stilling her instantly.

"Stop," he demanded, moving to lay her across his chest.

She whimpered, her blown pupils meeting his eyes.

He scented the air. Lorelei smelled sweet and intoxicating, but not like estrous.

"I need," she growled, fixing him with her glare.

"The doctor said no, Lorelei, and I don't think it's healthy for you right now," he tried. He didn't smell her slick or growl to induce it. He kept his voice flat, trying to calm her.

"I need!" she growled in his face, low and threatening, and Jameson remembered that in a rage, Lorelei had torn another Alpha apart. Nose to nose with him, she threatened to do the same.

Fuck, he didn't know what to do. Her body vibrated with rage, and a pissed off Omega was a deadly Omega. He purred louder, and her shrill cry echoed the room as she launched herself at him. She scratched and bit him, gnashing her tiny teeth and marking him where they made contact.

Jameson grabbed at her neck to subdue her, but rage blinded Omegas find strength they shouldn't. They were violent when feeling protective or threatened, and he didn't want to trigger her or hurt her either. He lay back and put his hands up in supplication. The furious growl changed to a purr, and she began rubbing her face on his body again.

She didn't want his comfort. That's not what she needed.

"I need," she said again, whimpering this time as she covered him with kisses and licked his skin clean of blood.

"Take what you need, Lorelei, but I won't fuck you. I'll lock you in here alone before I do that. Understand?" He meant it. His parents were here; she'd be safe alone. He'd leave the house if he had to. Maybe she just needed to touch him. He didn't know, but he had taken the nurse seriously, and nothing could make him hurt Lorelei more tonight.

His Omega calmed at his words, and her blown pupils met his. She went back to licking the bloody gouges she'd made. Her growl changed to a purr, and when her lips touched his cock through his boxers, he stilled.

Leaning up, she ripped them down the middle, exposing his softness. When she took the entirety into her mouth, it didn't stay soft for long. He groaned as she worked him, alternating rubbing her face on him and sucking.

"Lorelei, please," he begged, feeling his hard-earned control slip.

She took him to the base, bypassing the back of her throat to do it. Working his knot expertly, she had him ready to cum in minutes. Whatever she needed, he wanted to give it to her and did not hold back. When she did not try to ride him, he relaxed.

His balls tingled, and he felt his release coming. With a groan, he let it go. Lorelei removed her mouth from him and whipped his shirt off, leaving her bare. Jerking his knot, she emptied him onto her chest, and she jacked him dry before abandoning him to rub his cum into the skin of her face, chest, and thighs.

And then he understood.

Fuck.

He lay watching as she took what she needed, which was him. When she'd covered every part of her with his essence, she curled next to him, purring softly. Without another word, Lorelei went to sleep.

Jameson lay awake for a long time. His skin hurt from the ferocity of her attack, but he didn't move. All he could smell was Lorelei and his cum, and it soothed him, too, taking away some of the pain of the day.

She wasn't broken.

A broken Omega wouldn't demand his cum and use it to reestablish his ownership of her. A broken Omega wouldn't attack him and reestablish her ownership of him. She was angry, as was her right, but she was not broken.

He could work with angry.

He'd taken her from Xander to save her, to protect her, but it hadn't worked. If she could get past that, so could he. He'd find a way to be a better Alpha. With those thoughts running through his head, he finally fell into a restless sleep next to her.

Jameson smelled coffee and frying bacon far earlier than he had hoped to. Stretching, he nuzzled into Lorelei's hair, enjoying the soft groan it brought. She'd laid on him or next to him all night, but he wouldn't complain about her nearness.

"Mom's here," he whispered. "I smell breakfast if you're hungry.

Lorelei's groan grew louder, and her closed eyes wrinkled. "Breakfast or sleep?" she mused before her eyes opened slowly. "Breakfast, it is."

Jameson doubted she'd eaten yesterday. Her face already looked thinner, and he hated that. An Omega's high metabolism meant they needed more calories than even an Alpha. "Perfect," he said, not letting his worry show.

She rose stiffly, and he cringed at the way she moved around the room. She was hurting, and he knew it. Lorelei made no move to shower, just threw pants on her legs, replacing his nasty tee shirt to cover her from the thighs up. Dark circles marred the skin below her eyes, and she was pale.

The nurse said she had a concussion, and he had a new worry on top of the many others. "How's your head?" he asked, running his hand over the staples.

"Hard," she answered. "It'll be fine," she added, giving him a little smile.

"Do you want to talk about it?" he asked, dreading either response. He'd rather dig up the two dead Alphas, three if you counted Xander, and kill them again, but he'd do what she needed.

"No. It's not worthy of discussion, Jameson. They're dead." Her voice sounded hollow, but he wanted her to know he'd listen if she needed it.

"Okay, let's eat then."

Downstairs his father sat at the table, reading a paper. He shoved it under the placemat when he heard them coming, and Jameson knew it had something to do with Lorelei.

"There's our girl." His mother rushed forward, scooping her up like a child. "I will not ask if you are okay, but understand that you will be," she said.

"I know, Miss Annabelle." Lorelei buried her nose in his mother's neck, and he thought he saw her back shudder with a sob.

Maybe she'd talk to his mother if not to him. "Hey, Dad, can you help me adjust the carburetor on the truck? I can't get it right."

"Yeah, sure, son," his dad sighed, shoving the paper behind his back and rising to his feet. Earl grabbed his coffee and walked to the door, keeping the paper out of sight.

They walked through the living room and out into the dry morning air.

"I don't really need help with the truck, dad. I just wanted to give the girls a minute," he said, closing the front door behind him.

His dad laughed out loud, covering the sound quickly. "You don't think I know that, boy? That old diesel doesn't have a carburetor. I'm not going to lie, son, this is bad," he added, handing the paper to Jameson.

In the driveway, Jameson took it and read the headline, feeling fury wash over him. He closed the bond to Lorelei so she wouldn't be alarmed. The Hollins family had gone to the papers. Jordan

Hollins was quoted as saying that Lorelei had killed his brothers after they'd broken Jameson's bond. He went further, laying blame on The Alpha and the state for not giving her to them as soon as his brother was killed. It was all there. Every dirty claim could be read by all.

He didn't believe it. Lorelei had no new bite marks, and their bond was as solid as ever. But it was the South, and people would talk. Their talk would hurt Lorelei, and he wanted nothing but to take her away from it all.

"It's not true, Dad. Those fuckers couldn't break our bond; they didn't even try. They just fucking raped her. Fuck." Jameson dissolved into sobs and was collected and hugged by his father.

"How's she doing?" Earl asked, still holding his baby in a firm embrace.

"She doesn't want to talk about it." Jameson pulled away, scrubbing the tears away with his hand.

"Okay, that's okay. Lorelei has friends and your Ma. If she needs to talk, she'll go there. Probably isn't something she wants to talk about with her husband."

"Is it bad that I don't want to know?" Jameson asked. "I mean, I know. I know what they did, but I don't want to hear her say it." He took a ragged breath, meeting his father's eyes.

"It's not bad, JB. You're entitled to feel how you feel. But if she needs you, you'll be there, boy. Hear me?"

"Yeah, dad. I hear you."

"So, this case?" he asked, leaving the question open.

"Is bullshit. The Alpha is going to destroy the entire bloodline if they aren't careful. The high court will hear it tomorrow probably. Eve thinks they are just trying to challenge NS304." Jameson looked back at the house and saw the girls moving about the kitchen. "Eve Jennings is going to destroy them," he added.

"The Alpha's pregnant mate?" Earl's mouth dropped open, and he turned his stunned gaze to Jameson.

"Thanks to NS304, she passed the bar."

"Is that wise? We can afford a better attorney, Son. Let us hire the best." Earl closed his hand over his son's shoulder.

"Dad, you don't get it. Eve Hatfield Jennings is the best. She's a shark, and Lorelei is her sister. Eve is invested in the outcome," Jameson added, moving back toward the house.

"If you're sure."

"I'm sure, Dad. Believe me, that's one Omega I wouldn't ever mess with."

They stood a while longer, giving the women a chance to talk. When they reentered the house, food was piled on platters, and he moved to make one for Lorelei. It gutted him when she took her plate from him and ate standing at the counter instead of sitting at the table.

He'd taken biology. He'd had a class in dynamics in college; he fucking knew. No other Alpha could call her slick, so whatever they did to her would've been done by brute force. The nurse had only confirmed what he knew.

She stood at the counter, shoveling plate after plate of food into her mouth while she tried to get comfortable in her own skin, and it was painful to watch. She moved around, tidying up and putting away dishes, trying not to make it obvious, but Jameson saw. So did his mother, and her face fell when she noticed.

Lorelei engaged in conversation and gave half-smiles, but her pain was clear.

"I have to see The Alpha soon. Do you want to come with me, Lorel?" Jameson asked, watching her unstack the dishwasher. Lorelei had refused to allow his mother to do it.

"I'll stay here with Miss Annabelle," Lorelei answered, not looking his way as she busied herself wiping off the big table for the third time.

Jameson gave his mother a pleading glance. He didn't know what to do or say, but she would.

"Lorelei," Annabelle said. "Go have a long soak, sugar. Here," she added, rifling through her pockets and handing Lorelei a small bag. She gave no explanation and would accept no argument. "Nice hot water, honey."

Lorelei's eyes flit to his, then away. "Okay, Miss Annabelle."

243

"Call me mom, or I'll get the spoon," his mother said, bringing a smile to Jameson's face. Even damaged, Annabelle Battle wouldn't let Lorelei slide; she'd take a spoon to her if she had to.

"Yes, ma'am; I mean, mom," Lorelei gave a real smile, then, walking up the stairs to their room.

When she was out of sight, Jameson hugged his mother tightly.

"You give the best little boy hugs," she said with a long sigh.

"I'm not a little boy," Jameson said.

"You're my little boy." His mother swatted him as he pulled away.

"Thank y'all for everything."

"You're welcome. She'll be fine, and so will you. She's family now, and there's no tougher family than the Battle family."

Jameson went upstairs to change for his meeting. The bathroom door was closed, and he let Lorelei be. Opening the bond between them, he sent her what strength he had, then left for the Capitol building.

"The trial's tomorrow, Jameson," The Alpha said as soon as Jameson walked in the door.

"I saw it in the paper." Jameson walked over to the chair by the desk and sat down.

"Moonshine?" Lukas asked, pouring a shot.

"Uh? Sure?" Moonshine seemed to be all anyone talked about. He hadn't tried it, but the Omegas drank it like water. He assumed it was a honey wine like mead, but he hadn't delved into Lorelei's stash yet.

Lukas's face cracked into a wide grin as he poured a shot for Jameson and slid it across the desk. His smile grew wider when Jameson picked up the glass and pounded it.

"What the fuck?" Jameson asked, spewing the liquid fire all over The Alpha's desk. "What is this, and how do they drink it? Tastes like shuttlecraft fuel."

"It's an acquired taste," The Alpha said, sipping from his shot glass. "It's best if you sip it because it kicks like a tank."

Jameson couldn't believe those tiny Omegas drank it at all, let alone like it was sweet tea. Now he understood Lorelei's tolerance for whiskey. Next to this shit, whiskey was nothing.

"The paper's editor has been arrested for publishing false information, tainting the legal process, and perjury," The Alpha smiled again, the air hinting at violence.

"You can't kill everyone, Lukas," Jameson said. "The article was mostly true."

"I can kill everyone. It's in my job description. The news media is getting out of control, and I'm putting a stop to it." Lukas leaned back, taking another sip of his drink and watching Jameson. "How is Lorelei?" he asked.

Lorelei was like a sister to him, and what Jameson didn't understand was that his Eve would quite literally kill him if he didn't make this right somehow.

Jameson sighed deeply, scrubbing his hand over his face. "I'm not sure. She seems okay, but it's hard to say. She won't talk about it. Not with me anyway; my mother came. Thank you for calling her."

"Eve called them," Lukas started. "She insisted Annabelle could help. Lorelei's parents are both pieces of shit; they don't deserve to be involved. She'll talk to Annabelle if she needs to," Lukas added, steepling his fingers in thought. "This trial is going to be a circus, but the Hollins family doesn't have a leg to stand on. My chief counsel reviewed NS304 and said that, although there are some loopholes, it's mostly solid."

"You mean Eve?" Jameson chuckled. Lorelei had told her Eve was one hell of a lawyer, and he believed it.

"Yes, Eve. But before Eve, my former chief counsel reviewed it too. She's fixing the loopholes he left behind, but both agree it will stand.

"She doesn't want to see Lorelei dragged through this, and neither do I, but NS304 has to be defended, and its detractors silenced. Eve says Lorelei can handle it, and I want to believe her, but the trial itself will get nasty. I have no doubt. They'll question everything. Opponents of the law are rallying behind the Hollins family, donating money and time. I just wanted to warn you,"

The Alpha stood, walking around the desk and sitting on the corner facing Jameson. His Marine blues were crisp, and his white shirt sharp. "I want to say one more thing before I let you go. You are a much stronger Alpha than I gave you credit for, Jameson. I believe that, under the right circumstances, you could be a challenge.

"My second is not as strong by half, and I don't want a weak second. Should I fall, I don't think Jason could withstand challenges from men like Xander and Jordan Hollins. I've asked him to step down and am appointing you in his stead." The Alpha's green eyes met Jameson's brown ones and held them.

"While I appreciate the vote of confidence, Lukas. I don't want to be your second. I enjoy being a drone jockey and digging up dirt for you just fine," Jameson said. His eyes went wide when Lukas laughed in his face.

"You don't have a choice, Jameson. It's done. You'll still be a drone jockey and dig up my dirt. Now you'll have the additional responsibility of being my second in command. Good luck. Jason hated the job and told me to tell you thanks for relieving him of it. Now go home; once this trial is over and the Hollins family put to rest, I need you back at work."

247

The Alpha left, leaving Jameson alone. He took the bottle of moonshine and poured himself a shot. If Lorelei could drink that shit, so could he. He pounded downed it quickly, willing himself not to spit it out. The third shot wasn't nearly as bad; Lukas was right. It was an acquired taste.

Chapter 19

"Is Layla okay?" Lorelei asked when Jameson and his dad walked outside. She knew they were going to talk about her. That damned old truck didn't even have a carburetor.

"Layla?" Annabelle asked, her face scrunched in confusion.

"The mare," Lorelei said.

"After everything you've been through, you want to ask me about the mare?" Annabelle asked, her voice incredulous. "Oh, honey, sit down." The older Omega went to Lorelei, wrapping her in her arms.

"I can't sit, Miss Annabelle. I'm very sore today," Lorelei said, looking anywhere but at Annabelle.

"Tell me everything, leave nothing out."

And Lorelei did. She talked fast, and it came out in a rush. She knew the men wouldn't stay outside long, so she told Jameson's mother the whole sordid tale. Even what she wanted to hold back, under the stern look of a southern mama, it all came out anyway.

"I'm proud of you, Lorelei," Annabelle said when she was done.

"What?" Lorelei said, her brows knitting in confusion.

"You killed two Alphas; they deserved it. Good for you. They'll never harm another woman again. You're standing strong in the face of adversity; this too shall pass," she finished.

"Yes, but how many more times, Miss Annabelle? First Xander, then Jameson, then three men whose names I don't even know, Miss Annabelle. How many more times?" Lorelei asked, crossing the kitchen in frustration to pile food on platters.

"No more; it's done. Maybe this was your fate, Lorelei. You may not have wanted to be a call to action, but you are. Omegas are rallying. They want an end to this kind of behavior from Alphas.

"Yes, NS304 gives Omegas rights, but now it comes down to enforcement. I'm sorry it had to be you, but I'm not sorry it happened. It needed to. This is the end, Lorelei, and as awful as it is, you'll win."

"But it won't be just you who wins. Every Omega in the New South will win, and no, that isn't fair to you. But then none of this has been fair to you, has it? Be proud, Lorelei. Take this tragedy and make something good come from it."

"I wish it had never happened to you or Jameson. I can't imagine how much pain you both feel, but it happened. Now's the time to make it what you want it to be, and I have faith that you will do that. That's why I'm proud."

"An Omega in my day would never have the opportunities you do. Think of the way you are paving for your Omega daughters to walk." Annabelle walked to where Lorelei stood and placed her hand on her shoulder. "You and those girls from the Seventh are making the world better, Lorelei. And you'll continue to do so. I believe in you, and I believe in my son; now all you have to do is believe in yourself."

The front door opened and closed. Annabelle poured cups of coffee and had them waiting when the Alphas walked in. Lorelei kept her head down, trying to look busy as she scarfed down as much food as her stomach would hold. She'd woken up feeling hot today and knew the nurse didn't lie. Her estrous was coming.

Within a few days, she would be beyond most rational thought, and so would Jameson. She knew the trial would be soon; she just hoped it would be quick. Lorelei couldn't imagine starting this estrous with another Alpha fighting for the right to serve her. She knew it was bullshit, and so did Jameson, but that wouldn't stop the argument from happening.

Their bond was solid; even now, it hummed steadily between them. She could feel it like a physical cord. Rubbing her chest, she went back for more food. Jameson stood next to her, knowing why she couldn't sit. He offered her his strength and support. How many other Alphas would do that? Not many.

Back home, there once lived an old Omega at the far end of the county. She'd been raped by a band of nomadic Alphas, and her bonded Alpha never forgave her for it and banished her to live her life in solitude for something that wasn't her fault.

She died alone in her cabin, and a legend grew from her bones like ivy. Young Omegas used to hike out to see her remains and tell the tale of how she died.

Those old bones stood as a reminder of what all Omegas fear. Jameson had been angry, but not at her. He hadn't demanded to knot her last night to strengthen his claim. No, it was she who attacked him in a frenzy, demanding that he perform for her. He'd given her what she wanted but had been reluctant. Not out of disgust, but out of fear of causing her pain.

Jameson was a real Alpha. It wasn't just her who was a call to action; it was Jameson too. The New South could stand for a few good Alphas like him.

She watched as he ate, staying tuned into the conversation and joining in when required. She was lucky to have him; she knew that. He was successful, gorgeous, and strong, but he was also kind. She'd never dreamed she'd be where she was at this moment.

Full of emotions she didn't want, she cleaned the kitchen. She focused on putting away food and stacking the dishwasher instead of listening to her thoughts.

Funny how, from the ashes of a life burned to the ground, something good would come. After the events of the last few days, she realized she could love Jameson. She might not be there yet, but then again, she might be lying. Maybe she was.

Working faster, she wiped counters as she tried to come to terms with her feelings. How? How had it happened? She didn't know. How could she pick one moment in a long succession of moments that made her love him?

Still, she was feeling anxious. She needed to heal before her estrous hit, and it was coming. The powerful urge to clean her house in preparation was just the beginning.

"Go soak in the tub," Annabelle said, handing her a small bag that clinked when she moved it. "I'll finish up down here," she added, sensing her discomfort.

In their room, Lorelei made the bed and picked up their clothes. The room looked amazing. A team of experts wouldn't find evidence of yesterday's events with a microscope. It was pristine, but she tidied it anyway.

She shut the door to the bathroom and turned the water on hot. Opening the drawstring to the bag, Lorelei pulled out small bottles of oils labeled Bergamot, Lavender, and Frankincense, along with a note that said how many drops to add to her bath.

Sighing, she eased her sore body into the deep tub, loving the way it felt on her muscles. The oils worked immediately, soothing her aching core and calming her nerves. She needed to find out more about them. Her skin felt less taut, and her temperature cooled despite the warm water. Maybe Miss Annabelle was holding out.

Lorelei wondered if these oils would help delay her estrous long enough to get through the trial. As fast as the courts moved in the New South, she'd only need to hold on two or three days. Even without help, she thought she might have that long. Still, if something would make those days more tolerable, she'd take it.

Jameson entered their bedroom, and she heard him moving around as he changed clothes for his meeting with The Alpha. That he didn't make demands of her helped their situation.

Earlier, he'd shut down the bond between them, likely to talk to his father, but now it was open. She felt nothing but calm strength from him. She'd talk to him later about her estrous and ask him to stock up on water and supplies.

Eve, as her attorney, needed to know, too. Lorelei's approaching estrous could cause problems. Maybe this trial should be delayed. Her body needed to heal, and so did her mind- if it ever would.

Lorelei soaked until the water cooled, and her body felt better than it had in days. Dry and dressed in loose pants and the same shirt from the night before, Lorelei stood at the edge of the bed. Her fingers twitched, and she ached to make a new nest of the soft bedding in the baskets. But she didn't. She scoured the laundry, retrieved the clothes that smelled most like Jameson, and hid them under the pillows in the baskets.

Feeling more settled, Lorelei went downstairs to call Eve and find Annabelle.

The afternoon passed quickly. Eve arrived and met Jameson's parents, who, like most, were smitten with her immediately. As they talked trial strategy, Lorelei watched Eve gain Jameson's parents' respect. In a moment of privacy, she warned Eve about her impending estrous. The hope was that the trial would be short, but there was a real risk of running from a few days into a week.

During their conversation, Annabelle walked by, slipping a small, brown bottle into Lorelei's hands. "Rub it behind your ears and down your neck," she said. "We all have our ways," she finished with a wink, then left the two Omegas to their discussion.

Lorelei sniffed the bottle and found it smelled like the oil she had put in her bath this morning. She'd been able to sit afterward, and there was no longer soreness when she moved. Also, the burgeoning side effects of her impending estrous had lessened. She rubbed the oil on as directed and immediately felt better.

Eve took the bottle, sniffing it with a skeptical look. "Beats a menstrual cup filled with pine tar, I suppose," she said. "I'll do what I can to shut this thing down and finish it quickly," she added.

Jameson came home irritated. He explained Lukas had made him Second Alpha, and the entire room stilled.

"I suggested he wait until things settled," Eve sighed, shaking her head. "But he's hard-headed and doesn't listen. It's a well-deserved promotion. You're not all that bad for an Alpha, Jameson." Eve rose to leave.

"Stay for dinner," Annabelle said, pulling dishes from the oven.

"Another time, Ma'am," Eve replied, The Alpha will look for me, and God knows, it's better if he doesn't have to search too long.

Dinner flew by, and once again, Lorelei found herself soaking in the tub. Whatever Annabelle had given her was working miracles, and she could practically feel her body healing.

After her bath, she dressed again in the ratty T-shirt Jameson had put on her the night before. Even Lorelei could admit it was smelling ripe, but she didn't care. In the absence of taking him into her body, she surrounded herself with his scent. It was the best she could do.

Despite eating three plates at dinner and making the biggest milkshake of her life, she was still hungry. She'd caught Jameson casting wary glances her way, and she knew she'd need to explain, and now that time had come.

"My estrous is coming," she said as he reached to turn off the lights. "A few days to a week at most."

"Fuck," he said, sitting up in bed. The sheets pooled around his waist, highlighting his eight-pack. The deep lines of his Adonis belt dipped below the sheets, making her mouth water.

"Is there anything you can do?" he asked, scrubbing his hand over his face.

"I'm doing what I can; hopefully, it will help." Lorelei stood at the edge of the bed, watching Jameson intently. "I took a pill, Jameson. They offered me a morning-after pill at the hospital, and I took it. There won't be any babies, not this time."

"That's a relief, Lorelei. It is. I want kids someday, but not yet. Not like this, anyway. If I'm honest, I hope it's a while. Right now, I want to focus on you. On us." He sighed, meeting Lorelei's eyes. "I can ask Lukas for a suppressant. He might grant the request."

"I don't want a suppressant. I'm healing quickly; it'll be okay. Suppressants have nasty side effects and will make the next heat worse." Lorelei took a step toward the bed, glancing at the baskets of nesting material. It was by sheer force alone that she didn't grab them up and start a new nest.

"Eve's right, you know," she mumbled.

"About?"

"You're not bad for an Alpha," Lorelei's smile started small but grew wider at Jameson's expression.

"Thanks," he said, laughing. He shook his head, holding the covers out for her.

"Lie back, Jameson," she said, ignoring his gesture.

"Lorelei," he started.

"No. I'm going to tell you what you told me in the barn. I will not apologize, but I need you. I need what I can take from you, but I'm using you to make myself feel better. Still, I'm using you. Make no mistake." Taking the blankets, Lorelei pulled them back, exposing the hard planes of his body. Her breath caught in her throat, and her mouth watered at the sight of him.

He was hers, only hers. Another woman could never make Jameson's body work for her. She supposed he could do other things, but he was hard wired not to.

"I've used you to feel better more than once, Lorelei. I suppose it's no different, but I won't let you hurt yourself. Let me just hold you," he tried.

"That's not enough." Her eyes moved along the lines of his body, knowing it was hers and feeling the need to take from it. "I'm hungry; I've been hungry all day, and I've eaten and eaten but can't get enough. Maybe there isn't enough time. Maybe you should get the suppressant.

"I feel like this estrous is going to be horrible, Jameson. Be ready. There's nothing I can do but warn you." Lorelei took a step forward, easing herself onto the bed.

An Alpha's cum had more calories than a day's worth of meals. It tasted sweet and a little salty, and was designed to be an Omega's favorite treat. It would keep a starving Omega alive through the worst heats and satisfy their deepest cravings. It also soothed their need to be close to their Alpha, and that's what Lorelei needed now.

She groaned as her tongue traced the muscles cut into his thighs. Looking up the line of his body, she met his eyes. "You're beautiful," she said.

"Lorelei." Her name sounded like a prayer on his lips, and his heated eyes watched her like prey.

She made short work of it, attacking him with the voracity of a starving animal. She'd love him later, but she needed him now. Her belly growled deeply, approving of her decision to feed it well. Within a few minutes of his crown breaching her lips, he came down her throat while she sucked and massaged him until there was nothing left.

With a sigh and a contented purr, she crawled up his body, draping herself across his torso, and slept.

Chapter 20

"Base." The Attorney for the Hollins family stood, addressing the court.

"The Omega is a base, volatile creature with very little ability to process thoughts and actions."

Beside Jameson, Lorelei stiffened, and Eve took in a sharp breath she attempted to cover. They sat in the high court, surrounded by family and friends. There was standing room only, and the doors to the court were open so that those beyond could hear.

Benches were deep with a who's who of The New South. The power and prestige represented there had even the Justices looking their way. The Alpha sat behind Jameson and next to his father, the former Alpha of The New South. The Battle family came in force, as did many other influential southern families.

But Jordan Hollins had his following too, and they filled the benches behind him, casting scathing looks Jameson's way.

"Omegas are driven and ruled by need and instinct. They are incapable of higher thought. Omegas need to be protected and cared for, but they must also be managed," the lawyer continued, his expressive voice carrying throughout the room.

"An Omega with choice is an oxymoron. They are our mothers and our sisters; our daughters, our wives. But they are not our leaders. Their dynamic ensures they cannot be trusted with important decisions. They are the weaker dynamic and require the Alpha's assistance in most, if not all, things." The hush that sat over the courtroom meant everyone was listening, and it sickened Jameson. Lorelei might need him, but he fucking needed her more. Their relationship was equal parts need and respect, support, and care.

"An Alpha is the only dynamic that can serve and appease an Omega. Therefore, an Alpha should decide to claim them. It is a heavy burden, as the Alpha must be responsible for the decisions involving his Omega.

"Allowing Omegas to have status as individuals threatens the fabric on which The New South is built. It threatens the Alpha-Omega bond, and where does this lead? Nowhere good. The strength of The New South is predicated on the strength of its Alphas. Allowing Omegas' individual rights and freedoms weakens that, thus weakening The New South.

"On October fifteenth, Xander Hollins claimed Lorelei Hollins as his mate. She was an Omega in estrous, and he served her, claiming her as was his right as an Alpha. The Alpha of The New South killed Xander in cold blood, citing NS304 as his reason. None were present when Xander's claim was made and therefore do not know the circumstances under which it happened. Lorelei Hollins cannot testify because she was in estrous and not of sound mind.

"After killing Xander Hollins, The Alpha, Lukas Jennings offered the rightfully bonded Hollins Omega to another Alpha, allowing him to attempt to break Jordan's claim. This Alpha is now The Alpha's Second in command, and the Hollins family cries foul.

"NS10 gave the Alpha domain over the Omega, making her his property. NS134 allows this property to pass to an Alpha's next of kin in the event of his death. Lorelei Hollins is a Hollins and belongs to the Hollins family, and has been his lawful property since October 15th.

"NS304 states that an Omega has a choice with the Alpha-Omega bond, but it does not impart an Omega with individual rights. It allows for circumstances in which an Omega may work or study at university. Still, it does not grant them explicit legal status as an individual.

"Once Lorelei Hollins was claimed by Jordan Hollins, she ceased to have further choice in the matter and became Hollins' property. We don't know what Mrs. Hollins said as Jordan claimed her. No one does, and his claim should stand.

"As Lorelei Hollins was stolen from them, the remainder of the Hollins Alphas went to collect her and strengthen the Hollins bond. According to NS134, everything Timothy, Russel, and Jordan Hollins did two days ago was legal and binding.

"Lorelei Hollins was reclaimed and bonded. During this incident, she killed two of her bonded mates in cold blood, highlighting why Omegas cannot be allowed to decide their paths. The offense is punishable by death under the law.

"The Hollins family recognizes that Omegas are rare, and they just want their property back so that she can be treated as she deserves. The court must ask itself three questions. One: Was it legal to steal a bonded Omega and give her to another Alpha? Two: Could Jameson Battle legally and rightfully attempt to break another Alpha's claim? And Three: Is NS304 legal under the laws existing in The New South?

"If the answer to any of these questions is no, then Lorelei Hollins must be returned to her rightful mate, Jordan Hollins. Thank you." After a piercing look at the petitioner's side, the attorney sat down.

Jameson glanced around. The space in the back of the courtroom was filled with nearly one hundred Omegas. He could feel their unease. Lorelei sat in stunned silence by his side, and Eve's face was pale. Expectation sat heavily on the air, and a tense readiness came from row after row of warrior women. If this went sideways, it would not be good for anyone.

Eve stood slowly, cradling the swell of her belly. She came around the table, walking to the front of the room, and stood directly in front of the judges.

"Base," she said, her voice so low that the room strained to hear.

"Volatile," she paused. She wore a black suit with a royal blue shirt beneath. It highlighted her red hair, and Jameson could tell every eye in the room was hers now.

"Slow." She looked up, meeting the eyes of the three male Alphas hearing the case.

"Driven by instinct and incapable of rational, higher thought. That is what Mr. Spokes would have you believe. My name is Eve Hatfield Jennings, and I am mated to The First Alpha. I graduated at the top of my class at the University of Atlanta with degrees in dynamics and law. There were twelve Alphas, thirty-one Betas, and one Omega in my graduating class. I am that Omega." Sharp intakes of breath came from the opposite side of the courtroom, making it obvious not everyone had known who or what Eve was.

"If you are in this room, your mother was likely an Omega. Or perhaps you have an Omega sister. Are there fathers of Omega daughters here?" she asked, turning to the room as if waiting for an answer.

"Is your daughter slow? Does your mother function at a lower intellectual level than your father? Does your Omega sister require your assistance with her financial accounts or day-to-day life?

"Yes, Omegas are different. No one denies that. All the dynamics are different. There is a 1.6% difference in DNA between Alpha and Omega and between male and female. One. Point. Six. This is science. It's irrefutable.

"That one point six percent involves muscle mass, physical size, gender, and other features of the dynamics, not intelligence. Is your Omega wife unable to think for herself or make proper decisions?" she said, pausing. "One point six percent genetic difference between you and me. That's all."

Eve turned to the judges, looking at them one by one. She'd told Jameson that all of the judges were bonded, and based on their uncomfortable shifting, Eve was making a point.

"There are nearly one hundred Omegas in this room. If you look behind Jameson and Lorelei *Battle's* family, you'll see them. They are sitting there, nicely dressed and peaceful. They are taking this all in as this court holds their future in its hands." People shifted in their seats to look. The Omegas were easy to spot, if only because of their size.

"Most of the Omegas in this room are unbonded, and they seem to manage themselves just fine. The Alpha himself will tell you that they were instrumental in helping to quell an insurrection in the Seventh just months ago. Omegas. Omegas did that. Not Alphas and Omegas together, mind you. Omegas.

"Of the Omegas who made The Sixth District or the capital their home, some are already bonded. Not only are they bonded, but they've claimed their mates in return. Not only are they bonded and have claimed their mates in return, but one hundred percent of those bonded Omegas are pregnant." A gasp went up throughout the room. Anyone familiar with dynamics would realize how significant that statistic was.

"Let me rephrase. One hundred percent of the willingly bonded and claimed Omegas, who have undergone a natural estrous, are pregnant," Eve paused for that to sink in and allow the hushed murmurs to cease. She cast a glance at Lorelei for effect.

"One hundred percent," she said, turning to look over the crowd. She gave her belly another rub as if to accentuate her claim. "Scientists have struggled with the Omega fertility problem for years. Why don't Omegas conceive? Why don't they nest? Why don't they claim the mates who have claimed them? Why has the Omega purr all but disappeared? They've struggled in vain to answer these questions when all those Alpha scientists needed to do was ask an Omega.

"Omegas wanted a choice. They wanted to decide which Alpha would serve them sexually for the next fifty to eighty years; that's all. Basically, they wanted the ability to pick their long-term lover. Give them a choice and see what happens.

"One Hundred Percent.

"A baby boom is coming, ladies and gentlemen." Eve allowed herself a soft smile before turning back to the judges.

"On October fifteenth, Lorelei Nash Battle was at an Alpha-Omega mixer with The First Alpha and me. She had two drinks. One of those drinks was given to her by an Alpha named Xander Hollins and was later proven to have been laced with a drug. This drug caused her to become disoriented and slip into a short-term, *false* estrous. She slipped into this estrous only *after* Xander Hollis raped her up against a dirty bathroom wall.

"Xander Hollis attempted to claim Lorelei Nash Battle by biting her, very much against her will. At no time did Lorelei Nash Battle consent. We know this because *she* was there.

"Earlier that evening, she decided to allow Jameson Battle to serve her through her next estrous. She'd liked him." With those words, Jameson's heart stopped beating. Were they true? If so, he'd never known. Lorelei kept her hand in his and her face tilted down.

"Jameson Battle was everything she thought a good Alpha should be. He'd charmed her, made her laugh; he was a fine dancer and seemed intelligent. She was a little smitten. I know because she told me, but I was also there. Everyone in that room will tell you that sparks flew when they came together.

"Lorelei went to the bathroom a few minutes later and was raped and claimed against her will. Her life will never be the same. Never. NS304 gives an Omega the right to choose her mate. Lorelei Battle was stripped of her rights by Xander Hollins.

"After his legal execution for violating NS304, The Alpha had only one choice. Ruin Lorelei's future by allowing her to suffer or letting someone he trusted try to help.

"Jameson Battle saved Lorelei Battle's life that night. She knows it. Was she angry? Absolutely. Her choice was ripped from her. Twice.

"But Jameson's bond is as strong as they come. Jameson, stand a moment and pull down your collar, please." Jameson did as he was asked, offering his neck for all to see. Lorelei's claiming marks were both healed and angry. She'd chewed on him multiple times, and it showed. There's no faking those tiny teeth marks.

"The petitioner's attorney asked you to consider three questions. I only ask you to consider two. Who is Lorelei Battle bonded to? I think you'll find that the bond between Jameson and Lorelei is so strong that it could never be broken. I also ask you to ponder who is better to decide an Omega's path than the Omega themself. Lorelei Battle killed two of the three Alphas raping her in self-defense. None of those men had a legal claim to her, not under NS304, and not under any law that makes sense. Thank you," Eve finished, taking a seat beside Lorelei.

Through our bond, Jameson felt her peace. She was calm, even. Lorelei smelled more floral than usual today, and he knew his mother was responsible, but whatever concoction she'd made was working. Lorelei tipped her face to his, meeting Jameson's eyes. "It'll be okay," she said, shocking him.

"I know it will, dove. We've got this."

"The petitioner would like to call Jordan Hollins, please." The opposing attorney stood and followed Jordan to the stand.

"Were you and Xander close, Jordan?" Mr. Spokes asked without pause.

"Very." Jameson spared the other Alpha a glance. He looked much different from the night he'd jumped out of Jameson's second-story window. The cuts and scrapes were scabbed and healing. His short, sandy hair was shaggy, and his brown eyes bright. He looked harmless, and Jameson was sure that was the intent.

"You are the youngest brother, aren't you?"

"Yes," Jordan answered.

"And you want Lorelei to come home with you, correct?"

"Yes. She's my brother's Omega, and the last thing he ever did was to claim her. She's ours, and our family needs her to heal." Jordan's voice broke, and Jameson wanted to kill him.

"Did you try to rescue her from her current situation?"

"Yes. My brothers and I went to get her. She's ours. For all we knew, she was pregnant with a Hollins baby, and we needed to get to her. Jameson Battle had no right to take her from us."

"I see. Jordan, did you break Jameson's false claim on Lorelei Hollins?"

"We did. She is a Hollins and will always be a Hollins. Jordan's claim was strong, and Jameson hasn't broken it."

"Who killed your two brothers, Jordan?"

"Lorelei did. She shot them. But we forgive her. If she weren't pregnant with Xander's baby, she could be pregnant with Russel's or Tim's right now, and we might not even know it. We just want our family together again," Jordan finished, sounding pitiful. Beside Jameson, Lorelei stiffened, and he purred softly for her.

They'd both know this trial would be difficult and that things would be said they wished weren't. She calmed, her hand relaxing on his. Slowly, her head crept to his arm, and he circled her body with it, pulling her in.

"You should separate them," Jordan added, his eyes flashing Lorelei's way. "She isn't his."

Through it all, Jameson purred.

The purr was meant for Lorelei, but those around picked up its sound. No one missed the rancor with which Jordan Hollins spoke, either.

"Thank you, Jordan. That's all for now, your honors."

Eve stood, walking briskly to the witness stand; the fire in her eyes not to be dismissed. Her heels clicked on the marble floors, and her red hair flashed under the lights.

"Mr. Hollins," she started.

"I'd prefer a man ask me the questions," Jordan said, trying to keep the sneer from his face.

"Is that so?" Eve asked calmly. "Your honors, is there any reason I should not be allowed to cross-examine Mr. Hollins?" she asked, looking at the judges.

"Proceed, Mrs. Jennings,"

"Mr. Hollins," she asked smoothly, unruffled by the waves of anger flowing from the man on the witness stand. "How does an Alpha go about claiming his mate?" she asked.

"That's a stupid question. Everyone knows that," he said, looking around the courtroom.

"I would've thought so too, but you claim you broke Jameson's bond. That's very difficult once the bond has settled. How did you do it?" Eve asked, not looking at the man in the stand.

"Xander claimed her; his bond is ours genetically," he said.

"Yes, he claimed her. But that's not an answer," Eve said, bringing her eyes to Jordan's.

"Russel fucked her, and Tim came on her. I rubbed it on her skin until it dried," his voice wavered a bit. Jameson saw red, and his grip tightened on Lorelei's so hard that she whimpered.

Forcing himself to calm down and soothe his mate, he took up his purr again.

"So, Tim had sex with Lorelei?" Eve asked.

271

"No," Jordan sneered, looking down at Eve. "Russel did."

"I see," Eve said calmly. "Did he call her slick?"

"Slick?" he asked, looking momentarily confused.

"Yes. Slick. It's the fluid an Omega produces to ease the way, you know, for sex."

"That's a myth," he laughed.

"A myth?" Eve said, cocking her head to the side slightly.

"Everyone knows that's not real."

"How about the Omega's bite? Is that a myth, too?"

"Of course, it is. An Omega doesn't have the power to claim a mate. That's why they shouldn't have a choice."

"Interesting. So, there was some ejaculate and perhaps some penetration, but no slick. Did you bite Lorelei?" Eve looked down, pretending the question wasn't important.

"No, I didn't bite her."

"Did your brothers?" she asked, picking a piece of imaginary lint off her suit jacket.

"Nobody bit her; we aren't heathens," he scoffed.

Jameson wondered what the fuck was actually happening and if the man was even an Alpha. Alphas were born with the knowledge of how to claim a mate. They take classes, and their parents teach them, but it was also pure instinct. He wasn't sure what backwoods goat rodeo this genius came from, but he was killing him when this was over.

"Did Lorelei scream?" Eve asked innocently.

"Yeah, she screamed. She was scared, that's all," Jordan replied, looking smug. "She's just afraid, but she'll be okay once we get her home." Jameson wanted to scream that his wife wasn't a lost dog and that she might never be okay again, but he kept silent.

"Did she fight you and say no?"

"Yes, but that's natural."

Silence filled the room. Even the Hollins side knew it was wrong. Maybe they believed the story initially, but not now.

"Did any of you knot Lorelei?" Eve asked innocently.

"No. We didn't have time. We intended to later." Jameson shook with fury. Knotting an Omega bonded to another Alpha was tantamount to torture. The pain would be unimaginable. This was common knowledge, and why the deed was punishable by death.

"Mr. Hollins, is your mother an Omega?" Eve asked, her eyes concerned.

"Yes, of course."

"Is your father still living?" Eve asked, casting a look over her shoulder at Lukas.

"Yes."

"And the Omega claiming bite is just a myth?" Eve asked.

"Yes."

"Just like the female orgasm, I suppose. Thank you, I have no further questions."

The opposition called another witness or two, but Jameson floated on a sea of pain, unable to hear their testimony. He was angry that no one mentioned how much his wife had bled at the hands of these assholes or how much pain she'd been in after. How much pain she was probably still in.

He wanted to hold them accountable for every bruise on her body and every ache in her bones. They fucking hurt his wife. His. Fucking. Wife.

They just kept talking and talking about nothing.

"The Petitioner rests, your honors." The dull-eyed lawyer stood, pulling Jameson from his thoughts.

"The defense requests a lunch break, your honors," Eve said, standing immediately.

"Granted. Court will resume in one hour."

In an airless room filled with people, they ate. Lorelei, Eve, and James huddled in the corner. Lorelei's glassy eyes and fevered expression concerned Jameson. She'd said her heat was coming, and he worried they wouldn't make it through the case.

Surely to God, they wouldn't sequester her until the verdict, but he couldn't be sure. Once it became apparent what was happening, all bets were off.

Lorelei refreshed her potion and seemed better afterward.

"I'm going to speed this up, Lorelei. I don't think you have days. Maybe a day, but not days. I planned to call Jameson's family and an expert on dynamics, but I'm just going to call you.

"It will be obvious that you and Jameson are bonded, but that might be uncomfortable for both of you. I just don't think we have enough time to dick around. Okay?" Eve looked at both our faces for an answer.

"It has to work, Eve," Lorelei said. "I'll die before I go with Jordan fucking Hollins."

"Oh, it'll work. You just might not talk to me for a bit after. Look, these Alpha judges are bonded and claimed. I can see the bite marks on two of them, and the other wears a high collar. They know what's up." Eve finished, looking for their ascent.

"We do trust you. And we definitely need to hurry this up."

Eve nodded and rose, taking her lunch to Lukas.

"I love you, Lorelei. I do, and we'll get through this," Jameson offered, reaching for her hand.

"I know," she said, closing her eyes slowly. Jameson watched her heartbeat in the hollow of her throat. It was far faster than was normal, and her smell was becoming sweeter. If this case wasn't over today, they'd be in trouble.

They rose together and walked back into the courtroom. Lorelei kept her hand on Jameson's arm, and he kept purring.

"All rise." Eve scurried to their side, waiting on the judges.

"You may be seated."

Lorelei took the water pitcher and filled cup after cup. Her actions caught the judges' attention, and their faces grew worried as they sniffed the air.

"The defense would like to call Lorelei Battle to the stand," Eve said, rising to her feet.

Once Lorelei was settled, Eve began. "Did you consent to a claim from Xander Hollins?" she asked, getting right to the point.

"No," Lorelei said, leaning into the mic.

"Did Xander Hollins's claim on you ever cement or settle?"

"No," she answered again, firmly.

"Why not?"

"Because Jameson broke his claim before it could," Lorelei said, her voice low and even.

"And how did he do that?"

"Like, specifically?" Lorelei asked.

"Objection, your honors. There's no need to air explicit details of the claiming process in court." Jameson figured the Beta lawyer had finally realized his client was a piece of shit and wanted to quash the line of questioning.

"Overruled," the supreme judge said.

"He had sex with me, biting me over the other mark and knotting me."

"Was it painful?"

"Very," Lorelei answered. Jameson hadn't known that. He'd never meant to hurt her. "I could feel both claims. It was very uncomfortable. Jameson is a powerful Alpha, so his claim settled, and Xander's didn't."

"I see. Did you consent to this?" Eve asked, bringing up the question Jameson was sure everyone wanted to know.

"I was in a sort of estrous. It was short-lived and drug-induced, but it was still an estrous." Lorelei leveled James with a look. "I never told him no. Not once. Jameson would've served me through my next estrous anyway, had he been willing. I just hadn't had the opportunity to ask him."

Jameson wasn't sure whether that was a lie, and his stomach clenched.

"Who is your bonded mate, Lorelei?"

"Objection. Calls for speculation," Mr. Spokes jumped to his feet, waving his arms.

"Speculation? Your honors, I intend to prove to whom Lorelei Battle is bonded." Eve strode forward, looking very ready to take the other lawyer out.

"Overruled."

"Lorelei, would you care to stand in front of the witness box?" Jameson watched as Lorelei stepped delicately down, moving to where Eve pointed. Lorelei had chosen a gray dress that fell below her knees, pairing it with black, low-heeled shoes. She looked somber, standing alone under the harsh light in the room.

"Mr. Hollins, would you care to growl to the witness?"

"Objection."

"Overruled," the judge sighed this time, looking out across the room.

"I don't want to scare her any more than necessary, your honors," Jordan said, looking confused. For the first time, Jameson wondered how old the boy was because there was no way he was an adult.

"Go ahead, son. Step up and follow the directions," the older judge at the end of the bench said.

Jameson watched as the other man stood up, walking toward Lorelei. It was all he could do not to rush forward. However, he could not stop the low growl meant to threaten the other man. Eve turned her head, cocking an eyebrow. None of this was missed.

"Growl for Lorelei, please," Eve asked.

Jordan growled, and nothing happened.

"Growl a bit lower and perhaps a smidge deeper," she instructed. Jordan did as she asked.

The Omegas in the back of the room rumbled.

"That's it," Eve said when he'd growled for a solid minute. "Now, give us a purr."

"I've never purred before," said Jordan, his voice hardening. "Purrs are frivolous and unnecessary.

"Humor us and try," the old judge said, staring the young Alpha down.

Jordan's purr sounded pained, but eventually evened out. Lorelei stood in the face of it, her face expressionless and her back straight.

"Thank you, Mr. Hollins."

"Jameson, would you come closer?" Eve asked, already knowing the answer.

"Objection," The Hollins' lawyer rose to his feet, albeit slowly.

"Overruled."

"Mr. Battle, I know this may be embarrassing, but would you growl for your mate?"

Without hesitation, Jameson growled low. Lorelei's head fell back with a groan, causing him to growl lower. He smelled the sweet scent of Lorelei's slick filling the air, and his hands shook to touch her. He kept growling until the slick flowing could be heard splattering on the floor. Jordan stared, transfixed at Lorelei's reaction. His eyes widened, and his nostrils flared at the scent of her desire.

Jameson had had enough. He purred, and Lorelei went limp like a ragdoll. She fell and was caught, then cradled to his chest.

"Enough," he said. "She is mine, and there is no breaking my claim."

"The defense rests, your honors," Eve said, walking around to sit.

"The uh, the petitioner rests as well."

"What? No! You've got to ask her questions. She needs to admit that Russel and Tim broke Jameson's claim. We claimed her, and she's ours now!" Gone was the innocent young Alpha, and in his place stood a feral one.

Jordan Hollins scented the air, and his eyes went wild, and all pretense of being the boy next door vanished.

The gavel pounded, and conversations broke out across the room. "We will retire to deliberate." The judges rose and left.

"Get her out of here," Eve said, patting Jameson on the arm.

In a quiet room, he held her. Rocking her gently as he purred. His mother had come in and covered Lorelei with oil from a small brown bottle, but he didn't think it was enough.

Her scent was rapidly changing, and she burned like fire against his skin. She moaned, and tremors went through her tiny body. Jameson purred, soothing her as best he could. He pulled the strands of her hair, massaging her scalp.

Slowly, she unfolded from him. "I'm okay," she said, taking a deep breath. "I'm better. This is going to be a rough one; I can feel it." She cast her glassy eyes his way, and he wondered how they did it. Omegas were much stronger than given credit for; there was nothing weak about Lorelei.

Eve walked into the room with The Alpha at her side. "The judges are retiring for the night. We'll reconvene in the morning at eight. Are you going to make it, Lorelei?" she added upon seeing her friend's state.

"I'll be fine, thanks. We'll be there," Lorelei answered, straightening her spine.

"I can ask for a continuance," said Eve, looking at Jameson.

"No. I don't want to go into estrous, not knowing the outcome. I can't. We'll be here." Lorelei stood, straightening her skirt.

Jameson draped his arms over Lorelei's shoulders as they exited the courthouse. He lifted her into the truck and slid in next to her. His parents traveled behind him, and they made a slow procession back to his home. Lorelei said nothing; she stared at the window as the scenery went by. Her soft, blonde hair had escaped its updo and obscured her face.

"My brother is sending his accounts for you to review. I told him it would be a week to ten days before you could get back to him. He said not to rush."

"I can take a cursory look at them when we get home; it'll keep me busy," she replied, her voice sounding stronger.

"Okay. Don't forget to order furniture for your office; put it on my account."

"You don't have to do this," she said, looking his way.

"I want to. You deserve more than you've ever gotten. I'm going to give it to you, and you're going to accept it. End of story," Jameson's voice sounded gruff and commanding, even to him.

He caught her smile and the soft shake of her head as her expression softened. "Yes, sir," she said, not concealing the smile in her voice.

"Now you're getting it." Jameson turned his head so she couldn't see his own smile.

She elbowed him in the ribs.

"I'm going to drop you off and run back for supplies. If you're going to look into Darrian's accounts, you won't need me. Mom already said she's making lasagna," said Jameson as he pulled into their driveway.

"She doesn't have to do that. It feels weird having her in my kitchen," she added as he pulled her from the truck.

Jameson hid his grin. She'd transitioned into calling it her kitchen. Their house. Us. We. She was seeing them together, and he gloried in it. They'd been so close to having everything, and it had been taken away the night Xander Hollins attacked Lorelei- except maybe it hadn't.

"She makes a delicious lasagna, babe, roll with it." Jameson set Lorelei down to walk into the house under her own power, then backed out of the drive.

His father had slipped him a list of things to stock up on before he went on lockdown for her estrous. He wasn't sure what to expect. Alphas talk, but he still wasn't sure. His father's list helped, and he hurried to fill it.

Chapter 21

Lorelei took a deep breath and moved into the house. Jameson had gotten to her. His support over the last few days had eroded any resistance she'd raised, and she was done. Her estrous was coming, and she was tired of fighting him.

He'd won. Regardless of how they'd gotten here, here they were. He loved her. The bond doesn't lie. She changed out of the cursed dress in their room, throwing on soft leggings and one of his gym tees. His scent calmed her, soothing away the symptoms of her impending heat.

Biology fucking sucked. But it sucked equally. Jameson would abandon his post as Second Alpha to deal with her needy ass for the next five to seven days. And she was excited about it. She had dreaded every single estrous she'd endured, but not this one. Her heart rate sped up at the thought.

Everything he did, he did well.

Lorelei was a few months younger than Eve. And at twenty-four, she'd had precisely twenty-one estrous cycles. She'd never run from them the way Eve had. No, instead, she'd contracted with an Alpha each time to serve her through.

She didn't even remember their names. Twenty-one nameless, faceless men had ensured she'd gotten what she needed. But it isn't like they did it out of the goodness of their hearts.

This time, she had Jameson. This time and the countless times that would follow. He'd broken her. There was no more resistance, no more thoughts of running, and no more thoughts of death. She hoped the bond would make this experience something more than need, sex, and depravity.

She felt as eager as she did going into her first estrous. Anticipatory, even. That experience had ended in emptiness and disappointment, as had the others that followed. Not this time, she could feel that.

The smile on her face did not lessen when she ran into his parents in the kitchen. She was lucky. The Battle family had been nothing short of amazing to her, and she knew her life was far better than most.

Lorelei watched Annabelle build a monster lasagna while she and Earl sat at the kitchen table. Pen in hand, Lorelei went through the papers Darrian sent, marking receipts and making notes. Her body had calmed. Focused on her task, she didn't notice Jameson come in. Earl rose, and the two Alphas carried boxes of supplies up the stairs.

"Darrian has a problem," she said when Jameson joined her at the table.

Lorelei had papers spread everywhere, attaching colored sticky notes to the stacks. Detailed notes sat at her elbow.

Scrubbing her hands over her face, she rearranged the stacks before piling them back into boxes.

"What do you mean?" Jameson asked, taking the refilled box and setting it aside.

"I'm sorry, Jameson, I was thinking out loud. I'll talk to him about it privately." Her eyebrows crashed together as her concern mounted.

Darrian had a rat. Someone had embezzled millions of dollars from his investment firm. They'd done an excellent job of hiding it, but no one was better at finding lost money than Lorelei; it was one of her gifts. She'd taken several specialty courses in forensic accounting and had loved them.

Jameson met her eyes, and she could see his desire to challenge her, but he said nothing.

"Dinner!" Annabelle said, oblivious to the tension at the table.

"I could eat the whole pan," Lorelei growled, her eyes flashing at the food.

"You certainly can; I made two. What you don't eat tonight, you can freeze for next week," Annabelle said with a wink. "Now, son. We all know what's coming. You take care of our girl. Hear me?" she added, shaking a wooden spoon at him.

"Yes, ma'am," Jameson answered. Lorelei thought the blush spreading across his neck was adorable. An adorable Alpha. Who would've thought?

286

Dinner went well; no one mentioned the trial, and the atmosphere was light. Despite her embarrassment at being made to bathe the courtroom floor in slick, things had gone well. Better than well. Besides, other plans were afoot. Whatever happened with Jordan Fucking Hollins, justice would be served.

Lorelei ran a hot bath, soaking herself in the oils that staved off the anxiety and desperation building before her estrous. She didn't need those anymore. Jameson wasn't nameless, and he wasn't faceless. He loved her.

There would be no awkward offers of thanks and the inevitable handshake after the deed was done. He wouldn't leave her, and she wouldn't want him to. What would an estrous on that foundation feel like? She could only guess.

After her bath, Lorelei pulled on Jameson's tee and walked into their room. She could hear Jameson talking to his parents, their muted voices filtered up the stairs. Her skin wasn't hot, and her nerves were calm. Deep within her body, her womb was quiet.

Lorelei glanced at the mound of soft furs, blankets, and pillows. Her fingers twitched, and she could no longer resist their call. Purring, she pulled each item out, rubbing her face to judge its softness. Painstakingly, she built her second nest. Layering, twisting, and fluffing each individual fabric until it was perfect. And it was perfect. With a sigh, she crawled into it and slipped the cover over her head.

She awoke alone. Startled, she pulled the covers off the nest to find Jameson curled on the outside. She growled at him, not out of need but from anger. How dare he? She thought. How dare he not join her in their nest? Her growl deepened, then she forced it to stop.

"Jameson?" she said, shaking his shoulder to wake him.

"Hmmph?" he answered.

"Why the fuck are you out there when you should be in here?" She tried and failed to keep the growl from her voice.

The sleepy smile that split his face was glorious. With a yawn, he stretched, rising on one elbow. "You didn't invite me," he said.

"You're kidding, right?" she said, stopping her growl again.

Jameson shook his head, opening his eyes to meet hers.

"It's our nest. You're always welcome," Lorelei said.

"Good to know." His smile grew impossibly wide. "I'll make coffee. How are you holding up?" he asked.

"I'm good. We'll be okay for a while." Lorelei's skin was warm but not painfully so. Her sense of smell was sharper, and she could smell every nuance of Jameson's scent, and he smelled delicious. The heady scent of exotic spices tickled her nose, making her inhale deeply. A shiver went down her spine as she took in the sight of him.

"It hurts to look at you," she said, her breath catching in her throat. She was on edge and prayed he wouldn't tip her over. If

288

they fell into bed now, all bets were off, and they probably wouldn't rise from it for a week.

"I'm sorry?" Jameson said, confusion rippling across his beautiful face.

"It's not an unpleasant pain," Lorelei added, tracking Jameson's movements like she would a game animal. Her eyes narrowed on him, and she scented him in the air again. Her only chance was that he would move, because she certainly couldn't.

"I'll meet you downstairs," he said, his eyes growing heated. Behind the heat was understanding; he understood she was hanging by a thread. She appreciated he didn't try to cut the string.

Jameson got up, and Lorelei's eyes snagged on the sharp edges of his body; there was no softness to him. All edges and hard angles, the light cast shadows on the planes his muscles made. Her mouth watered at the sight and she kind of doubted she was actually all right.

He flexed as he walked into the bathroom, making her laugh. With a wink over his shoulder, he went to dress, and Lorelei's breathing slowed.

Alphas. Lorelei shook her head before going to her closet to dress. Their fate would be decided soon, but she wasn't worried. After talking with her friends yesterday, one way or another-everything would be fine.

Chapter 22

She watched Jameson with hungry eyes as he went into the bathroom, and he knew something had changed. Their bond felt different. Stronger. Steadier. Something had flipped in her mind, and the bond reflected that. He shaved and dressed in silence, hearing her moving around in the room beyond.

He hadn't realized how much of their bond was filled with darkness and angst until it was gone. It made him wonder. He didn't want to look at it too closely. He'd done what he'd done, and he didn't regret it. Not then, and not ever.

He'd come upstairs last night to find her sprawled out in her nest, fast asleep. He'd taken a picture with his ComLink. Her face had been slack, and her body relaxed; she was the picture of Omega surrender he'd had in his mind from the beginning. He'd seen nothing more beautiful in his life, and despite his desire to slide in next to her, he couldn't. She needed her rest, and he didn't think he could stop himself from fucking her. They needed to get through today. That was all. One more day.

She was still in the closet when he slipped out of their room. His parents were meeting them at the courthouse, claiming some early errand in town. Jameson found plates of bacon and scrambled eggs on the counter and took them both to the table.

Lorelei came down the stairs dressed in a navy-blue pantsuit with a cream shirt beneath. She looked every bit the sharp professional that he knew her to be.

She'd found a problem with Darrian's finances. Darrian had a dozen accountants who had found nothing, but he had known. He'd known there was an issue, but no one could find it.

Lorelei looked through Darrian's papers with tired eyes and found the issue in a few hours. Lower functioning creature, Jameson's ass.

They ate in silence, drinking coffee and mentally preparing for the coming day. Jameson held her hand on the way to the courthouse, rubbing his thumb idly on the pad of her palm. They'd not said more than a few words to one another, but the silence was comfortable.

He wasn't worried about the outcome of this trial, not even a little bit. He'd kill Jordan Hollins before he came within two feet of Lorelei. Period. End. Nothing short of death would part them, and with the strength of their bond, they wouldn't be parted for long.

Sighing, Jameson parked the truck and helped Lorelei down. He felt her stiffen and looked over his shoulder. Protesters by the hundreds had gathered. Brightly colored signs proclaimed NS304 a step forward, while others proclaimed it a step back. Two sides converged, both chanting limericks that blended into incoherent words.

Lorelei kept her head down. With a hand on the small of her back, he ushered her past the press of bodies. Some reached out to touch her, and some tried to spit. Hurriedly, Jameson escorted her to the stairs where The Alpha's men stood guard. Guns at the ready, the protesters were kept at bay. The experience shocked Jameson. The Alpha was not known to tolerate protests, peaceful or not. For the second time in one day, Jameson wondered.

Eve met them at the courthouse door, then led them into one of the small waiting rooms next to the high court.

"I received word this morning that the verdict is in," she started without preamble. One thing Jameson appreciated about his wife's sister was that she did not mince words.

"Is that good or bad?" Lorelei asked, her voice resolved.

"It's definitive. Whatever decision they reached, there was not much dissent or discussion." Eve reached over, rubbing Lorelei's knee. "How are you holding up?"

A long look passed between the Omegas. Almost to the point of discomfort for him, because they communicated silently with that look.

"Well, sister," Lorelei said with a vicious half-smile. "Very well," she added with one firm nod.

The smile on Eve's face reminded Jameson who these Omegas were. These were the Omegas that slid through mountain passes like smoke on the wind. They were savage. All their savagery could be hidden under pantsuits and an Omega's scent, but he knew.

And suddenly, Jameson wasn't as sure of himself anymore. His spine straightened as they shared one last feral glance. His mother was right; there would be no taming Lorelei. Maybe he could contain her, maybe not.

A knock sounded, and The Alpha joined them. The grim determination in the man's eyes was equally scary as that he saw in Lorelei's. He was missing something; he knew it.

Not long after, a knock sounded at the door. As one, they rose, filing into the courtroom to hear three men pass judgment on Jameson and his wife.

The courtroom was packed. If it were possible, even more people filled the large space. Faces pressed against the glass in the observation suites above, and they had to press forward to the front. Jameson fought to catch his breath as the air was stifling and stale.

Lorelei patted his arm. She patted *his* arm. Giving him a smile and a faint nod, she pushed forward, taking him with her. The anxiety that started in the waiting room lessened a little.

"All rise."

The entire room had already been standing in anticipation.

"Be seated."

The shush of bodies settling was loud, and the justices waited until it fell silent before beginning.

"Times are changing," the justice started, looking out across the room. "Perhaps for the better. NS304 was written in the heat of battle, and despite its clarity, needs some revision. But we have not been tasked with that cause. The defendant presents a compelling argument, and more needs to be done to evaluate the claim that Omegas flourish and thrive when given a proper choice.

"The Petitioner, Jordan Hollins, was arrested and charged with Violations of NS304, first-degree rape, interference with a bonded Omega, and interference with an Alpha in regards to a bonded Omega. These charges are serious, Jordan Hollins. Most never reach the high court for a hearing as their cases are handled expeditiously by The Alpha of The New South," he said, casting a worried glance toward said Alpha.

"The Alpha-Omega bond is sacrosanct," he continued. "The New South's foundation is predicated on this bond and what this bond means to everyone, Alpha, Omega, and Beta alike.

"This court is unanimous in its decision," the chief justice paused, looking from the papers he held in his hand. "No outbursts in the courtroom will be tolerated," he stopped to glare at both sides of the aisle.

"On October Fifteenth, by the articles of NS304, Xander Hollister illegally claimed Lorelei Nash Battle and was dealt justice by The Alpha. Xander Hollins' claim was uncemented when Lorelei Nash Battle was legally claimed by Jameson Beauregard Battle. The Battle claim was made willingly and may stand.

"The charges of Interference with a Bonded Omega, Interference with an Alpha in regards to a bonded Omega are affirmed.

"As Jordan Hollins assisted in, but did not commit the act of rape against Lorelei Battle, the charge of first-degree rape has been reduced to second-degree rape." A sharp intake of breath in the courtroom had the gavel banging. "One more outburst, and the court will be cleared." Immediately the room silenced.

That fucker got away with it, Jameson fumed. Second-degree rape carried a sentence of ten years. Jordan Hollins would be out before he was thirty; it was unconscionable. Beside him, Lorelei went limp. He went to shore her up, but a glance at her smile made his blood run cold. Lorelei was smiling, and it was not at all pleasant.

"The charge against Xander Hollins of NS304 violations is affirmed, and his punishment is deemed legal. The charge against Jordan Hollins for violating NS304 is as follows. The court does not find that Jordan Hollins violated NS304, as it stands, and that charge is vacated. He is sentenced to fifteen years."

"Your honors, as Mr. Hollins' part in the alleged crime was minor, the Petitioner requests a suspended sentence," Mr. Spokes rushed to stand.

"Denied," the lead justice said with a loud bang of his gavel.

Soldiers moved in, taking Jordan into custody.

A small hand touched his arm. "I'm boiling. I need to reapply the oils," Lorelei said, fanning her face with a folder. "I just need a minute," she finished, looking flushed and uncomfortable."

"I'll take her," Eve said, standing. She placed a supportive hand on Lorelei's arm and helped her to stand. Jameson fell in behind them, but the crush of departing Omegas separated him from Lorelei.

"It must be considered a win, Jameson," The Alpha said, stopping his march behind the myriad Omegas. "Eve is hashing out the variances that need to be addressed in NS304. The Justices reached out to her personally, offering to help. This won't happen again. If it does, it will never go to trial. I guarantee that," he finished. He ignored Jameson as he stood on his toes, trying to keep Lorelei in sight.

"Give them a minute," he said. "She's in good hands."

Jameson eased back, letting the river of Omegas through. "Why don't you pull the truck around so that she doesn't have to walk through the press?" The Alpha added, clapping Jameson on the shoulder.

"Good idea, Sir." Jameson nodded and began pushing toward a side door that would give him easier access to the parking lot. He pulled the truck through the crowd just as Jordan Hollins was escorted through the crowd to jeers and chants of support.

Despite what Lukas said, Jameson couldn't help thinking The Alpha was mistaken. What the Hollins' men did would happen again. Alphas were Alphas and never is a long time. He opened his door, pushing his gigantic frame into the mix. People moved aside for him, clearing the way.

He meant to say something snide to Jordan Hollins as he passed by, something that he could think about for the next fifteen years. But the arrow that pierced Jordan's chest stole his chance. The tip entered his back and went through his heart, drawing Jordan's eye. The second arrow pierced his throat from behind, silencing any cry he might have made.

Screams filled the air as Jordan Hollins stood, staring with disbelief at the tips of the arrows protruding from his front.

People ran.

Some ran forward and some away, but they all ran. Jameson stood, unable and unwilling to do anything but stare.

A flutter of paper in the breeze caught his eye. A banner reading 'Justice' came to the ground, and his heart stopped. He glanced up, but no one stood in the many windows and balconies overlooking this spot. No trace. No sign. Like smoke, the shooter was gone.

Lorelei ran to him, placing a delicate hand on his arm; her concerned eyes searched his. Her face was not flushed, and her eyes were calm. There was no flare to her nostrils or fear in her scent. The heartbeat at the base of her neck was steady, and her chest rose and fell slowly.

Eve rushed to The Alpha and stood by his side. "Search the premises!" he bellowed, and his soldiers went. People flowed around him like an island in the tide.

Jordan Hollins finally fell.

It happened so quickly.

What Jameson knew was that any single one of those Omegas could've made that shot. He knew that Eve Justice Hatfield Jennings was an expert with a bow, and his wife was even better. Lorelei had nocked and shot eight arrows in under thirty seconds and not missed once. He hadn't seen it, but he knew it to be true.

He never paid attention to what went on behind his seat in the courtroom, and who's to say one of the many Omegas hadn't left ahead of the rush. Or not.

Two shots.

For Justice.

Two shots.

Jordan would have known what was coming. The first shot wouldn't have killed him right away. He would've had a second or two to understand.

Justice.

Eve's former name was Justice. Was it a death sentence handed down or a calling card?

Lorelei pulled him along.

These exotic Omegas were killers; it could have been any one of them. But Jameson thought he knew.

Lorelei climbed into his lifted truck, sitting on thirty-eight-inch tires, giving him the brightest smile he'd ever seen.

"Let's go home, Jameson. We'll just be in the way here."

Soldiers climbed over the stairs like ants, surrounding the soon-to-be dead Hollins. Windows were thrown open, and balconies searched. Jameson's eyes scanned the façade. The Alpha barked orders, and Eve answered a reporter's questions, looking unruffled and calm. But then she would, wouldn't she?

During the troubles in the Seventh, the Omega Force left a swath of bodies, and none seemed worse for wear for it, either. The Chief Justice of the High Court was right. Times were changing.

With a sideways glance at Lorelei, he slid into the seat next to her, her mood almost giddy.

His parents met them at home, and they had a celebratory dinner. Jameson seared thick steaks, and Lorelei pulled the grits off the stove that had simmered all day.

He would catch his parents' glances at Lorelei and each other. They knew too.

In the end, no one cared.

Jordan Hollins was a waste of the Alpha gene, as were his brothers.

Lukas Jennings said he would destroy the Hollins' bloodline, and maybe he had.

Were his shouts a little too loud and his outrage a little too strong? Perhaps.

Dinner turned into drinks, and drinks turned into moonshine. Lorelei passed around a squat mason jar of the stuff, insisting they all drink.

One sip turned into another, and Jameson finally saw the allure. As he took the jar for the umpteenth time, he knew his neighbor would find him under a picnic table in the morning. Jameson didn't care.

Lorelei laughed as if it were the very first night they met. Her smile was bright, and her eyes happy. Jameson wouldn't judge, not when she looked so beautiful by the light of the fire.

The next morning his poor, hungover parents peeled themselves off the floor and limped home. Jameson opened his eyes as the afternoon light filtered through the curtains in the living room. He lay with an empty mason jar at his side and a pillow behind his head. He doubted Lorelei was hungover.

Tough Omega that she is.

Hard pounding at his door made him curse the Seventh, Moonshine, and his lovely wife, not precisely in that order.

He crawled to the door, hauling himself up and only swaying just a bit when he stood.

"What? God. Hush," he whispered, opening the door and shielding his eyes from the fall sun.

A delicate twitter sounded, and Eve Jennings covered her mouth and looked anywhere but at Jameson. The Alpha stood at her side, his smile wide and his voice booming. "Get into the shine last night, did you?" He clapped Jameson on the back a little too hard. "Where's your wife? This involves her, too."

Jameson stood, his bloodshot eyes glassy and his mind dull.

"Go find Lorelei and have a quick, uh, shower," Eve chuckled. "I'll put on coffee."

Somehow, Jameson stumbled up the stairs and into their bedroom. Lorelei lay in their nest, sprawled out and smiling. Her makeup was smeared from laughter and alcohol, and the trace of a smile graced her lips. She was more beautiful than the rising sun, and the sight of her sobered him.

Her smell was thick. Sweet. His cock twitched as he took in her flushed cheeks and rapid heart rate. Whatever Lukas Jennings wanted, he'd better talk fast.

"Babe," Jameson groaned, shaking her awake.

"Mmhm?"

"Eve and Lukas are here. They want to see us," he said.

Her eyes popped open, and he was indeed correct. Jameson's little Omega showed no signs of a hangover after drinking God only knows how much of that shit she called alcohol.

Her eyes trained on him immediately, growing heated; her pupils were large, but not yet blown. There was a little time.

"Shower," Jameson croaked, stumbling into the bathroom and turning the water on full cold.

He heard Lorelei's tinkling laugh and her soft sigh as she rose. "I should've stopped you at the third round, Jameson. Sorry," she said, and Jameson detected not one iota of sorrow in her voice. Sorry, not sorry, he thought. He was never drinking again.

Lorelei was downstairs sipping coffee and looking perfectly fine when Jameson slid down the stairs. He took the cup she offered him gratefully, noting the sly grin on her lips.

"Sit, Jameson," The Alpha bellowed, and Jameson knew he did that shit on purpose. "I remember my first round with moonshine. I looked about like you do right now. It gets better," he laughed.

"I'm never drinking again," Jameson said, voicing his earlier thoughts.

"Ok. Sure," Eve chuckled, sipping her coffee delicately.

The Omegas did not look at each other. In fact, they seemed to make a point not to. "Getting down to it, aren't you, sister?" Eve said, glancing at Lorelei.

"Nearly there," Lorelei responded.

Eve raised her coffee cup in a toast. "Enjoy!" she said with a wink.

"Oh, I plan on it," Lorelei answered, slapping Jameson on the back.

Jameson groaned. He was the next to die; he knew it. Hungover and already dehydrated, he'd never survive his wife's estrous. But what a way to go. His own smile curved his lips.

"Let's get to it then," the Alpha interrupted. "And add a jug of water to both your coffees," he said, laughing and thinking himself funny. "That's an order."

Knowing a good idea when he heard one, Jameson rose. He took a gallon jug of chilled water, first offering it to Lorelei, then taking some for himself. They shared the jug, and within seconds, it was gone.

"The Hollins' compound was raided last night," he started, causing Jameson and Lorelei to pause their movements.

"There was so much wrong with Jordan's testimony that something had to be going on," Eve said seamlessly.

"Special Ops found a small haven of cultists. Two Omega females, one Beta female, and one Alpha female were rescued," The Alpha continued, and any hint of Jameson's hangover vanished.

"Rescued?" he asked.

"Turns out Peter Hollins, the Hollins boys' father, was a scientist of sorts. He developed the drug Xander used on Lorelei and was experimenting with it. The Hollins boys were half-brothers, not full. Peter Hollins used fertility drugs, artificial insemination, rape, and torture to make those boys; there was a sister there, too, a Beta female. Being related didn't stop Peter's experiments or ministrations.

"Peter has been put to death, and the compound wiped out. Anyone involved is no longer breathing." The Alpha gave a happy smile.

"The women are in the hospital. Not all of them are expected to survive. None of the Omegas were bonded. The Hollins boys either didn't know, didn't care, or were complicit in the horrors of that place. My bet is on the latter," Eve chimed in, leaning against her mate. "It's over. All of it," she finished.

"That it is, little one, that it is." The Alpha rose, holding his hand for Eve to follow. "I expect to see you at the office in seven to ten days, Jameson. No slouching."

Jameson watched Eve punch the Alpha's arm with a smile.

"You kids have fun," Eve said, leaving with a grin and a wink.

"Are you okay?" Jameson asked, moving to Lorelei's side.

"Better than okay," she answered. "It's over."

"Is it?" he asked, meeting her eyes and holding them.

"Yes. Yes, Jameson. It is."

He sighed, letting out the pent-up stress he felt. "Breakfast?" he asked.

"I'm starving," she said, moving to the kitchen.

Lorelei reheated grits while Jameson fried bacon and eggs. A day-old loaf of homemade bread sat on the counter, and they snacked on it as they cooked. After sharing another jug of water, Jameson felt almost human. After breakfast, he felt great.

"I'm going to shower," Lorelei said, pushing away from the table with a rounded belly full of food. "I smell like a distillery."

"Yeah, you do," Jameson teased, not looking up from the front page of the paper.

The article was about Jordan Hollins's death. The New South was stunned, even though Jameson wasn't. There were no suspects. Video surveillance failed to reveal the killer or killers.

Somehow, though there were cameras on every corner, they'd caught nothing.

Smoke.

There was no one left in the Hollins family to cry foul. The supporters on the other side of the aisle vanished when the compound was raided and hadn't been seen since.

Jameson put the paper down and drank another gallon of water while finishing the loaf of bread. When Lorelei didn't return, he went in search of her.

She stood dripping and naked in the middle of their room. Goosebumps dotted her wet flesh, and her hands were clenched at her sides. The eyes that snapped to his were black- all pupil. None of the deep, dark brown of her irises showed. She growled, stalking forward at his entrance.

Lorelei sniffed the air, then ran her nose up Jameson's arms as high as she could reach.

"Mine," she growled, swiping him with baby claws.

"Yes, yours, dove. Always yours," Jameson pinned her arms so she couldn't claw at him. With one hand, he undressed, holding the pissed-off, growling, sweet-smelling, water-soaked Omega in his arms. He wasn't ready. But ready or not…

Her growls heightened when he shifted her to remove his pants. Her eyes snapped to his cock as he freed it, and her growling stopped. Taking the opportunity, he grabbed a jug of water he'd placed by their bed a few days ago.

"Drink," he demanded, offering her a growl of his own.

Whimpering, she took the jug and drank until it was gone.

"Choose to let me in," he said, his voice growing harsh. Lorelei stumbled backward into her nest, reaching wordlessly for him.

He strode forward, climbing in and covering her with his body. She felt glorious against him. He growled low, calling her slick as he kissed down her body, nipping her peaked breasts and feeding on her bare skin. He would not lie, ready or not; he couldn't wait.

Her cloying scent called to him like nothing ever had, and his dick was so hard it was painful. He'd never been in a rut and wasn't there yet, but when her estrous hit full bore, he was done. He hoped he remembered even half of it.

When he slipped his tongue down the delicate curve of her slick soaked core, she sang for him, and he growled, taking in every gush she offered. Flicking his tongue over her clit, he made her claw at him. His Omega was a sharp-edged thing.

He loved it.

He loved her.

Jameson traced the lines of her core with his tongue, knowing that soon only his body in hers would calm her. He was the only thing between her and unbearable pain, and he would serve her well. While he could, he would enjoy the taste and feel of her under his tongue. Taking the hardened nub in his mouth, he pulled it gently, loving the feel of her coming apart for him. She came, gushing fluid to nourish him and ease his way.

Her body shook as she reached for him. Her whimpers and cries changed, and he knew all playing was over. She needed.

Him.

In one swift move, he sheathed himself inside her. She was made for him. Her body took him perfectly. He was large, even for an Alpha, yet he fit. Already, her tight, greedy pussy milked him for his seed. Her moans and pleas for him grew more frantic. He snapped his hips against her over and over, coaxing out another of her glorious orgasms.

She might have screamed his name and clamped her sweet pussy on his cock, but he wasn't giving her his knot. Not yet. She needed more. Her body cried out, and the smell of full-blown estrous saturated the air. Grabbing her face in his hands, he kissed her lips like a man starving. Her tongue met his, thrust for thrust, and she clawed at his back, crying out and demanding more simultaneously.

He felt himself slip into that hard-earned spot past her cervix and groaned. She arched into him, raising her mouth to his. He took her delicate throat in his hands, pushing her back onto the bed.

Her eyes snapped wide when he squeezed, putting enough pressure on her neck to make her eyes roll back and close. He thrust into her wildly, hammering her with the very thing she begged for until she came again. When her orgasm gushed around him, he pushed in deeper, once, twice, then gave her his knot, coming hard into the deepest part of her.

Jameson released her neck, bending to kiss Lorelei's face, lips, and shoulders. Every time he thought he'd seen her at her most lovely, he was proven wrong. Here, naked in their nest and covered in sweat and his cum, she was a goddess. No star shone brighter in the southern sky.

She rolled her hips into him, forcing his knot deeper still. He flipped their positions, draping her over his torso while he waited for the knot to abate.

And she purred for him.

Her purr was sweet and rich. With eyes closed and face relaxed, her purr joined his until their song was orchestral. Then she grimaced, and he felt her walls tighten around him.

His knot released, and their fluids rushed between them; scooping up the rich mixture, he fed his wife before entering her again. And again.

Jameson lost himself to the rut not long after, and the next days were a blur of endless need for both of them. He came to from time to time only to find he was always inside of her. Her mouth would be locked on his cock and swallowing his cum, or his tongue buried in the depths of her pussy. He made her cum until her core shook from weakness, and he served her until his cock was raw.

It. Was. Glorious. Five stars. Recommend.

In the rare moments she slept, he slept too, only to be awakened by her demanding growl and her sharp claws marking his skin with her displeasure. He forced water down her throat and quick bites of food down his.

There was no way to track time. The days passed in a blur of pleasure so blinding he thought he might never truly see again until one of the times he fell asleep; she didn't wake him.

Chapter 23

Lorelei forced her eyes open. Her face was a crusted mess, and her eyes were matted shut. She knew why. She didn't want to think about it, except she kind of did. Her smile came unbidden, and damned if she would stop it. That. Was. Incredible.

Hands down, best estrous ever.

She was never giving Jameson up.

Eve had offered to kill him for her and set her free, and she'd actually thought about it.

Not happening.

Life with Jameson was far, far better than life without- choice be damned. He *was* her choice.

She'd never felt so cared for in her life. A few times in the past, she'd waken from her estrous alone, the Alpha gone with her need for him. Jameson lay in the ruin of their nest, arms slung over his face while he slept deeply.

Lorelei ran her hands down her body, noting she'd lost little to no weight. Jameson was a good Alpha. The best Alpha, even.

Her smile grew, then faded when she tried to move. She couldn't. Her body hurt in places she didn't know she had, but it was a glorious pain. Groaning, she slid out of the nest, off the bed, and onto the floor. She lay there spread-eagled for a bit, staring at the ceiling while letting the cool air from the fan chill her flesh.

She had to pee. Badly. God knows when was the last time she'd done so. With a groan, she tried to will her boneless body into the bathroom.

"Lorelei?" Jameson said, his voice hoarse but concerned.

"Yeah, Babe?" she answered, her voice no better. God, they were a train wreck- a fantastic, beautiful, can't look away train wreck.

Her words were met with silence. Then Jameson's worried face peered over the edge of the bed at her, causing her to give a weak wave and glance at the bathroom.

Jameson heaved himself up, trying to hide his groan and failing. He wobbled a bit before straightening and bending to scoop her into his arms. Lorelei noted he was a mass of claw marks, teeth marks, and goo. She almost felt bad.

Almost.

Cradled in his arms, Jameson took Lorelei to the bathroom, setting her on the toilet. She'd be embarrassed about it, but she didn't have the strength for that.

While she peed, he started the shower. She usually liked his smell on her and vice versa, but this miasma of current smells was a bit much. From the toilet, the shower looked terrific.

Lorelei found herself picked up again and placed gently on the shower's corner seat. There was no stopping the long groan she let out as the hot water hit her skin. When Jameson's hands touched her, her eyes fell closed.

Every nook and cranny of her body felt the sweep of his hands and the caress of soap. He adjusted her on the seat until he could reach every part of her. Her soapy hands rested on his hips, and she purred as he worked.

He washed and conditioned her hair, pulling at the long blond strands until she was a puddle. His purr never stopped as he cared for her, and she knew that staying with him was the best decision she'd ever made.

"I love you, Jameson," Lorelei said, smiling when his hands stilled on her scalp. "I don't know when it started, but I know why. You're a good man Jameson Beauregard Battle, but you're an even better Alpha. Thank you."

He pulled her into a hug, turning her so that the soap rinsed away. "I love you too, dove. Thank you for choosing me. Maybe you didn't in the beginning, but you did in the end."

She ran lazy hands over his body, trying to clean him as best she could, but she was so tired. Between the two of them, they managed to get Jameson a modicum of clean. In the bedroom, they stripped the bed and fell onto the bare mattress.

Tomorrow was another day. They'd deal with sheets then.

Funny how the biggest worry Lorelei had at that moment was dirty sheets. With her body humming and pleasantly sore, they

313

slept the rest of the day away. Wrapped around each other, there was no greater worry between them than linens, and that's exactly how it should be.

Chapter 24

A week later, they sat around a bonfire at the Battle Ranch. Surrounded by friends and family. They laughed, shared moonshine, and talked.

Jameson had gone back to work, taking on the duties as The New South's Second Alpha that he claimed to hate, but Lorelei knew he secretly didn't.

The bond between them sang happily as their fingers twined together. Eve and Lukas sat across from them, and Darrian, Annabelle, and a scattering of the Battle brothers.

As usual, Earl was in the fields, moving this thing or that as the fall sun approached the horizon, calling him home. Eve and Lorelei had jumped on horses and disappeared before Jameson's truck slowed in the drive. He and Lukas shared a long look and a knowing smile. Those girls were trouble.

Eve hadn't worried about her pregnant belly when she jumped on her horse bareback, and she'd scoffed at the suggestion she should. Lorelei had thrown herself at the red mare's neck before sliding onto her back. The thing wasn't even broke, yet off they ran into the mountains together.

Untamed. All of them.

Every now and then, their laughter echoed through the valleys filled with Carolina Pines.

Like smoke.

Jameson wondered what dead things they'd drag back.

The dead thing was a wild boar.

As dinner was laid on the table, Lorelei came into the yard with it draped over the red mare's neck, blood dripping down her sides.

"I didn't do it," she claimed, raising her hands high in surrender. "Layla did it," she pointed at the horse innocently, and Eve chuckled, looking away. The only weapon Lorelei carried was a short-handled knife.

"The horse did it?" Jameson asked, hands on his hips. He scowled at his wife, eyebrows pinched so closely they formed one angry line. He pinched the bridge of his nose with two fingers, shaking his head.

"Yes," Lorelei answered, her rotten grin wide. "This thing attacked her, and she killed it. One kick, she has perfect aim. The pig was as good as done."

"Uh-huh. What about that stab wound between its shoulder blades?" The Alpha asked, walking over and poking the hornet's nest.

"Bless your heart, sweetie," Lorelei said, batting her eyelashes at The First Alpha of the New South and grinning. "That's just a scratch," she added.

"Right," groaned Jameson. "A scratch."

Lorelei dumped the dead thing off the wild mare, then all the wild things headed to the barn.

"Well, Jameson. Hang that up in the meat shed," His mother sighed, shaking her head. "We were almost out of bacon." Annabelle tipped her moonshine back, grinning at her son.

The Mother's curse had been fulfilled with him. Now on to the next, she thought. "When are you going to marry her, JB?" she asked.

"Ma," Jameson groaned. "Soon, okay?" he said, hoping that would be enough.

"How about tomorrow? I'll call preacher Sullivan; he'd be happy to come and make this official." The sly grin his mother gave him made Jameson sigh. Omegas. There's nothing easy about them, despite what the dynamics classes teach.

"Sounds perfect, Mom," Lorelei said from behind him as she wrapped her arms around Jameson's neck.

"Really?" he asked.

"Really," she said, leaning down to kiss his cheek. "I meant what I said, Jameson, no take backsies."

They stared at each other for a long moment.

"Get a room," one brother said, laughing and breaking their spell.

"Tomorrow it is, dove." Jameson pulled Lorelei around his chair, settling her in his lap. They hadn't had sex since her estrous ended. Between trying to catch up on calories and having raw body parts, it hadn't been a priority. Their needs had been sated, but it was in their eyes tonight.

A cough broke another lingering look. "I had a question for you, Lorelei; you and Eve both," Darrian paused, looking uncomfortable. "Are there any single Omegas I might court? I don't think I can handle anything like you two. Perhaps someone a little tamer?" he finished, looking sheepish.

"Tamer?" Lorelei asked, narrowing her eyes at him.

Eve laughed, not bothering to hide behind a hand.

"I've meant to tell you I found your accounting problem," she added, looking thoughtful. "Three million dollars were skimmed from your accounts. It was very sophisticated. Whoever managed your transactions installed a program on the device that diverted ten percent of every purchase to an unregistered bank account.

"On paper, it looks like fees or losses. It's not something you would have noticed. Most investments charge fees like these, and there's always loss with the stock market. The problem came last month. You had a client sell out completely, and a million dollars was skimmed from that account alone," Lorelei added, tilting her head in question. "Whoever has access to that level of investment funds," she said. "That's your culprit. As the bank account the money went into is unregistered, I can't find out who it belongs to."

Darrian's face fell. "I can't believe you found it. I mean, I thought there might be a problem, but no one found anything. Ten percent would've been easy to miss; you're right. It adds up, though. Only one other person had access at that level," he stopped, taking a deep breath. "Meghan. It had to be Meghan," he finished, looking sad.

"I'm sorry," Lorelei said.

"Don't be. Thank you for finding it. I'll come to your office this week and bring what records I have. There could be more evidence, and I'll need it to fire her."

"If you need a lawyer, let me know," Eve said, meaning it.

"I will, thanks. So, back to the question at hand... A nice, sweet, peaceful, docile Omega?" He had the nerve to look sheepish.

"Oh, Darrian. The docile ones are damaged," Eve said, looking at him with a serious expression.

"We're all damaged, EJ," Lorelei whispered. "Some of us just survived it," she added.

Jameson gripped her thigh, rubbing a comforting circle on the pad of her hand.

"What about Grace?" The Alpha said, his voice low.

"No," Eve said.

Lorelei sucked in a breath. "Not Grace, Lukas. She's beyond damaged; she's broken."

"I can deal with damaged," Darrian said. "I just can't imagine sleeping with one eye open every night," he added with a laugh that trailed off when no one joined him. "What?"

Lorelei sighed. "We think Grace needs to be put down," she whispered. "It's the only kindness left for her."

Eve nodded her head, and The Alpha did not contradict their assessment.

"What? No! You can't put an Omega down because she's broken. She's not a fucking dog." Darrian stood, pacing angrily by the fire.

"You don't understand, Darrian. She has no will left. She eats what's placed in front of her and sleeps when put to bed," Lorelei said, her eyes sadder than anything Darrian had ever seen.

"She isn't one of ours, Darrian. She was rescued from that horrible place in the Seventh, where the resistance was housed. Grace was caged and doesn't speak," Eve answered.

"Would she come willingly?" Darrian asked, his face fierce and oh-so-determined.

"No, Darrian. You don't understand. She has no will, no drive, no desire. There's nothing to save," Lorelei said. "She truly is a shell."

"It's an option, EJ," The Alpha said. "We can't keep her on heat suppressants forever. Perhaps Darrian can do something we could not. It's this or death for Grace."

"Give the girl to Darrian," Annabelle said, and all eyes snapped to her. "He was always the best with the spiritless, abused colts. What?" she added when she saw the disbelieving looks around her. "He was. Surely it's better than putting a young Omega down?"

Lorelei sighed, meeting Eve's eyes and holding them. Maybe they were right. Eve and Lorelei both came back from being broken. Maybe Grace could, too.

"Let us speak with her, Darrian. I promise nothing," Eve added with a long sigh. "She's been hurt enough, and death may be all that's left for her. She's suffered enough."

"I won't accept that, Eve. As long as she's alive, there's a chance for her. Don't give up yet. The only way a possibility ends is with death. She deserves a chance." Darrian stood begging for a woman he'd never met. He'd always been one to give endless second chances, so it didn't surprise anyone who knew him.

"You don't understand, Darrian." Eve started. "She deserved better a long time ago."

"Talk with the girl, EJ," The Alpha said, shutting her down.

"Okay," she said, placing her hand on his.

The fire burned low, and the moonshine ran out. Lorelei and Jameson retired to the pink room she'd once stayed in alone. They'd come to see his parents, who had insisted on inviting everyone. Annabelle was a sneaky Omega.

"Are you really going to marry me?" Jameson asked, tugging at Lorelei's dark shirt. He loved how it brought out the depths of her eyes.

"Yes, Jameson. I am. You're not backing out now, are you?" she laughed, tracing her hands up his chiseled chest.

"Never." His lips crushed hers, and he picked her up, settling her across his hips.

They crashed into the bed, all hands, lips, and need. Lorelei fought him off long enough to scrape together enough linens to make a giant pink nest. She seemed unable to have it any other way.

When Jameson pushed inside Lorelei, he knew he was home. Home is a place. Home is the walls and furnishings that welcome you back from a long day at work or a night out on the town, but home is also a feeling. Lorelei was his home, and she would be until the end of their days. Jameson was lucky, but so was Lorelei, and they both knew it.

She arched into him with a groan. "It's been too long," she said with a smile as she met his eyes. "I missed you."

Her lips met his, their tongues twining. And when Lorelei brought her hands to the curve of his ass, she urged him on.

Jameson refused to give in to her demands this time. He wanted to enjoy every moment of having her beneath him. Her body gripped his like a vise, and she groaned again. Reaching down, he slid his finger across her clit, making her cry out.

He covered her mouth with his, muffling her pleas for more. She fell apart around him, soaking his cock with her desire. He took as much as he could and brought his fingers to her lips, where she sucked them dry.

He did it again.

The sight of his fingers covered in her essence and claimed by her mouth undid him. Good intentions aside, he pressed into her faster. When he hit that spot, she screamed his name. He emptied into her, giving her his knot and everything else along with it. She was his. God. What a road. Every bit of it had been worth it to share this moment with her.

"No one is more loved than you," Jameson said, emotion bleeding into his voice.

"Right back at'cha, babe," she said, struggling for her breath.

He smiled, shaking his head.

Untamed and Untamable. He wouldn't change her for the world.

Dear Reader,

Whew! I hope this series is as fun to read as it is to write! Jameson breathed himself to life on a smoky late summer day, and his story fell onto the pages. There was only one match for him, and ~~as bad as I felt about torturing her,~~ I knew she could handle it.

NS304 faced its first challenge; will there be more to come? Who knows? Certainly not me. What's next? An Alpha's Grace, the third Omega's of the New South book, will be along shortly. I had intended to work on another project, but you know all about good intentions.

If you liked The Omega Challenge, drop a quick review, and don't forget to follow me on Facebook and Instagram for updates!

Also by Sharilyn:

Trauma: stand-alone contemporary women's fiction

Healer Series: **Series Complete**

Cerridwen's Tears

Healer

House of Fire

The Scarlet Heron

The Flame Keeper

Goddess Bound

Goddess Rising Series

Goddess Rising

The Eight Series:

Airmed

Ravena

Teagan

Omegas of The New South:

The Omega Rule

The Omega Challenge

An Alpha's Grace

An Omega's Choice: Predators and Prey

An Alpha's Ruin

An Omega's Dance

An Alpha's Price

The WidowMaker trilogy:

Widowmaker

Gravedigger

Queenmaker- coming Summer 2026

Follow Sharilyn on Facebook, Instagram, Goodreads, and her plain old website.

www.sharilynskye.com

About Sharilyn:

Sharilyn spent most of her early years on the Grand Strand of SC, annoying local police officers and pretty much everyone else with her fast cars and loud music. She graduated from the University of South Carolina and now lives on a small farm outside Morgantown, West Virginia, with her family and a menagerie of cats, horses, and visiting wildlife.

Sharilyn writes urban fantasy, fairy tales, Omegaverse romance, and women's fiction. Each title in her Omegaverse series, Omegas of The New South, spent weeks on Amazon's best-sellers list. An Omega's Dance and An Alpha's Price were USA Today and Amazon Best Sellers, and her Healer series has a following that borders on cultish. (She adores you, you crazy Lara Hennessey fans!)

She loves showing Quarter Horses, trail riding, reading, drinking coffee, driving her vintage Corvette, and being annoyed by her kids. If she's missing, check the garage or look for the horse trailer. If one is missing, no worries; she'll be back. Probably.
www.sharilynskye.com